Antiques Disposal

"The book is so funny, I honestly couldn't put it down. It's so entertaining, pages simply fly by. Hey, did I mention there are recipes for chocolate brownies in it? Now how can you go wrong with that?
—*Bill Crider's Pulp Fiction Reviews*

"A zany antiques mystery . . . A classic gathering of suspects leads to an unexpected denouement."
—*Publishers Weekly*

"Here's something to brighten your day . . . very funny, with lots of great dialogue. There's even a Nero Wolfe homage, along with a cliffhanger ending . . . good news for us fans."
—*Bill Crider's Pop Culture Magazine*

"This humorous cozy is framed by life in small-town Iowa and teems with quirky characters. It will appeal to readers who enjoy Donna Andrews' Meg Langslow mysteries."
—*Booklist*

Antiques Knock-Off

"If you like laugh-out-loud funny mysteries, this next Trash 'n' Treasures installment will make your day."
—*Romantic Times Book Reviews*, 4.5 stars

"Scenes of Midwestern small-town life, informative tidbits about the antiques business, and clever dialog make this essential for those who like unusual amateur sleuths."
—*Library Journal*

Antiques Swap

A Trash 'n' Treasures Mystery

Barbara Allan

KENSINGTON BOOKS
http://www.kensingtonbooks.com

KENSINGTON BOOKS are published by

Kensington Publishing Corp.
119 West 40th Street
New York, NY 10022

All Kensington titles, imprints, and distributed lines are available at special quantity discounts for bulk purchases for sales promotion, premiums, fund-raising, educational, or institutional use. Special book excerpts or customized printings can also be created to fit specific needs. For details, write or phone the office of the Kensington Special Sales Manager: Attn. Special Sales Department. Kensington Publishing Corp., 119 West 40th Street, New York, NY 10018. Phone: 1-800-221-2647.

Kensington and the K logo Reg. U.S. Pat. & TM Off.

ISBN-13: 978-0-7582-9306-0
ISBN-10: 0-7582-9306-2
First Kensington Hardcover Edition: May 2015
First Kensington Mass Market Edition: March 2016

eISBN-13: 978-0-7582-9307-7
eISBN-10: 0-7582-9307-0
Kensington Electronic Edition: March 2016

10 9 8 7 6 5 4 3 2 1

Printed in the United States of America

In memory of
Patricia Ann Collins
1925–2012

Brandy's quote:
There are two ways to be fooled.
One is to believe what isn't true; the other
is to refuse to believe what is true.
—Søren Kierkegaard

Mother's quote:
Fool me once, shame on you.
Fool me twice, still shame on you!
—Vivian Borne

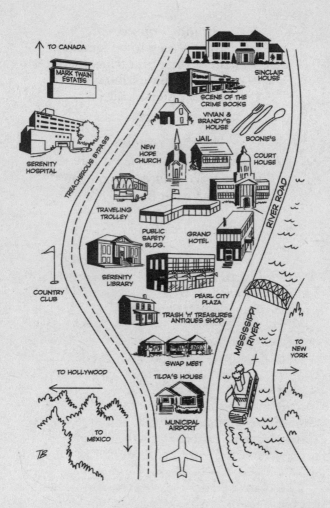

Chapter One

Opening Lead

(In the game of bridge, first bid by defenders.)

You know that expression, "Be careful what you wish for"? Well, in my case, it's "Be careful what *Mother* wishes for."

Mother being Vivian Borne, seventy-threeish, Danish stock, widowed, bipolar, local thespian, part-time sleuth, full-time gossip, and sometime county jail resident.

And me being Brandy Borne, thirty-two, divorced, Prozac-popper, audience member, reluctant sleuth, subject of gossip, and onetime loser (breaking and entering) with a record in the process of being expunged, since I was helping solve a murder at the time.

The third member of our sleuthing team is my blind diabetic shih tzu, Sushi, who accompanied me to my little hometown of Serenity, Iowa, after my divorce two years ago.

Only . . . wait for it, longtime readers . . .
Sushi is no longer blind! That's right, no more
spooky white Exorcist orbs. No, we did not make
a trek to Lourdes (meaning you did *not* miss a
series entry entitled *Antiques Pilgrimage*).

We did trek to New York, however, to attend a
comics convention several months ago (*Antiques
Con*), where Mother and I auctioned off a valuable 1940s Superman drawing acquired in a storage unit auction (*Antiques Disposal*). With part
of the proceeds, we funded an operation for
Sushi to remove her cataracts (a result of her dia-
betes) and implant new lenses, and now I assume
she can see perfectly. I say "assume" because a
dog can't exactly read an eye chart. Do dogs
really see in black-and-white? Well, I guess with
an eye chart they do. . . .

It's been fun watching the little fur ball explore a world she hasn't seen for years. Sushi is
now a Super Dog, minus only the cape, her
other senses honed to perfection. I don't mean
to imply her sleuthing powers have increased,
but it's true that the little mutt seems to know
when I'll be going into the kitchen for a bag of
potato chips even before I do!

But Sushi can sometimes be a little stinker,
and her reprisals were numerous and varied, according to the degree of her ire: peeing on my
pillow (ten on a scale of ten), chewing a new
pair of shoes (eight), leaving a little brown car-
rot inside the house in plain view (six). One
through five were various barks, growls, or dirty
looks. Just where the little tyrant learned such
vindictiveness, I have no clue.

As for Mother's aforementioned wish, it was for our TV pilot to be picked up, a reality show shot at our new shop, an expansion of our old antiques mall stall underwritten by the pilot's producers.

Perhaps the best way to bring you up to speed is to reprint a recent interview with Mother conducted by a young male reporter from the *Serenity Sentinel.* So hold on to your hats—especially the Red Hat Society kind.

Serenity Sentinel: *Why you?*

Vivian Borne: *Dear, not meaning to be critical, you understand . . . but it's always best to begin an interview with a complete sentence. Such as "Why were you and your daughter chosen from among the many 'wannabes' for a reality TV show?"*

SS: *Why were you?*

VB: *Phillip Dean—a veteran cameraman turned producer—thought that the antiques business run by myself, Vivian Borne, V-I-V-I-A-N B-O-R-N-E and Brandy Borne, B-R-A-N-D-Y, Borne Again . . . no religious connotation intended . . . would make a perfect series because—*

SS: *I heard the show was called* Antique Sleuths.

VB: *Dear, it's not polite to interrupt. If you want to be a responsible member of the Fourth Estate, you must—*

SS: *Fourth what?*

VB: *—pose your questions in the* form *of a question.*

SS: *That* was *a question.*

VB: *The name of the show is* Antiques Sleuths, *in the plural, not* Antique Sleuths. *You do perceive the difference?*

SS: Now you're *asking the questions.*

VB: (sighs) Yes, because it has become clear that I need to commandeer this interview, if anything of substance is to be conveyed.

SS: Go for it.

VB: The concept of the show is that a mother and daughter, who have solved numerous mysteries in real life, as amateur sleuths . . . that would be my daughter and myself . . . also solve the mysteries behind various unusual antiques brought by clientele into their, which is to say our, Trash 'n' Treasures shop.

SS: But right now there's only a pilot. I mean, right now there is only a pilot, right?

VB: I congratulate you on that recovery. That is correct. Most of the pilot was filmed last week, with a little more footage—"B roll," they call it in the industry—to be shot this Saturday at a local swap meet. The finished product will be shown to several cable TV networks.

SS: So it's not a done deal?

VB: No . . . but we're hopeful. We have an undeniable advantage, factoring in my considerable history in local theater, not to mention my experiences off-Broadway.

SS: I'm not to mention that?

VB: Well, certainly you may mention it. Why would you not? Next question.

SS: You've recently moved your antiques business to a house where two murders took place. Isn't that creepy?

VB: Dear, I don't think the demise of those poor victims—murders separated by many years, both of which we *solved, by the way—need be referred to as "creepy." Let us just say it lends a certain resonance to the undertaking.*

SS: *So does "undertaking." Sounds like you're capitalizing on the infamous notoriety of the house. I mean, are you capitalizing on—*

VB: *Certainly not! It just happened to be vacant when we were looking for an appropriate venue for our expanded business, and the prospective television show. We would not think of tastelessly exploiting the tragic history of that structure.*

SS: *Then why does your website say, "Come and visit us at the Murder House"?*

VB: *Does it? Well, that's a minor lapse on the part of our web designer. I'll give him a real talking-to.*

Had enough? I have! But I do think Mother came off better than the interviewer.

Where were we? Ah yes—Saturday morning, and Mother and I were getting ready to open for business at the Murder House—a designation that was not our doing, a local nickname dating back to the axing of the patriarchal owner some sixty years ago, and a copycat killing last year, about which I won't go into, for those among you who haven't (as yet) read *Antiques Chop*.

Maybe it was my mildly mind-altering Prozac, or possibly a numbness that's set in due to the number of murders Mother and I have solved since my homecoming two years ago, but I've come to *like* that historically homicidal house, perfect as it was for our expanded business.

The large two-story white clapboard with wide

front porch and modest lawn was situated down-town just after commercial Main Street begins its rise into East Hill residential. Built around the turn of the last century, the place had a down-stairs parlor, a music room, a formal dining room, and spacious kitchen; four bedrooms and a bath occupied the upstairs.

In setting up our shop, Mother and I decided to slant each room toward its original pur-pose—that is to say, all of our kitchen antiques were in the kitchen, bedroom sets in the bed-rooms, linens in the linen closet, formal furni-ture in the parlor, and so forth—even the knickknacks were placed where you might ex-pect them to be (only with price tags).

Our customers often had the vague sense that they were visiting an elderly relative—a grand-mother or kindly old aunt—with so many lovely things on display. Only at Trash 'n' Treasures, you didn't have to wait to inherit something; for the listed price (or maybe a haggled-over lower one), you could walk right out with whatever caught your eye.

The spacious entry hallway was where we put our checkout counter, so that we could greet customers, and also keep an eye on the down-stairs rooms. Mother and I believed a certain amount of pilfering was better business than se-curity cameras hovering high in every corner announcing: "We don't trust you."

Besides, even a state-of-the-art system couldn't compare to our secret weapon: the all-knowing, now all-seeing shih tzu, who with her Sushi sense could detect a nervous shoplifter, following him or her from room to room with an accusatory glare. (Now if someone would only steal that darn smiley-face alarm clock!)

Before moving our business into the house, Mother asked Serenity's resident New Age guru, Tilda Tompkins, to meet us there and conduct a reading to make sure we weren't going to upset any spirits—especially murdered ones—thereby courting bad karma. A disgruntled ghost slamming a door was one thing . . . knives hurtling through the air was quite another.

Mother, Tilda, and I had sat in a circle on the floor of the empty parlor holding hands, while the guru closed her eyes, chanting softly, summoning any willing visitor from the other side.

But, much to Mother's disappointment, no one answered. Oh, there was a *sneeze*. But it turned out to have come not from a departed one who'd died of pneumonia, rather from Sushi, thanks to some antique dust she'd breathed in.

The next day, still uncertain, Mother asked Father O'Leary to come bless the house, which he did, even though we belonged to New Hope Church. For flood relief, Mother had organized a charity bazaar at St. Mary's, which brought in a lot of money (*Antiques Bizarre*), so we'd racked up some good Catholic-style karma there.

Father O'Leary intoned a prayer in the entryway, then went from room to room, sprinkling the air with Epiphany water, and marking each door in chalk with the initials CMB—"Christ bless this house." If Linda Blair happened to drive through Serenity, and stopped to do some antiquing, she'd be just fine, though some of our collectibles were real head-turners.

And, so, with our bases covered from New Age spiritualism to old-time religion, we moved our antiques in, and Trash 'n' Treasures was ready to rock 'n' roll.

Anyway, Saturday morning.

Mother and I and Sushi were waiting in the shop for Joe Lange to arrive and "take the conn" (as the longtime Trekkie put it) so that we could attend the swap meet down on the riverfront.

Joe was tall and loose-limbed, with nice features that were somehow a wee bit off—one eye higher than the other, mouth a touch too wide, nose off-center. He was a committed bachelor (in the sense that he'd been occasionally institutionalized), and was an old pal of mine since our community college days, when we were assigned as lab partners in biology class. I'd been faced with a crucial decision: either strangle the irritating nerd, or befriend him. I chose the latter. After graduation, Joe joined the Marines and fought in the Middle East, while I married an older man in Chicago. On some level, we were both getting away from our mothers.

And now, veterans of our various wars, Joe and I were both back home, more or less where we started, including *living* with our mothers. To varying degrees, I suppose, we were both damaged goods. If you're wondering, we weren't an item. Joe showed no signs of interest in sex, either female or male.

Mother was saying, "Dear, I wonder if we're

making a mistake, entrusting our shop to that poor troubled soul. One day it may come back to bite us in the you-know-what."

She was wearing a new Breckinridge summer outfit—pink slacks, and a pink-and-white checked blouse; the only out-of-date item in her ensemble were the huge-framed magnifying eyeglasses.

I shrugged. "Joe did all right at the shop while we were in New York."

I had on my fave DKNY jeans and a gauzy floral shirt by Joie, an Internet steal.

We had left Joe in charge for two weeks, and received nary a customer complaint. His sales had been respectable, too.

"Yes," Mother said, then qualified her nod. "But it's just about *that time.*"

She was referring to Joe's summer "drug holiday," when his doctor took him off his antipsychotic meds for a few months, because of their potency. The problem was that my friend then reverted to Marine status, and went into full survival mode, often camping out in the caves at Wild Cat Den State Park.

Hiding out was more like it.

The front door opened and Joe stepped in, wearing his desert camouflage utilities. (Once— okay, maybe a couple of times—I have referred to his attire as "fatigues" and caught heck for it.) He wore no helmet or hat, and thankfully wasn't carrying any military weapons.

"Reporting for duty," he said crisply.

I exchanged wary looks with Mother.

"Joe, dear," Mother said in the kind of voice a negotiator uses to talk someone down off a ledge, "do you think you might be able to stand watch here at the shop for a few hours? Brandy and I need to attend the swap meet."

"Roger that," he said. "You'll return at . . . ?"

I checked my watch; it was ten now. "Oh-two hundred." Then added, "Give or take an 'Oh.' Would you like us to bring you lunch?"

"Negatory." He patted a tan bag slung over a shoulder. "Packed my own rations."

Leaving Sushi behind, Mother and I made our uneasy exit. Outside, I asked, "You think Joe will be all right?"

"As in, is he up to handling a few customers without scaring them silly? Or, how likely is it he will take them hostage and wait for air support?"

"I was thinking more like . . . will he court-marital anybody with slippery fingers?"

I blinked away the image of middle-aged Serenity ladies lined up for a firing squad.

Mother raised a finger of her own. "My last instruction to the boy was to uphold the Geneva Convention!"

"I'm sure that was helpful." I sighed. "No chemical or biological warfare, anyway. Does our liability insurance cover post-traumatic stress disorder?"

"In him or us, dear?"

Parked in front of the shop was Mother's vintage 1960s black Caddy convertible (more about that later), and I climbed in behind the wheel, Mother riding shotgun. She had lost her license due to numerous infractions, including but not limited to: taking a shortcut though a cornfield to make curtain time for a play she was starring in; running down a curbside mailbox shaped like an open-mouthed spotted bass; and driving with a suspended license (to get chocolate-mint ice cream in the middle of the night).

I drove the short distance to Riverfront Park, which was across the railroad tracks. The park had been recently beautified by a wrought-iron fence, in keeping with the restored Victorian redbrick train depot.

In past years, the city council, understanding that Serenity's biggest asset was the Mississippi River, lavished money into enhancing the half-mile riverfront by adding a state-of-the-art playground, restroom facilities, a new boathouse (along with improved slips), and an assortment of beautiful trees, flowerbeds, and general landscaping. Plus ample parking for residents and visitors alike.

Even so, one had to get up at the crack of dawn to snag a parking spot for the summer swap meet, which drew folks from a hundred miles around. But Mother had come up with an ingenious plan for when we were finished shopping: she had entered the Caddy in the antiques car show, which was piggy-backing the swap meet. When the time came to head back to the shop, laden with purchases, having walked the entire length of the park, corns aching (hers), feet swollen (mine), our ride would be right there, waiting for us.

We parked among the other classic cars and vintage relics, made a little small talk with event organizer Mr. Blackwood, and headed off toward the swap meet area. The day was glorious, the temperature in the mid-seventies, humidity low, sun shining brightly in a clear blue sky, with just enough breeze to dry any bead of sweat.

Summer in the Midwest brings all kinds of weather, which Mother and I like to describe as cities.

"Brandy, what kind of weather have we out there?" she would ask.

"Chicago," I might reply, meaning, windy. Or "Houston," hot and humid. Or "Seattle," rainy.

Today was "San Diego." Which, if you've ever been to that wonderful city, means *perfect*.

But this was Iowa, so blink and you might find yourself in another "city". . . .

We had a dual purpose today in attending the swap meet. In addition to finding interesting items for the shop, Phil Dean was going to shoot additional footage of us browsing the vendors, the last of his B-roll wish list.

I'm sure he hoped Mother, Serenity's favorite diva, would do something outrageous for the camera; and I felt confident she wouldn't disappoint.

You may be wondering what my role on the proposed TV show was. Well, basically, to be her straight man. The Crosby to her Hope. The Martin to her Lewis. Only I didn't sing as well as either. Maybe I was Abbott to her Costello.

Anyway, Mother was asking, "Where were we to meet Phil?"

"In front of the fried butter stand."

Okay, so sometimes we don't eat so healthy in the Midwest. Considering this delicacy was created at the Iowa State Fair—famous since 1911 for its annual life-size cow sculptures fashioned from 600 pounds of pure creamery butter—

isn't *fried* butter the next logical step? And before you turn up your nose at the sweet concoction, you should try it. Maybe your *mouth* will turn up (as in a smile).

FRIED BUTTER

1 stick butter, chilled
funnel cake batter mix
1 tsp. cinnamon
vegetable oil
honey glaze

Prepare cake batter as instructed, adding cinnamon. Cover chilled butter with batter. Heat vegetable oil to 375–400 degrees. Fry batteredbutter in hot oil 1 to 1½ minutes. Remove to paper plate to drain, then drizzle with honey.

(**WARNING**: Fried Butter is not for everyone, as some serious, even fatal, side effects have been reported. These include—but are not limited to—dizziness, numbness of extremities, nausea, increased sweating, blurred vision, thirddegree burns, shortness of breath, stroke and/ or heart failure. Do not consume if you have a cholesterol level over 200, are allergic to butter, have hepatitis B, glaucoma, lupus, or have traveled to parts of the country where certain fungal infections are common.)
Enjoy!

We found Phil, toting his Sony HD camera, next to the long line of fried butter enthusiasts.

In his early forties, the former director of photography of such popular reality TV shows as *Extreme Hobbies* and *Witch Wives of Winnipeg* was today playing an extra role besides that of producer/director, reverting to his original calling as cinematographer. His regular cameraman had already departed for LA with the pilot episode's main footage.

Phil—muscular, with thick dark hair tinged with silver at the temples, a salt-and-pepper beard, and intense dark eyes—refused to dress like the producer he'd become, still wearing his scuffed white Nikes, torn Levi blue jeans, and wrinkled plaid shirts. Which, to my thinking, was smart, as his good-natured casual style put the local extras (often nervous before the camera) immediately at ease.

Accompanying Phil was Jena Hernandez, a young, petite, dark-haired woman wearing a halter top and shorts; the attractive Hispanic was Phil's assistant director, also handling continuity, and makeup and hair. (Crew members covering multiple positions were essential in staying within our pilot's limited budget.)

The first day on set, which is to say our shop, Jena had immediately clashed with Mother (no surprise there), becoming easily exasperated with her eccentric star's theatrical demands. The talented young woman was ready to quit, when I took her aside.

"Look," I said gently, "I understand that you're frustrated, stuck in this hick town dealing with a wild woman . . . and, for you, this is just a stepping stone to better things." I paused, then went on. "But if you can't handle *her,* how are you going to manage Hollywood actors with much bigger egos, and who have the power to fire you?"

Jena studied my face. "What should I do? Ignore her?"

I laughed once. "Oh, no. That'll only makes things worse. Think of her as a child. If you want her to do something, you have to cajole, flatter, and manipulate."

"Thank you."

"You're welcome."

Smooth sailing ever since.

Phil was asking, "Anybody got an antacid?"

I could tell by the melted butter stains on his shirt that he'd partaken of the fried delight while waiting for us. Probably not that many fried butter stands in LA.

Mother, who always carried a small pharmacy in her purse, obliged, and Phil popped the pill in his mouth and swallowed sans liquid.

Mother turned to Jena. "How do I look, dear?"

"You look lovely, Mrs. Borne."

"More powder?"

"Your skin is perfect."

"Too much rouge?"

"Just the right amount."

"Perhaps a different shade of lipstick?"

"That one complements you well. You look ten years younger. Twenty."

Mother beamed. "Thank *you,* my dear! What a lovely young professional woman you are."

And I winked at Jena, and she winked back, as Mother turned her attention to Phil.

"What's on the call sheet today, dah-ling?"

His wince was barely perceptible. "I've got several vendors already lined up for you to visit."

"I have pages?" Mother asked officiously.

Sorry to disappoint, but most reality shows are at least loosely scripted, a process made looser by Mother, since she often ignored the "pages" she was demanding.

Phil shook his head. "This will be improvised."

"But the play is the thing!"

I said, "Mother, it's like Second City—'something wonderful right away.' You'll be fine."

"Well, obviously, dear—but what about *you?* You have no training!"

Phil waved that off. "You and Brandy won't even be miked."

Which suited me fine—I hated wearing that battery pack on my fanny with its cold cord snaked up my shirt.

Mother frowned. "Not even a *lavalier?*"

"No."

"Well . . . what will I say? What is my motivation? One can't improvise properly without a premise from which to create."

Phil said, "Your motivation is to get this pilot in the can. The premise is you're shopping."

"For what? Antiques? Collectibles? Am I to bargain like an Arab trader? Meaning no ethnic slur. Am I to introduce myself as the star of our new show? I can't build a house without bricks, man!"

I snorted. "I'm sure you'll think of something, Mother."

Phil sighed. "What you say really doesn't matter, Mrs. Borne."

"Well, *of course* it matters!" Mother huffed. "We're establishing my character here! Not to mention there will be *lip-readers* in our viewing audience."

The producer/director/cameraman was on the verge of losing his laid-back composure—and I'm sure the one-fourth pound of butter in his stomach was no help.

Jena touched Mother's arm. "Vivian . . . just be your wonderful, charming, vivacious self."

That girl would go far in Hollywood.

Mother beamed. "Well, *that* I can do, dear! Standing on my head."

And she could, too. Stand on her head.

Mother faced Phil, a thoughtful finger to her cheek. "For purposes of improv, shall we say I am browsing, on the prowl for new items for our shop?"

"Let's," Phil said.

Followed by Phil and Jena, Mother and I strolled down a blacktop path between rows of facing vendors, stopping at one selling linens in a tent, and another hawking antique dishes on a table under the sun. Phil seemed pleased with the shot he got of Mother and me looking over merchandise, chatting about potential buys. True, Mother was a tad over-the-top, but no more than usual.

But when we visited the last pre-set-up vendor selling nautical curiosities, trouble arose between the dealer, one Mr. Snodgrass, and Mother.

Mr. Snodgrass lived down the block from us, and I'd known him since I was in elementary school. Back then, he'd often yell at me for taking a shortcut through his perfectly manicured lawn.

And his name really was Snodgrass—I didn't change it to an appropriate echo, Charles Dickens–style, though I believe his name did have a lot to do with his lifelong obsession with grass (the green kind).

Anyway, Phil had just finished shooting a little segment of Mother and me picking out an old brass clinometer (a navigational instrument used for recording a ship's sideways tilt) when Mother handed the slice-of-pie-shaped antique back to the dealer.

"I thought you were buying this, Mrs. Borne," Mr. Snodgrass said, somewhat flummoxed. "I've already rung it up."

He'd been old even back when I was in the third grade; these were the same rheumy eyes and bulbous nose, the lines between his bushy eyebrows and around his mouth deeply grooved from years of yelling, "Stay off my grass!"

Mother said, "Then after I've paid for it, I'll be returning it for a refund." She leaned forward and almost whispered: "We really have no use for such an item in our shop—it's not like we have a nautical room."

The man's face reddened. "All sales are final, Vivian."

Mother put hands on hips; her feet were already dug in. "I hate to quarrel with a dear old neighbor like you, Rodney . . ."

Rodney Snodgrass. I wouldn't kid you.

". . . and I *do* hate to get you on a technicality, but it's not a sale until I actually *give* you the money."

Mr. Snodgrass had the expression of a bull in an old cartoon, seeing a red cape—you know, right before steam comes out its nostrils and ears.

Having seen this particular cartoon a number of times, I turned to Phil and whispered: "Need me anymore?"

"No," he smiled weakly. "Brandy Borne, you're wrapped."

That was TV talk meaning I was finished for the shoot —the whole darn pilot. Free at last, great God almighty, free at last. . . .

I patted his arm. "Safe trip back to LA."

"Wish us luck selling this thing."

I raised a finger. "Be careful what you wish for."

After smiling a good-bye to Jena, I made my escape. Mother never missed me. Anyway, there was a purchase I wanted to make. It wasn't for the shop, but my stomach.

I made a beeline back to the fried butter stand.

Yes, I knew it wasn't good for me. That it was impossible to look pretty or dignified or to maintain any other respectable state of human appearance while eating a fried stick of butter.

Which is why I retreated with my treat behind the stand, to an old oak tree, where I sat, Indian-style, with plenty of napkins in my lap.

I was about to bite into the hot, gooey confection, when another carnival-food addict—also seeking cover—rounded the tree.

Caught yellow-handed, we both laughed.

"What would your wife say?" I asked.

"What would the stockholders say?" Wes Sinclair responded. He wore a pale yellow polo shirt, tan Bermuda shorts, and expensive slip-on shoes, sans socks.

I laughed again (more of a snort). "I can practically hear the market price dropping on your company."

He settled next to me in the grass, a literal wealth of Serenity money and history right next to me, eating fried butter.

Wesley Sinclair III was a fourth generation blueblood, or anyway his was as blue as blood got in Serenity, Iowa. His great granddaddy had founded the corn processing plant south of town, which recently became a Fortune 500 company (493, but who's counting?) under Wesley's savvy leadership, the thirty-two year old having taken over as CEO after his father's death.

Wes and I were the same age, and had dated a few times at community college after his partying too much got him flunked out freshman year at Columbia University. He came to his senses after his sophomore year and went back to Columbia, graduating with honors.

With that easy manner and a great sense of humor, and with his reddish-brown hair, boyish face, and well-toned body, Wes was a guy I could have easily fallen for. But back then, he had a self-destructive recklessness that made me nervous, the only part of him that said "rich kid"—

that he was somebody untouchable from harm. Besides, I never would have been accepted by his (obviously) socially prominent parents.

He was saying, "Haven't seen you around much, since you got back in town."

"That's because you and Vanessa don't eat at McDonald's and shop at Walmart."

Vanessa was the sorority beauty he'd met at Columbia and married upon graduation.

"Sometimes we do," Wes said with a grin. "Vannie and I don't *always* eat at the club, you know." He meant the country club, where they didn't serve fried butter, which was maybe why he bit so greedily into his, squirting himself and me with the melted liquid.

"Hey!" I said, laughing but a little irritated. "This was a spotless shirt."

"*Not anymore,*" he said in an Inspector Clouseau accent. We'd gone to a couple of those movies together, back in the day.

Trying not to laugh, I slugged him in the arm.

Rubbing the spot, pretending it hurt, he said, "So send me the dry-cleaning bill."

"Don't think I won't. Some of us aren't independently wealthy."

"Low blow. Aren't you making any money from those books of yours?"

"Enough to afford a stick of fried butter."

We ate for a moment in silence. Eating fried butter takes concentration.

Then, Wes, wiping his glistening chin, said, "What's this I hear about you dating Tony Cassato, now that he's back in town?"

"We'd just started dating before he suddenly left," I said with a shrug. "We're kind of picking up the pieces."

I didn't care to add anything more—early days for Tony and me, after our time apart.

Wes was saying, "Well, that's great. That's fine. Tony's a good man."

"Yes he is."

"Serenity is lucky to have him back on the force, even if he's no longer chief of police. Is it true he was in Witness Protection for a while?"

I nodded.

"Rumor is he testified against some mobsters in New Jersey, where he's from," he said, watching me carefully. "And there's a really crazy rumor that your mother had something to do with resolving his differences with . . . I mean, it's nutty, but . . . some godfather back there? I mean, come on—that's crazy, right?"

"Sure is." See *Antiques Con.*

"So . . ." Wes gave me a sly sideways smile. ". . . Will his presence cut down on the murders you and your mother have been getting involved in? *Solving?* I read the *Sentinel.*"

I gave him an embarrassed smile. "Honestly, it's not our fault. It's ridiculous, isn't it? I mean, what are the odds that a town our size has had so many, uh . . ."

"Murders? Pretty outrageous."

"So it's gotta end some time, right?"

He grinned. "If not, you should contact Guinness."

We fell silent for a few moments. Maybe we were both thinking about how our lives might have been different if our casual dating in community college days had become serious. Of course, I wouldn't change anything, not for all the tea in China or Wes Sinclair's money. My marriage had gone awry, but my ex and I had a great son, Jake, who means everything to me.

Maybe Wes had gone through similar calculations, because he sighed and said, "Well, I should go find Vanessa."

"And I need to locate Mother."

"Probably shouldn't have seconds on fried butter."

"Probably not. Unless you've got a defibrillator handy."

He chuckled and stood, offering me a hand, which I took. But my legs had gone numb and tingly from their crossed position, and as I rose I fell against him, and he grabbed me, and I grabbed him, both of us laughing, and then a woman asked, "Having fun?"

A woman named Vanessa Sinclair.

The dark-haired beauty stood with hands on hips, wearing a pink floral sundress more befitting an afternoon wedding than down-home swap meet.

Having regained my balance, I said, "Oh, hello. We were just—"

"I have *eyes*," she snapped, her anger shimmering like heat off asphalt.

Wes spread his hands. "Honey, you remember Brandy. We're old friends from community college."

"Hey," I said, wiping butter off my hands with a paper napkin, "this is innocent."

"I'll just bet it is," she said with a sneer, distorting her pretty features. She was talking to me, but looking at Wes.

I took a step forward and said, "Honestly, Vanessa, I lost my balance and fell—"

"Into my husband's arms!"

I shut my trap.

Vanessa turned on her husband. "Isn't it enough that I joined your stupid *bridge* club? How would you like me to *quit?*"

That was a strange threat—is that where an angry wife drew the battle line? Over a card game?

She poked his chest with a French-manicured finger. "This is the *last time* you embarrass me in public, Wesley Sinclair the *Third*. Do it again, and I *promise* you, you'll regret it!"

And Vanessa wheeled in her jewel-encrusted sandals, and strode off.

Wes, chagrined, ashen, turned to me. "I'm . . . I'm so sorry, Brandy. You didn't deserve that."

"Neither did you." I looked over his shoulder at the small crowd that had gathered. "*All over, folks!* Nothin' more to see here."

And the gawkers dispersed, exchanging frowns and muttering comments.

"Thank you for standing up for me," Wes said.

"For us," I said, and shrugged. "Anyway, so she doesn't want to be in your bridge club. So what? Mother tried to teach me that game, but it was way too hard."

He sighed. "It's not that. Vanessa *enjoys* the club. It's a social thing."

Status, he meant. Now maybe I understood the threat.

"That's Vanessa all over," he said, shaking his head. "Funny thing is, by the time we get home, she'll have forgotten all about this."

I doubted that; the woman seemed pretty po'd.

He lowered his voice. "She's under a lot of stress lately. You'll have to forgive her."

"Pretty stressful existence, huh? Being rich and beautiful." My response came out cattier than I meant it to.

"No, it's . . ." We were still standing under that tree, alone at the busy swap meet. Very softly, he said, "Brandy, we're trying to start a family, and it's . . . tough going."

"Oh. I'm sorry. It's none of my business. Had no idea."

I don't know why I said that. Everyone in town knew, thanks to certain big-mouth gossips—one of whom lived in the same house as me.

He went on, very quietly, almost inaudible. "She's been taking a lot of hormone pills, and, well, let's just say . . . just about *anything* sets her off."

I was waving both hands at him, like I was guiding somebody backing up a car to stop. "Really, Wes. You don't have to explain. . . ."

"But you *deserve* an explanation." He took my hand. "We've been friends a long time, Brandy, and that means a lot to me."

"*Really?*" It just came out. I mean, I already had a boyfriend. But not a boyfriend who was maybe the richest man in town.

"If it weren't for you, I . . . I wouldn't have gone back to Columbia."

I smirked. "You saw yourself stuck here in Serenity, with some girl from the community college, you mean."

"Don't be silly. Don't you remember? It was *you* who told me to get my act together." He took my hand and squeezed it. "That night you read me the riot act? Remember?"

I frowned. "Uh . . . over shots at the Brew?"

He nodded.

"I kinda remember. Sorta kinda. Maybe."

Suddenly embarrassed, Wes released my hand. "Well, I better go find Vanessa."

"Good luck," I said.

After he'd gone, I sat back down in the grass, mulling the unpleasant scene his wife had made.

Was there something different I could have done? Maybe reached out for that tree, caught myself, and not tumble into Wes's arms? I hadn't done that on purpose.

Had I?

Either way, I figured Vanessa would have been furious; just seeing us together would have been enough.

And I had another strong feeling—that her promise to Wes that "he would regret it," sounded more like a threat.

Or maybe it *was* a promise. . . .

A Trash 'n' Treasures Tip

At a swap meet, you can find everything and anything under the summer sun—from antiques to auto parts, household cleaners to clothing, darning needles to diapers. One vendor was doing brisk business selling discounted male enhancement drugs before the swap meet association shut him down, making him dysfunctional.

Chapter Two

Kiss of Death

(In the game of bridge, a score of minus 200.)

I wandered the swap meet vendors looking for Mother, and finally found her in a stall buying a book—the *Better Homes and Gardens Blender Cook Book*, its front copy promising "Tasty blender recipes for every course." Circa early 1970s, I guessed, judging by the greenish-tinged cover photos of unappetizing dishes. Sickening! Hilarious!

Imagine—an entire meal made easy in that wonderful glass gizmo with sharp blades, helping propel a lucky lady libber out of the confines of her kitchen and into a meaningful (if low-paying) career. I hoped Mother was planning on selling the cookbook at the shop, as opposed to trying the recipes out on me.

Note to self: hide the blender.

Mother, laden with plastic-bagged finds, asked, "Dear, where have you been off to?"

"Can I have an antacid?"

"*May* I have an antacid, and I gave the last one to Phillip. Are you all right, child? Your face looks as green as this book cover."

"Don't feel so good." And it wasn't just that cookbook cover.

Her concerned expression turned accusatory. "Don't tell me . . . you ate that disgusting *fried butter*, didn't you? For shame."

"Okay, I won't tell you."

She sighed. "Come along, dear. It's time we got back to the shop, anyway. Don't want to leave G.I. Joe in charge for too long. Besides, my bunions are killing me."

Mother also had corns and tarsal tunnel syndrome.

I relieved her of some of the bags, and we made our way slowly through the crowd toward the car-show area, to retrieve our Caddy.

Our San Diego day had disappeared, replaced by we-have-a-problem Houston: hot and humid. Which only added to my butter-churning discomfort. And at the next plastic-lined trash receptacle, I made an undignified deposit, by way of saying adieu to the fried confection.

"I wonder, dear," Mother said, with a minimum of *I told you so* in her tone, "if you'll remember this unfortunate aftermath the next time we encounter a fried butter stand?"

Having cleared the immediate vicinity of

shoppers, I straightened in embarrassed relief. "I wonder, too," I admitted.

The car show was winding down, the crowd having thinned due to the sudden heat. But one hardy person was hovering around our convertible, a middle-aged man with obviously dyed brown hair, his shirt and jeans too tight, as he tried with scant success to hold on to his youth.

"This baby yours?" he asked.

"Yes, indeedy," Mother said, smiling proudly. "Isn't she a beaut?"

"Certainly is. Classic lines. Would you consider an offer?"

Mother and I answered at the same time: "Yes!" (me), "No!" (her).

"Well, I'm having trouble sorting through those mixed signals," he said. "Which is it, girls?"

"No," Mother said emphatically.

I touched her arm. "Now, wait a second—let's at least hear what the gentleman is offering."

"Well," Mother replied, doubtfully, "I imagine that couldn't hurt. . . ."

He gave the car a careful look, walking around it, head cocked this way and that, rubbing his chin, then finally returned to say, "Five thousand."

"Pish-posh!" Mother pish-poshed. "She's worth *three* times that, anyway!"

The man shrugged, reached into a pants pocket and withdrew a business card, then handed it to Mother.

"Offer stands, should you change your mind . . . unless I find a comparable one elsewhere, that is. . . . Ladies."

And with a little salute, he walked away.

I turned to Mother. "You *know* we can't keep the car. Between high insurance and terrible mileage, it's costing us a small fortune."

She frowned. "Dear, I don't entirely disagree. But I'm not going to give it away—*especially* to a complete stranger. If I ever sell, I have to *know* that person will love her as much as I do."

"We are talking about a *car*, right? He wasn't offering to take me off your hands."

Mother pursed her lips. "It's not just *any* car . . . but a gift from . . ." She lowered her voice. ". . . a very special admirer."

A very special admirer who happened to be the semi-retired godfather of New Jersey, in return for a favor she'd done him. Yes, *that* kind of godfather (*Antiques Con*).

I sighed. "All right, Mother. I give up . . . for now. But that buggy burns gas like, like . . ."

"Like someone who eats fried butter?"

I knew better than to try topping that one.

We began piling the packages in back, with me getting behind the wheel to drive us back to the shop . . .

. . . where a police car was parked out front.

"Oh, dear," Mother said, fingertips to her lips. "We really shouldn't have dawdled. Appears Joe has gotten himself in a fix."

How could he have managed that? We hadn't been gone long, and business would be slow the afternoon of the swap meet. . . .

I parked behind the squad car, hopped out, and hurried up the sidewalk and into the house, half-expecting to find Joe handcuffed by the police, summoned by some hysterical customer who had been ordered to attention or about-face or something.

But my friend stood casually behind the cash register, trading military lingo with a uniformed police officer on the other side of the counter.

Patrolman Tony Cassato was saying, "Heard he'll be retiring to Camp Living Room, before long."

In his midforties, Tony was barrel-chested, with a square jaw, bulbous nose, and steely eyes, handsome in a man's man kind of way. Also a woman's man kind of way, if I'm the woman.

"A two-digit midget," Joe said with a nod.

At my sudden, wild-eyed entrance, both men looked at me quizzically.

Straightening, Tony asked, "Anything wrong, Brandy?"

Frozen in the doorway, I replied, "That's what I'd like to know."

Mother, on my heels, bumped into me.

"Everything . . . all . . . *right?*" she asked, out of breath.

Tony gestured with a big paw. "Everything's fine. I just stopped by to ask how the filming went."

Brightening, Mother said, "The pilot is wrapped, as we say in the biz. Now all we can do is hurry up and wait."

Joe said, "That's what they say in *my* biz."

I bent down and picked up Sushi, who had come trotting out from her bed behind the counter.

Joe, gathering his duffel bag, said, "Well, guess I'll be bookin' it. You Bornes need backup again, just call."

"Just a moment, Joseph," Mother said.

While she raided the till to pay our military-minded helper, Tony took my elbow and guided me into the parlor, which was vacant of customers at the moment.

"How about dinner?" he asked, gazing down easily from his six-foot frame. "The Sombrero, maybe?"

They had the *best* guacamole. "Good choice," I said, scratching the head of the dog in my arms. "When's your shift over?"

"Seven. Pick you up at home?"

I nodded. "Any word on your chief of police application?"

After Tony's sudden departure last year, Brian Lawson had been installed as interim chief, which gave the younger man the inside track. And to complicate matters, Brian was my former boyfriend. To further complicate them, Tony (as you may recall) was my current one.

Tony shook his head. "Won't know until the end of the month."

"How *are* you and the interim chief getting along?"

Tony shrugged. "We try to keep out of each other's way. We're professionals."

"But the men are used to taking orders from you."

Another shrug. "It can be awkward . . . but

not really a problem. I do my best to stay out of the middle."

Sushi, bored with the scratching, squirmed out of my arms, then trotted out of the parlor, passing Mother who was entering.

"Dear," she said, "I hate to break up your little tête-à-tête . . . but we do have boxes to unpack."

Tony touched my arm, whispered, "See you later."

"Can't wait."

I walked him to the door, almost traded kisses but settled on knowing smiles instead. Then Tony was gone and I was joining Mother by the counter where she was using a box cutter to open the considerably larger of two cartons.

"What's in those?" I asked.

"Swag, dear."

"Like in curtains?" Our shop windows already had drapes.

"Not *that* kind of swag! These are T-shirts to sell when our show goes on the air."

She held one up, displaying the front: I ♥ VIVIAN, and on the back ANTIQUES SLEUTHS.

"Mother," I said, wide-eyed, "what if the show *doesn't* go on the air? It's just a pilot! Then we're stuck with a bunch of shirts."

She put hands on hips and raised her chin. "Dear, that's just the kind of negative attitude that keeps you from achieving your true potential."

My response was a witty grunt. I nodded to the smaller box. "And what's in there? Vivian and Brandy bobbleheads?"

The slightly magnified eyes behind the lenses grew even larger. "No, but that *is* a fine idea! *Now* you're thinking! Uh, that smaller box contains *your* T-shirts."

I lifted an eyebrow. "Obviously you're assuming I'll sell less shirts than you."

"I'm just being realistic, dear. Television is about personalities! And I *have* one."

I reared back as if just hit by a cream pie.

Before I could recover, the phone rang on the counter. I answered it, forcing my voice into pleasantness. "Trash 'n' Treasures . . ."

"Brandy? This is Vanessa."

Oh, crap! Vanessa as in Mrs. Wesley Sinclair III.

In a rush of words, I said, "Vanessa, I want to apologize again for—"

"Brandy, I'm calling *you* to ask if you'll forgive *me* for my rude behavior today."

Wait, what?

She went on, "I was *way* out of line. Wes explained the whole thing to me." She paused. "I was wondering if you could come over to our house. . . ."

I didn't have the time or the wardrobe for that. "Vanessa, really, you don't need to apologize in person or anything . . ."

"No, no, that's not it. I have some collectibles that you might be interested in for your shop. You could buy them or I could even consign them. Just some things that need to go."

"What are they?"

"Old beer signs, mostly—some going back to

the nineteen-fifties. I understand a few of these are really quite rare."

"Well, yes, I am interested. We could *use* some man-type stuff in the shop."

"Great! Is there any chance you could come over now? You know where we live?"

"Oh, sure, of course." The renovation of the Sinclair homestead had been a topic of town gossip for years.

"See you soon," Vanessa said cheerfully, ending the call.

Mother, her interest piqued by hearing my end of the conversation, sidled over like a cat sensing a mouse. "Now whatever was that about?"

"Just a minor misunderstanding," I said. And, side-stepping the swap meet incident, I said, "Vanessa Sinclair wants to sell us some vintage beer signs."

"Whoa!" Mother's eyebrows climbed above her large glasses, threatening her hairline. "*Voon*-der-bar! Rich folks have high-end trinkets! I'll get my purse."

I held up a *stop* hand. "Aren't you forgetting that someone needs to watch the store? Joe is off on maneuvers."

Mother frowned. "Oh, horse doodle! I've always wanted to see the interior of that house."

The Sinclair place was one of the few interesting homes in town she hadn't managed to invade. But so far, she hadn't been able to finagle her way inside.

Her usual ploy was to ring the doorbell collecting for some charity, pretending to feel faint before asking to come in for a glass of water. But either the Sinclairs had never been at home for her road-show production, or perhaps they had seen who was loitering on their doorstep.

I patted Mother's arm. "Look, I'll go over there now and take photos of the beer signs, then come back so we can research their value on the Internet. *Then* . . . after the shop closes . . . we'll go back out there together, and make Vanessa an offer."

Mother clapped her hands. "Goody goody!" she sang, adding a few more of the Johnny Mercer lyrics, first pointing to me, then to herself.

Oh brother.

With Mother appeased, I headed out to the Caddy.

One might assume that Wes and Vanessa, with their considerable wealth, would live in a modern mansion in the most exclusive area of Serenity. But they didn't—Wes had inherited his grandfather's Mulberry Avenue home, known as Sinclair House. Not that the homestead was anything to sniff at—the three-story, beige-brick French provincial had once been the grandest residence on that side of town, dwarfing its much more modest neighbors.

As I mentioned, Sinclair House had been a topic of town gossip, because Wes and (really) Vanessa—evidently dissatisfied with the home's lack of twenty-first century sprawl—had spent a fortune on new additions. And these additions came at the expense of the neighbors on either side of their property.

Vanessa made the two owners offers they couldn't refuse, particularly with the latest Sinclair wings breathing down on them, and then promptly tore those houses down.

Which was a shame, really, because both were fine architectural examples of the Prairie School style, designed by Walter Burley Griffin in the 1930s. Their destruction not only infuriated Mother and her cronies at the Historical Preservation Society, but neighbors across the street, who had to put up with ongoing construction noise and dust and traffic backup.

But all was quiet at the moment on Mulberry Avenue, Vanessa at least temporarily sated by her latest expansion.

I pulled the Caddy into their driveway, passing beneath a pretentiously ornate black wrought-iron archway with a large *S,* then along a circular drive and up to the pillared porch.

Two huge Grecian urns overflowing with flowers stood on either side of the front door like sentries. I located the doorbell and pressed it.

Chimes sounded like Big Ben, and I repressed an amused smirk, in case I was being watched from a window.

Then the mistress of the mansion opened the door, and greeted me warmly. "Brandy! Thanks for coming by on such short notice."

She had changed out of the pink floral sundress into something more casual—at least her idea of more casual: a silk yellow blouse, white dress slacks, and black flats. An ensemble retailing at around a cool thousand.

"No problem," I said, slipping past her as she held the door open.

Her perfume was Dior—too expensive for my pocketbook, but I recognized it from when I rubbed myself with a sample insert from *Vogue* magazine.

I followed Vanessa through the huge black-and-white marbled entryway, skirting a center mahogany table, its gleaming top home to a large blue-and-white Chinese vase with a beautifully arranged assortment of fresh flowers.

As we passed the lavish living room, I paused for a look. The vast room, with its eclectic, expensive furnishings, could rival any movie star's Beverly Hills mansion.

"Lovely," I said. "Did you do the decorating yourself?"

"Yes," she said with a proud little smile. "If I love it and I want it, I get it."

She said this lightly, jokingly, but I sensed it was her credo in life.

We walked on, passing a formal dining room with a sparkling chandelier and expensive oriental rug, into a kitchen as big as our living room. Bigger.

The kitchen was one of the new additions. It had a slightly Southwestern feel with its terra cotta–tiled floor, colorful wall tiles, and bright floral curtains. A center island had its own sink and oven, over which hung copper pans of every size and style.

I walked over to the breakfast nook that looked out over a swimming pool and tennis court.

"You're just a nine-hole golf course short of a country club," I kidded.

Behind me Vanessa, stone serious, said, "Funny you should mention that—I'm negotiating with the people in back of us. Shall we take the elevator?"

"There's an elevator?"

She gestured with a hand. "Over there—so much easier for older relatives and friends . . . and the caterers, when we entertain downstairs."

In a corner of the kitchen, we took the elevator to the lower level, stepping off into another gigantic room, this one filled with every kind of home entertainment imaginable: huge wall-mounted TV, pool table, vintage pinball machines, an old jukebox, as well as a well-stocked wet bar.

Party Central!

Behind the bar was an etched mirror of a nude woman with flowing long hair, which, along with the black walls and blood-red carpet, gave the room a slightly disturbing San Francisco bordello feel.

Vanessa asked, "Would you like to see our latest acquisition?"

"Sure." Nothing would surprise me now. Monorail? Teleporter?

She walked me over to a door, and we entered a darkened room.

She flicked on the lights.

"You have your own movie theater!" I gasped.

"Uh-huh. Like it?"

What was not to like? The huge silver screen, the red theater curtains, ceiling-mounted projector, wall-mounted speakers fore and aft, recliner-like theater seats on graduated risers, the movie-reel print carpet . . . and the midnight-blue ceiling even had twinkling electric stars. . . .

It's good to be the king. And queen.

Not quite knowing what to say, I blurted, "You certainly have everything."

"No one does, really," she said with a wistful shrug, but didn't elaborate.

Filling the awkward silence, I asked, "Where are the beer signs? Not that I expected them in here . . ."

"Oh. Yes. Wes's man cave. Follow me."

Ah, the mystique of a male's private domain.

We went through a door next to the bar into a "cave" that didn't really contain extravagances on the order of the rest of the house, but was undeniably comfortable-looking. A brown leather couch and matching recliner were positioned in the center of the room in front of a medium-size flat-screen TV on a stand. To the left a large, round oak table with four chairs, and to the right were various storage cabinets. The carpet was an old-fashioned rust-colored shag.

The focal point of the room was a brick fireplace with wide mantel, on which rested a collection of beer steins made of porcelain or pewter, each depicting different woodland scenes, like running stags or grazing boars.

On the wall surrounding the fireplace hung the vintage neon beer signs. While most were familiar even to a non-beer aficionado like me (Budweiser, Pabst Blue Ribbon, Miller High Life), others seemed rather obscure (Kronenbourg, Schoenling, Almus).

Vanessa said, "Some of these go back to Wes's Columbia days, when he was decorating his frat room at Delta Sigma. Turned into a collection."

Those were memories that went way back. "You're sure he wants to sell them?"

She nodded. "He's into buying autographed sports jerseys now—here, let me get something to show you. . . ."

While I took in the beer signs, Vanessa walked away for a moment, then returned with a large frame, turning it toward me so I could see the stretched and mounted shirt under the glass.

"This was Mickey Mantle's," she said, pointing to the signature below the familiar New York Yankees' logo.

"Wow," I said. "That *is* impressive."

She made a *you're telling me* face. "These frames take up a lot of wall space. Wes also has jerseys from DiMaggio, Ted Williams, and Barry Bonds."

"Must've cost a lot," I said stupidly, feeling like a lowly flea in the company of a magnificent ant.

Her eyebrows went up and down. "You don't *want* to know. Anyway, I told him the beer collection had to go."

I held up a cautionary palm. "And Wes agreed? Just . . . I want to make *sure.* . . ."

When I was in high school, Mother sold my collection of Barbie dolls without telling me, and I've never forgiven her. (Number #317 on the list.)

Vanessa nodded. "Reluctantly, I'll admit. But even he says it's time to let them go." She cocked her head. "We *could* reach him on his cell, if you like—he's at his office, catching up on some work."

"No, no, no," I responded quickly, not wanting to give the impression that I didn't trust her. "Anyway," I added, "it's a moot point till we come to terms on a price."

For the next five minutes or so I used my digital camera and snapped the beer signs both from a distance and up close. Then I told Vanessa I'd be back with Mother after five, and we'd make her an offer.

Like the ones she'd made her neighbors, hopefully ours would be one she couldn't refuse.

Vanessa led me through a man cave door into the garage, where a white Mercedes minivan was parked.

"When you come back, go on in through the garage," she instructed. "I'll have it open."

We walked around to the front of the house where my Caddy was parked.

"Great wheels!" she said. Finally I'd managed to impress her.

"Thanks. But, really, it's Mother's."

"You know . . . I heard a strange rumor about that car."

"Oh?"

"That it belonged to a godfather. You know . . . the Sopranos kind?"

"Well, isn't that ridiculous?" I said pleasantly. Mother was such a blabbermouth.

"Even *more* so, since what people are saying is that your mother got this 'godfather' to cancel a, uh, *contract* on Tony Cassato . . . and that's how our ex-chief of police was able to come back."

"So absurd." *Antiques Con* wasn't out yet.

She touched my arm, smiling a little. "I guess you're glad he's back. If you don't mind my saying."

I smiled back. "I am. And I don't."

"You know, I really do admire you, Brandy." Darned if she didn't seem to mean it.

"Really? Why is that?"

She smiled again, shrugged a little. "Takes a special kind of person to be a surrogate mother for her best friend."

Vanessa was referring to the baby I carried last year for my BFF Tina and her husband Kevin—Tina hadn't been able to conceive after her bout with cancer.

"Was that . . . difficult for you?" she asked.

"Well, pregnancy is no picnic."

"I mean . . . giving up the baby."

"Well . . . yes," I admitted.

Which was why I had avoided seeing their baby much.

She said, "I could use a friend like you."

I laughed nervously. "Hope you're not in the market for a surrogate . . . 'cause that's a definite been-there, done-that kind of deal."

She laughed just as nervously. "Goodness, no. I still have options open."

I turned a hand over. "Well, seriously . . . if those options don't pan out, I could give you the name of the doctor who—"

"I have my *own* specialists," she responded sharply.

I'd overstepped with my new friend. "Oh, sure . . . of course you have."

Her voice softened. "But . . . thank you, anyway, Brandy."

"Okay." I shrugged. Grinned. "Well, I guess I'll head back and show Mother the photos. Hit the Internet. See you a little after five."

At the shop, I transferred the photos to the computer, and for the next hour, I googled similar beer signs, Mother hovering over my shoulder.

Most examples had a value ranging from four to five hundred dollars, but the sign from France—Kronenbourg 1664—was rare. I found only one for sale on eBay.

"It's worth thousands," Mother said excitedly.

"Doesn't mean anyone's going to *pay* that much. Prices are always inflated on eBay. And with only one of 'em posted, we don't have enough to go on."

Mother nodded. "You're right, dear. On *Pawn*

Stars, the customers are *always* wanting eBay prices—makes The Old Man furious!"

The bell above the shop door tinkled, and a rumpled little guy in his sixties came in wearing a wrinkled shirt and slacks. Perhaps five foot two, with wispy white hair, he wore old-fashioned adhesive-repaired plastic-framed thick-lensed glasses that diminished his eyes to raisins.

I knew him only as Dumpster Dan the Pop-bottle Man (as kids had for years taunted him). He was a fixture around town, cheerfully pushing a shopping cart through alleyways, sifting through Dumpsters for discarded bottles and cans for return deposit. Mother told me he'd once been a brilliant research chemist at Sinclair Consolidated, but at some point had had a nervous breakdown.

"Well, Dan," Mother said, greeting him, "and how are we faring on our rummage quest today?"

He came toward the counter with a little spring in his step. "Fine, Mrs. Borne, just fine."

"Oh, Dan, *Vivian*, please."

The man smiled shyly, showing perfect, perfectly yellowed teeth. "Vivian, you're kind."

"I strive, dear, I strive. Now, what can I do ya for?"

Dan was carrying a dirty, frayed-cloth shopping bag, and he reached into it. "I can do something for you. Here's a treasure I found in the trash that I think you might be interested in."

"What is it?" Mother asked excitedly. She loved surprises and was a grab-bag aficionado.

He placed a porcelain floral teapot on the counter.

Mother picked it up. "Yes, this *is* lovely," she said, studying the pot. "But Dan, dear, besides having no lid, I'm afraid there's no value . . . you see, it's cracked. A hairline, but a crack."

The man leaned forward. "Oh . . . I didn't *notice* that."

That I could understand, with those glasses.

"You know," I interjected, "even as is, it would be perfect for holding pens here on the counter . . . don't you think, Mother?"

"Why, uh . . . yes, yes, dear, I agree. Just what we were looking for, now that you mention it."

"Would you take four dollars for it?" I asked Dan.

His raisin eyes grew grape-size. "Four dollars!"

"All right, five."

"Huh? Oh, yes! Absolutely!"

And I fished in the change drawer and withdrew a fin, as we detectives call a five-spot.

As a beaming Dumpster Dan departed, Mother turned to me. "That was a good deed, dear."

"Hmmm. I hope we didn't just set a precedent with Dan that we'll come to regret."

Mother smiled. "Well, you know what they say . . . no good deed goes unpunished!"

I gathered the counter pens and put them in the teapot, which was so shallow that they all fell out. Punishment had come in a hurry.

At five, we closed up the shop, turning on the alarm; then Mother, Sushi, and I got into the Caddy at the curb, and soon were driving beneath the iron archway of Xanadu—me at the wheel, not Mother. Or Sushi.

"Now, let *me* do the negotiating, dear," Mother said.

To which I agreed: she was the consummate horse trader. No ancient Arab merchant in a bazaar stall was shrewder.

I stopped the Caddy in front of the opened garage, and we exited the car, me holding Sushi. I hoped bringing the little devil along with me would be all right with Vanessa. After all, with doggy, there's always a chance of doody.

Next to the white minivan was a pile of cardboard boxes and packing materials that Vanessa had gathered since my earlier visit.

We went through the door leading into the man cave, where the beer signs had been gathered on the large round oak table.

Mother, examining them, said excitedly, "These are even *better* than your photos, dear! Not to belittle your photographic skills."

"I'll see if I can find Vanessa."

The door to Party Central was open, but she wasn't in there, and I didn't feel I should take the elevator up and wander around, so I returned to Mother.

"I'm sure she'll be back soon," I said, and put Sushi down, trusting she'd stay out of trouble.

But the little mutt immediately disappeared behind the couch.

I went to fetch her, and said, "Oh!"

Mother asked, "Oh what, dear?"

"She's . . . she's already here . . ."

Vanessa, on her back, her beautiful dark hair caked with blood, stared at the ceiling with those violet eyes wide, yet seeing nothing.

A Trash 'n' Treasures Tip

When attending a swap meet, arrive early if you want a good parking place. One enterprising person I know used to park her car in a choice spot the day *before* and use a friend to take her home then back again. A word of warning: last year when I tried that, I got towed.

Chapter Three

Beer Card

(The seven of diamonds.)

While Mother used her cell phone to call the police, I went outside with Sushi to await their arrival, knowing full well that Vivian Borne would use the time to examine the body and crime scene.

I felt particularly shaken—not because I had any emotional feelings toward Vanessa, as I barely knew the woman. *But I had just been with her.* And she had been so friendly, and open, and . . . alive. It was an upsetting reminder of just how quickly a life could be snuffed out.

When, after only a few minutes, a siren-blaring squad car pulled into the drive, I was relieved to see Tony behind the wheel. That relief was undermined when I realized the officer beside him was Mia Cordona, with whom I'd had a rocky relationship of late.

Mia and I had been close childhood friends, but drifted apart over the years. I always sensed that Mia was disappointed in the direction my life had taken—or maybe that was indirection. And she was probably justified in feeling that way.

Tony reached me first, and that he had to hold back touching my arm or shoulder was apparent. I still wasn't used to seeing this former chief in a patrolman's uniform.

He said, "You're all right?"

"Much as can be expected. I was just *with* her. . . ."

"That's a tough one." He glanced around. "Where's Vivian?"

"Inside." I pointed to the door toward the rear of the garage. "The body's in Wes Sinclair's, uh, you know . . . man cave."

Mia—dark-haired and attractive, her uniform not entirely concealing her curves—said, "That mother of yours better not've disturbed the crime scene."

I shrugged. I suppose I could have been offended, but she had a point. And Mia was understandably even less enamored of Mother than of me. After all, Mother had once, however unintentionally, blown an undercover operation of hers.

"Go on, Mia," Tony said. "I'll be there in a moment."

As she disappeared into the garage, I said, "Tony, someone should find Wes. Vanessa told me earlier he was at his office."

Another nod. He seemed to be working hard

at being all business. "I'll send a patrol car over there with the news. Nasty way to hear, but beats a phone call. You gonna be all right here?"

"Sure."

Then he headed inside, too.

The paramedic truck arrived, its siren summoning any remaining neighbors out onto their porches to rubberneck and gawk. Human nature sometimes isn't my favorite thing. That was enough to send me retreating farther into the garage, where I confiscated two folding chairs for me and Mother, since she'd be ejected from the crime scene any moment now.

The door to the man cave opened and Mia shoved Mother forward, a little harder than I'd have liked, with a "And *stay* out!"

"*Well!*" Mother intoned, in her best Jack Benny huff. (Younger readers who don't know the name are free to google.) "I was *only* trying to help. How many murders have *you* solved, young lady?"

As two paramedics hurried past Mother toward Mia, still poised in the doorway, Mia said, "This time your help won't be needed!"

The paramedics froze, misunderstanding, and Mia shook her head, muttering, "Not you, sorry," and gestured for them to enter.

A disgruntled Mother strode over to me, gathering the shreds of her dignity about her like a tattered cloak. I was seated holding Sushi, and the spurned sleuth plopped into the chair next to me. "Those Keystone Kops will only contaminate the crime scene."

I said, "Mother, Tony's in charge. It'll be fine. It'll be very professional. We really *aren't* needed."

Mother responded to this with eye-rolling skepticism.

A second police car arrived, bringing a two-man forensics team, and Mother rose and pointed the way like Babe Ruth gesturing to the centerfield fence.

After they, too, had disappeared into the man cave with their equipment, Mother said, "She was still warm, dear. No rigor mortis. Couldn't have been dead more than a few hours." Brightening, she went on: "You may have been the last one to see her alive! Apart from the killer, that is."

"That's what worries me."

And I told her about the altercation at the swap meet, which could make me suspect numero uno.

"Dear," she said, with a dismissive wave, "I think it likely that a woman of Mrs. Sinclair's social standing had many others in her life with far more valid reasons to kill her than you. Yours was just the freshest."

"Oh, I'm *so* relieved," I said with a smirk. "But what do you mean by—"

I was interrupted by the squeal of a silver Jaguar pulling into the drive, weaving around the emergency vehicles as if they were cones in an obstacle course, finally coming to an abrupt, sod-tearing stop in the lawn.

Wes jumped out and ran toward the open garage. When he saw me, his wild eyes had an accusatory look.

Good Lord! Did *he* think *I* had killed Vanessa?

Stunned, I shook my head, and his expression softened into a putty mask.

"In there," I said, pointing.

He nodded, drew in a breath, then hurried in through the garage.

The coroner arrived, the caboose on this train, and Mother called out cheerfully.

"Well, hello there, Hector!"

The roly-poly, bald, bespectacled man winced, nearly dropping his black bag.

"Ah . . . hello, Vivian," he mumbled. Sighed. "Where is the victim?"

This time a beaming Mother pointed the way.

After he'd vanished within, Mother tsk-tsked. "Poor man is rounder than ever. Been dating the Hamilton widow, who's clearly been plying him with home cooking. Mark my words, some day that coroner's going to be his own best customer."

I turned to look at her. "Would it kill you to be a little more respectful?"

She raised her eyebrows. "Phrasing, dear. Anyway, don't blame me, blame Mrs. Hamilton."

"I'm not talking about being respectful to our coroner. His weight problem is his own . . . problem. I'm talking about a woman being killed."

"Dear, I understand the sentiment, but it's misplaced. Respect won't do Vanessa Sinclair any good, but catching her killer will. Well, actually, it won't, since she is, after all, dead. But her family and friends would appreciate seeing the perpetrator brought to justice, I'm sure."

Mother's phlegmatic reaction at a crime scene was not uncommon; on some level, I suppose it's a protective mechanism, because she's not really a cold person. But she does have a cold hard streak of Danish pragmatism.

Tony was coming toward us.

"Brian Lawson wants to see you down at the station," he said, lifting his cell phone.

Mother, who always relished the opportunity for a command performance with the interim chief, said, "We'd be most happy to comply."

"*Just* Brandy," Tony said, stone-faced.

"Well, *I* found Vanessa as much as my daughter did," a miffed Mother retorted. "It was a two-person catch!"

"Just Brandy . . . for now." Tony looked down at me. "That is, if you're up to it. Are you?"

"Not really," I sighed. "Couldn't it wait until tomorrow?" I was upset and tired—it had already been a long, trying, upsetting day.

Mother turned toward me. "Dear . . . as my associate in certain endeavors, you know very well the need for witnesses to report while the facts are fresh. Better to get it over with."

Tony touched my shoulder, breaking protocol. "Look, I'll tell Lawson you'll be at the station in an hour. Go home first. Get yourself together. Maybe have something to eat."

I nodded. "Sounds like a plan. Will you be at the interview?"

He shook his head. "I'll be tied up here for a while." He squeezed my shoulder before letting go. "You'll be fine. It's not like you're new to this kind of thing."

An unspoken *unfortunately* hung in the air.

I nodded numbly.

As Tony returned to the crime scene, Mother and I, Sushi in my arms, returned to the Caddy. After doing some fancy maneuvering around the various vehicles, I managed to get the big black boat out into the street.

On the few minutes of our drive home, Mother—Sushi on her lap now—gave me her crime-scene analysis. I did not protest—I'd been involved in enough of these incidents with Mother to know that (a) there was no stopping her, and (b) my own curiosity would get the better of me.

"She'd been hit on the head, dear," she said, as if reporting rain out a window. "Must have been quite a blow to produce all that blood. But I didn't see the weapon, so the killer must have taken it with him—or her."

"It's a big house. You only had a look at the man cave."

"Yes, but with the crime scene so near that open garage, it's more than likely he or she came in and went out that way. Now, I haven't searched the yard, but . . ."

"Maybe that's a job for the police."

I could feel Mother's indignant eyes upon me. At least she didn't say, "Perish the thought!"

What she did say was: "Very well, but the more you know before your interview at HQ, the better prepared you'll be to avoid any clever trap."

"Brian wouldn't do that to me."

"Wouldn't he?"

We had arrived home, an old-fashioned two-story white house with a wraparound front porch and stand-alone garage.

Mother was saying, "Perhaps it would be wise to call Wayne and have him by your side."

Mr. Ekhardt, our longtime lawyer, had himself been around a very long time. Nearly ninety, the semiretired criminal lawyer—who famously got a woman off for self-defense after shooting her philandering husband in the back five times—still hung on to a few clients like us. He'd been Mother's attorney long before I set foot on the planet.

I worked the key in the front door. "Mr. Ekhardt's probably already in bed."

I held the door open for Mother, while a lagging-behind Sushi was sniffing the lawn, checking for signs of canine trespassers. Satisfied her domain had not been befouled—or was that disappointed?—she trotted up the porch steps and inside.

I loved the smell of our house, which always seemed to fade a few seconds after entering; it wasn't pleasant or unpleasant . . . just the scent of *home*.

Mother, setting her purse on the Victorian table by the foyer, said, "Dear, why don't you have a little lie-down. I'll feed Sushi and give her her insulin injection. You can have a little something to eat after."

I said I couldn't possibly eat or sleep, though a hot bubble bath might help. Then I trudged upstairs.

Sometimes when I was little, particularly after

I'd been bad, Mother would lock herself in the bathroom for a long soak, and I would hear her cry out, "Calgon, take me away!" Just like in the old TV commercials. When I'd come back to live here after my divorce, I went looking for the bubble bath—turns out they still make it. So I tried the stuff. Relaxing, all right, but it never took me far *enough* away.

Half an hour later, feeling better if not exactly refreshed, I returned downstairs wearing a fresh pair of DKNY jeans and a floral silk Equipment blouse I'd snagged 75 percent off at Nordstrom Rack, my damp hair pulled back in a low ponytail.

Mother was in the kitchen, standing at the stove, stirring a pan, the aroma of Great Grandma Osher's Danish pea soup wafting toward me. Suddenly I felt like I could eat something.

About our kitchen—everything in it (except for the stove, fridge, and dishwasher) is 1950s vintage, purchased at garage sales and flea markets. Or almost everything. After Mother got shocked by an old waffle iron ("Yipe!"), we gave up the notion of being 100 percent authentic when it comes to small electrical appliances.

Mother pushed the step stool with its red vinyl seat over to the counter, and pulled out a recessed cutting board to use as a small table—just as she had done for little Brandy, who hadn't wanted to eat at the big table. Then she poured the steaming hearty soup into a green jadeite Fire-King bowl.

GULE AERTER (Yellow Pea Soup)

2 cups yellow split peas
1 quart chicken stock
1 pound chopped Canadian bacon
2 stalks chopped celery
3 chopped leeks
3 chopped carrots
3 chopped medium potatoes
1 chopped large onion
1 pound chopped Vienna sausages
salt and pepper to taste

Combine all ingredients in a large pot and simmer one hour.

Serves 4 hardy Danish men, or 6 dainty Danish women.

While Mother left me alone to slurp my soup with a red Bakelite-handled spoon, Sushi stood watch below, hoping for a bite of sausage (and, yes, her vigilance was rewarded).

Finished, I put the empty bowl in the sink and went to join Mother in the living room, where she was seated on our particularly uncomfortable Queen Anne needlepoint couch.

"Dear, I've put together some things for you to take to the interrogation—I mean, *interview*."

"Like what?"

She gestured to the tote bag at her feet. "Everything you'll need—a cushion for the hard chair, tissues, a sweater . . . they keep it so cold in there . . . and a thermos of coffee, because theirs is undrinkable swill. And of course, my secret recorder necklace to record what *they're* recording."

As a police interviewee of long standing, Mother was well versed in the necessary preparations for a grilling.

I waved that off. "Thanks but no thanks. I won't be there that long."

"Don't be so sure, dear. Brian Lawson is likely to give you the third degree for dumping him."

"I didn't dump him."

We'd split up over my decision to be a surrogate mother.

"And anyway," I said, "that's not why I'm being called down to the station."

"Just the same," Mother said, "it's better to be prepared—like a good scout!"

"That's the Boy Scouts, and anyway, I was a Brownie."

"Don't say you weren't warned!"

I just shook my head, gathered the car keys, and went out so quickly Sushi didn't have time to do her little take-me-along dance.

The police station was located in the heart of downtown, or maybe the spleen. Anyway, it was next to the new county jail, across the street from the old courthouse. A person could get arrested, brought to trial, and remanded to the clink all within a one-block radius. Talk about efficiency!

Night was descending like a bad simile as I parked the Caddy in the station's lot, then entered the one-story redbrick building.

I strode up to Heather, the female dispatcher

behind the bulletproof glass. She had reddish-brown hair and red glasses, and was Mother's latest snitch in a long line of snitches, all of whom had either been fired or transferred for revealing inside information. Heather had not benefitted from her predecessors' experiences.

Mother was a master at exploiting the weakness of any perceived stool pigeon. Some examples of her bribes include: offering a part in one of her plays; obtaining an autographed photo of a favorite movie star (which Mother signed); or, as in Heather's case, a promised appearance on our upcoming cable show, which of course wouldn't be coming up unless the pilot sold.

"Hi, Heather," I said. "Would you tell Brian I'm here?"

"Sure, Ms. Borne. Shame about Mrs. Sinclair. . . . Where's your mother?"

Natural assumption. This was a murder case, wasn't it?

"She didn't get invited," I said.

Heather laughed. "Bet she loved that!"

As Heather swivelled to a phone, I retreated to a corner chair next to a drooping rubber tree plant. The plant's continued existence depended on Mother and me administering much needed TLC anytime either of us cooled our heels in the station's waiting room.

But I didn't have time to do anything more than remove a few dead leaves before the steel door to the inner sanctum opened and Brian stepped out, wearing a light blue shirt and navy slacks, his chief's badge attached to his belt.

In his midthirties, Brian was boyishly handsome, with brown hair and puppy-dog brown eyes.

But those eyes looked more pit-bullish now as he summoned me with a scolding parent's crooked finger.

I followed him down the familiar beige hallway, where photos of long-ago policemen hung crookedly on the walls (Mother often paused to straighten each one), then was led into one of several small interview rooms.

Hey! It was *freezing* in there, and the windowless room was claustrophobic, the furniture consisting of two bolted-down metal chairs with a table between.

Brian gestured for me to sit, and my bottom settled onto a chair that was harder than a cement slab.

Let's hope Mother was wrong about the coffee, at least. . . .

I asked for some, and Brian brought me a Styrofoam cup of black liquid with an oil-slick surface. *Yuck!* Why hadn't I taken that tote?

Brian settled into the chair opposite me, placed a small recorder on the table, and turned it on. "Interview with Brandy Borne," he said, followed by the date and time. Then: "Why were you at the Sinclair residence this afternoon?"

"Vanessa called the shop wanting to sell some beer signs."

"Uh-huh. Maybe you should start with the fight you had with her at the swap meet."

How did he know about that?

I shifted in the uncomfortable chair. "It wasn't

a fight. Just a brief verbal scuffle. A misunderstanding."

"That right?"

"That's right. She saw me talking to Wes, and
jumped to the wrong conclusion."

"Then you're *not* having an affair with Wes
Sinclair?"

"What? *Affair?* No! Vanessa apologized when
she called me about the beer signs. I think it was
a kind of . . . peace offering."

Brian shut the recorder off, stood, then left
the room.

After a few long minutes, he returned and
resumed the interview, switching the recorder
back on.

"I've just spoken to Wesley Sinclair," Brian
said, "and he doesn't know anything about selling those beer signs. Furthermore, he said he
never agreed to do so."

Was Wes in one of the other interview rooms?
And was he trying to implicate me? Despite how
cold it was in there, I began to sweat. *Really*
could've used a tissue . . .

A Brian who seemed colder than the cubicle
was saying, "Vanessa embarrassed you at the swap
meet, in front of dozens of people, and you
went over there to have it out with her. You just
invented the story about the beer signs."

"No! That's ridiculous."

"Brandy, no one's saying this was premeditated."

"Premeditated?"

"You argued with her and things got out of
hand."

"She was alive when I left."

"Can anyone corroborate that?"

"I don't know! No one else was there. Maybe a neighbor? Have you asked?" I pointed to the recorder. "Will you turn that damn thing off!"

Brian sighed. Then did.

"Why on earth are you treating me like this?" I demanded. "You know very well I didn't kill Vanessa. Whatever I am, I'm no murderer. Come on!"

The door opened and Mia stuck her head in. She didn't look at me. "A second, Chief?"

He stood and abandoned me to the cold again, and I could hear him and Mia talking in low voices out in the hall.

When Brian came back, he said curtly. "You can go."

"That's it?"

"Yes. You're no longer a suspect."

I folded my arms. "For the *record?*"

Brian sat back down, turned the machine on. "Brandy Borne is not a suspect *at this time.* A neighbor, Gladys Fowler, saw Ms. Borne leaving the Sinclair home while Mrs. Sinclair was standing outside."

He shut the machine off.

"Thank you," I said.

He leaned back in his chair. "I'd still like an explanation about the beer signs."

"What's to explain? Since Wes said he didn't know anything about Vanessa selling them, she must have been doing it out of spite. But I didn't sense anything phony about her friendliness." I shrugged. "Anyway, the beer signs don't have anything to do with the murder."

He thought about that. "All right. You can go."

"Is that how it is between us now?"

"Brandy," he said, and as impassive as his face was, the sadness in his eyes was something he couldn't hide, "there isn't anything between us now."

I had no sooner arrived home than Mother called out from the music/library room, "Dear! Do come tell me about your interrogation."

I dutifully went in where I found Mother hauling out the old schoolroom blackboard on wheels that she kept behind an ancient standup piano. The appearance of the blackboard—on which she invariably compiled her list of suspects—signaled the music/library room had just become (once again) an incident room.

I plopped down on the piano bench. Neither one of us could play the old out-of-tune upright, with the exception of "Chopsticks" and "Heart and Soul." But the collection of trumpets, displayed on a bookshelf, was a different matter. I had played the silver 1940s King in band throughout high school, and Mother could blat out a (somewhat) recognizable "Boogie Woogie Bugle Boy of Company B" on the old coronet.

I asked, "A little soon for the blackboard, wouldn't you say?"

"No I would not. Never too early to revisit an old friend, dear. Now spill."

I recited chapter and verse.

Mother, in full I-told-you-so mode, looked down

her nose at me. "Didn't I *say* you'd receive the third-degree treatment from that man? Hell hath no fury like an interim chief spurned."

"Yes, Mother, and I wish I'd had a sweater, and a cushion, and some tissue, and brought my own coffee, and all I could think of was that I hoped someday to learn that I should always listen to you."

She smiled, ignoring the sarcasm underlying the last phrase. "And the recorder necklace?"

"I skipped that accessory."

She frowned, just a quick one, then more pleasantly asked, "Are you going to tell Tony about how Brian gave you the Abu Ghraib treatment?"

I shook my head. "Already too much tension between those two." I pointed a finger. "And don't you dare tell Tony! That's one place I can't have you overstepping."

Brightening, she said, "That reminds me! Tony called and said he'd be coming over anytime now. You must've had your cell phone turned off."

"I did. Thanks. I'll talk to him here in the living room. Ah . . . do you mind if we have a little privacy?"

"But of course, dear. I am bone-tired after a long day!" She yawned and stretched, not terribly convincingly for a diva.

After Mother disappeared upstairs in a staggering manner that sent "The Song of the Volga Boatmen" playing in my brain, I got up and turned on the porch light. Then I returned to the Victorian couch and tried to make myself comfortable with Sushi and a blanket.

Soosh heard Tony's car pull into the drive before I'd completed that task, and gave a sharp bark. I rose and went to open the front door, and when Tony stepped in, still uniformed, looking a little tired himself, I leaned against his chest, his strong arms holding me, and finally let out some tears. Tears over Vanessa's brutal murder; tears over how cruelly Brian had treated me; tears because I really *was* bone-tired.

Tony walked me over to the couch where we sat, and he held my hand until I'd finished blubbering and sniffling.

"Better?" he asked gently, offering me his handkerchief, one of many of his I'd collected over time.

"Yeah. I'm . . . I'm okay now. Sorry."

"No need to be. As rough days go, you've put in a whale of a one." He gave me a tiny smile. "You know, I'd forgotten just how uncomfortable this couch was."

"Shall we move to the floor?"

He nodded.

We slid down onto the oriental rug, putting the needlepoint pillows behind our backs. Sushi, who adored Tony, settled on his lap. Good taste, that pooch.

Tony was saying, "I heard that a neighbor of the Sinclairs got you off the hook."

Had he heard anything else about the interview?

"That's right," I said.

He took my hand. "Brandy?"

"Yeah?"

"Promise me you'll stay out of this one."

"You know I'd like to."

"But you can't, huh? Because of Vivian?"

"You know Mother. She's already off to the hounds." I nodded toward the blackboard. "Tony, I'll stay out of it. As for Mother, I'll do what I can to discourage her, but there's only so much one human can do."

His lips formed a thin tight line, which barely broke to let out: "Her meddling could hurt my chances."

"To be chief of police, you mean?" I hadn't considered that.

He nodded.

"Because you and I are seeing each other?"

His forehead creased. "Brandy, we already have my being a married man hanging over us."

"Yes, but you and your wife are separated. . . ."

"It's a small town. People can be petty and mean. Everybody knows we're close. And I can't be put in a position where someone thinks I've given you or Vivian information on this case."

I nodded. "If I explain that to Mother, I'm sure she'll understand."

"Really?"

". . . Pretty sure."

Tony's cell rang. "Cassato." He listened a moment, then straightened. "You've already got the warrant? . . . Good . . . Okay. See you over there."

Ending the call, he stood, gazing down at me. I felt small, like I was six years old.

He was smiling. "I guess our little discussion about you keeping out of this case was premature. It's a moot point now."

I gave him a quizzical look.

He explained: "We're arresting Wesley Sinclair for the murder of his wife."

I was too stunned to speak.

But from the top of the stairs Mother called out, "I just *knew* he did it!"

A Trash 'n' Treasures Tip

A crowded swap meet is an ideal place for purse snatchers to operate, so leave your big bags at home. I wear a cross-body purse with a zipper that sticks.

Chapter Four

Insufficient Bid

(A bid not higher than the preceding one.)

The next morning, Sunday, I wanted to sleep in, but not surprisingly Mother had other ideas. She came into my Art Deco–appointed bedroom around nine-thirty, sing-songing, "We're all in our places with sun-shiny faces!"

In other words, we were going to church.

Burrowing in deeper under the covers, I groaned. "Please, Mr. Custer," I sang back at her, intoning an ancient pop song, "I don't want to go."

"That's in very poor taste, dear. Rise and shine!"

"I . . . I had a rough night."

And I had. A nightmare-ridden one. In the most vivid of them, a handcuffed, foot-shackled Wes was being hauled down a long dark corridor to an awaiting electric chair. I forced myself awake and then returned to slumber to look for better dreams, without success.

That I hadn't updated my memorable nightmare to lethal injection, or taken into consideration that our state didn't have capital punishment anymore, is just one of the things that drives me crazy about dreams. If I knew these things awake, why didn't I in the dream world?

Mother sat on the blond maple framed bed, springs squeaking, and a beneath-the-covers Sushi growled her displeasure.

"I've made coffee cake and scrambled eggs just the way you like them."

She wanted to go to church in the worst way. And by worst way, I mean not to commune with the Lord, but to be the center of attention. This would be our first public appearance since finding Vanessa, after all.

I said, "I don't feel like going. Why don't I just drive you?"

"Then you'd already be there, dear, so it would be ridiculous not to attend. Plus, it would save you a trip back picking me up."

True. And I could always sleep in our pew. Not exactly comfy, but what the heck.

She bolted to her feet, startling me, and exclaimed, "Now, chop chop!"

And waltzed out.

An hour later, in a pastel floral skirt and white blouse, I left the house with Mother, who wore a summery yellow slacks-and-top outfit. Sushi, apparently an atheist or anyway dognostic (sorry), had gone back to bed, as part of that dog's life you hear so much about.

We belonged to New Hope, a nondenominational church not bound by any hierarchy other than its own elected board, with an emphasis on the teachings of Christ ("Rather a novelty," Mother once commented). The congregation was formed some years ago by displaced Methodists, Presbyterians, Baptists, Lutherans, Catholics, and others who had become disenchanted with their former churches—a Jewish family even attended occasionally—and I had long ago dubbed New Hope "The Church of Common Sense and Mild Scoldings." If anyone wanted hell and brimstone, they needed to go elsewhere. This was more heck and pebbles.

But New Hope was really the Church of Pastor Tutor, a kind and gentle man, whose calming personality, good humor, and abiding patience held together the various former this-and-thats into one house of worshipers.

New Hope was located about a mile from our house and we used to walk there, on sunny days anyway, until Mother got her double hip replacement. The building had once been an old redbrick fire station, slated for the wrecking ball; but Mother and her preservation cohorts had once again ridden to the rescue of a local relic. Later Pastor Tutor and his followers raised the necessary funds to turn it into a church.

I found a place for the Caddy in the already-packed parking lot. We got out and headed toward the main door just as the old fire station bell sounded—a five-minute warning that service was about to begin.

Church for some years had started at eleven, but Pastor Tutor long ago noticed his flock getting antsy as noon approached, and noted as well the regular stampede when the service was over. All these good Christians wanted to beat other congregations to the local eateries for Sunday dinner. So starting time was changed to ten-thirty.

Then the Baptists at Calvary—who had the largest, most proactive membership in town—retaliated by moving their service to ten-fifteen. This shot across the bow took no casualties, as the Calvary pastor ran to the long-winded side. And while those poor souls were still on their knees getting saved, we still got to the restaurants first, claiming all the best tables not to mention wheelchair parking.

As Mother and I entered the sanctuary, a noticeable murmur rose among those already seated—some half-turning, craning their necks—word apparently having circulated quickly about Wes's arrest, and our connection to the murdered woman. No surprise, as the socially prominent Sinclairs were members of New Hope.

As the organ music began, drowning out the whispering, Mother and I took our usual place in a back pew, next to four of Mother's gal pals from the Red-Hatted League—a mystery book club offshoot of the Red Hat Society—who we always sat with. (More about these avid mystery fans later.)

When we first joined the church, I had been surprised that Mother preferred sitting way in back, but then realized she enjoyed being behind everyone. That way she could see who was there, keep track of who was playing hooky, what people were wearing, and whether their wigs or toupees were on straight, plus which ones bowed their head during the sermon, not in prayer, but slumber.

Several times Pastor Tutor tried mixing up the seating to encourage his flock to enjoy fellowship in the company of different members. But his sheep always strayed back to their pew of preference. And woe betide the person who sat in someone else's preferred pew. You don't want to cross a regular churchgoer.

After the opening hymn, I had trouble keeping my eyes open—yes, the back pew was my preference in case I needed to finish a sleep cycle—but I was alert during the Prayers for Members portion of the service. Plump Pastor Tutor—a short bespectacled man in a simple black robe with purple shawl—offered a few carefully chosen words about the Sinclairs, of the "our thoughts and prayers are with them" variety.

Then the choir performed a contemporary number, after which the sermon began, Pastor Tutor reading from Matthew 7:1-5 (*Judge not that you be judged*), and 19:19 (*Love your neighbor as yourself*).

Pastor Tutor had a wonderful manner of never looking at the congregation, but behind and above them, so that no one ever felt uncomfortable under his gaze, in case his teachings/scoldings hit too close to home. Nor did he mean to embarrass them had they nodded off.

Which I was getting ready to do, when Pastor Tutor segued into 1 Timothy 5:13, saying, "And they learned to be idle, wandering about from house to house; and not only idle, but tattlers also and busybodies, speaking things which they ought not."

He was trying to head off the inevitable gossip about Vanessa and Wes, which was a valiant attempt, but about as likely as the second coming of Christ happening next Tuesday.

Knowing how close to home this hit, I looked sideways at Mother, who wore an angelic expression, the sun shining down on her from a skylight above in a halo effect. Who says God doesn't have a sense of humor? Everyone else seemed to be sliding down in their seats.

Pastor Tutor concluded his sermon, after which came the last hymn followed by the benediction. And it was a sheepish flock (couldn't resist) that filed out of the sanctuary, no one daring to acknowledge Mother and me with anything more than a simple hello-how-are-you. If Mother was disappointed by the lack of attention, she didn't show it.

In the hall outside the sanctuary, we stood in a quiet line to shake Pastor Tutor's hand, and upon our turn, he asked us to stay behind for a moment; we stepped to one side. Perhaps the pastor felt a need to further instruct us (that is, Mother) on the evils of gossiping.

Then, when everyone else had gone, he turned to us, clearly concerned. "I'm here for counsel should either of you feel the need to talk about what has happened . . . it must have been terribly upsetting for you both, yesterday. And of course Vanessa was one of our own."

"Oh, we're just fine, Pastor," Mother chirped.

Her cavalier attitude seemed to startle him.

Not me—Mother was not an unfeeling person, merely one who compartmentalized. Regarding another murder I accused her of being insensitive about, she had said, "Dear, blubbering won't help that poor victim. The best thing that can happen is to bring the killer to justice."

And yesterday she had said much the same thing. Only this time the killer—Wes Sinclair—had already been arrested, with justice waiting around the corner.

Trying to smooth over the awkward silence, I said, "I thought today's sermon was very insightful, Pastor Tutor. I'm sure both Mother and I will find it very helpful."

He nodded solemnly. "I felt it necessary to remind our New Hope family that careless words can be hurtful at a time such as this." His sigh was deep, the weight of his congregation on his shoulders. "And when someone of prominence in the community dies—and another is incarcerated—tongues do tend to wag."

"I agree," Mother said, then raised a qualifying finger. "But *sometimes* wagging tongues can be constructive."

"I must disagree, Vivian."

"Really?" Adding cryptically, "Even if those wagging tongues lead to the truth?"

Tutor's frown was in contrast with his next words. "Perhaps even then."

"As it says in the Good Book," Mother sermonized, "truth will out."

His eyes widened. "I believe that's Shakespeare, Vivian, not Scripture."

"Oh, that's right! *The Merchant of Venice.* Well, you know the Bard is sacred to us thespians!"

Tutor seemed to be studying her, like a scientist looking through a microscope at a troubling slide. Then he said, almost to himself, "You know, before the tragic news reached me, today's sermon was to focus on the Tenth Commandment."

"Ah!" Mother said. "An often undervalued teaching, if a tad politically incorrect by current standards."

My stomach growled, and—not relishing a theological discussion between Mother and a real pastor—I said, "Well, okay, then—guess we'll be going."

As we walked out to the parking lot, Mother said, "Little bit brusque, dear, weren't you?"

"I'm sure Pastor Tutor will forgive me."

"I'm sure he will," she said brightly. "Anyway, we were done."

"What was all that about the Tenth Commandment, Mother? Which one is that, anyway?"

"The one about not climbing over fences to get at the greener grass, dear."

I thought Mother might be miffed that there wasn't anyone left in the parking lot to talk to her about the murder, and her role in its discovery. But everyone had headed home or to a restaurant.

And she seemed uncharacteristically quiet on our drive downtown to the Button Factory, where we always ate post-church with her gal pals.

The eatery was located on the riverfront, in a refurbished building that had once been (ahead of me, are you?) a thriving button factory—one of half a dozen such businesses that sprouted up along the Serenity banks of the Mississippi during the mid-1800s because of the (then) abundant supply of clamshells. But then plastic came along and replaced the pearly white buttons, and the factories closed and all but one shuttered.

"The girls" were already seated at our usual round table in a little alcove set apart from the main dining area. The restaurant wasn't supposed to take Sunday reservations, but the management made an exception for the Red-Hatted League, because Mother had cast the owners' teenage stagestruck daughter in one of her theatrical productions at the Serenity Playhouse. The girl's performance did not rate a standing ovation, but Mother got a standing reservation.

Along with Mother and me, the group included Alice Hetzler, a former middle school English teacher, who still treated me like her eighth-grade student; Cora Van Camp, a retired court secretary, who knew everybody in town's legal business; Frannie Phillips, a part-time nurse at the Serenity Hospital, who specialized in giving the *worst* shots; and Norma Crumley, a socialite and world-class gossip.

Norma was at least ten years younger than the rest (myself not included), and was a newbie to the group. Shortly after the rumormonger's addition, I questioned Mother about it. I mean, with Vivian Borne in the group, who needed another gossip?

"Dear," she told me, "after Norma's husband divorced her, all the poor woman's married friends crawled back into the woodwork."

"Then they weren't really her friends, were they?"

"No. They were *his* friends. They only put up with the unpleasant woman because of him."

"Then why do *you* want to put up with her?"

"Because dear, she's a font of information."

"Even after her married friends abandoned her?"

"Plenty of widows and divorcées around, and Norma has social-circle connections to which I'm not privy. Or is that to whom?"

Had Mother purposely chosen these friends in their unrelated fields, so that she could tap their knowledge in solving her cases?

Absolutely. And I had to admire the deviousness and forethought.

The ladies were studying their menus; while the restaurant had a delicious Sunday brunch buffet, no one in the little group but me ever took it.

As Norma had once sniffed, "If I want to fetch my own dinner, I'll stay at home."

A waitress appeared and took our orders, and I excused myself to head to the buffet to beat the long line that would soon be formed by other churchgoers now filing into the restaurant.

At the food bar, I filled my plate with breakfast items, only to reach hot lunch dishes at the end that made me question my selections. This was a lesson I seemed incapable of learning, like so many Sunday morning lessons. And the only Button Factory restraint I burdened myself with was limiting the buffet trips to one.

By the time I returned to our table, the others had been served their first course of salad and/or soup, so I didn't feel bad about digging in.

Cora, petite retired court secretary prone to bird-like head movements, said, "I have it on good authority that Vanessa recently consulted an out-of-town lawyer about how to break that nasty prenuptial agreement Wes imposed upon her."

I asked, "*How* nasty?"

"I hear it states that she got not a centavo unless they had a child."

"That seems pretty medieval."

"Well, it's a Sinclair family thing. Family business."

Mother was silent; her modus operandi here was to sit back and listen, and benefit from her friends' chattiness . . . and my natural curiosity.

Frannie, slender, part-time nurse with short, wiry gray hair, chimed in, "And I happen to know from someone in OBGYN—I won't say *who*—that Vanessa could never conceive due to . . ." She dropped her voice to a conspiratorial whisper. ". . . a botched abortion she had in college."

Norma, overweight socialite wearing too much makeup, commented, "Their former cleaning lady now works for me, and let me tell you . . ." No whispers for Norma. ". . . she said they had *wiiiild* parties at that mansion of theirs."

I asked, "What kind of wild parties?"

Norma blinked at me indignantly. "Well, I wasn't about to *pry!*"

Only Alice, retired English teacher with dyed brown hair showing an inch of white outgrowth, had nothing to offer.

Maybe Mother should consider replacing her.

Mother, satisfied that she'd gathered everything pertinent these sources had to offer, deftly turned the conversation to a topic close to her heart: herself. Specifically, how she had come to find the body. As she described the bloody scene, the girls were unswayed in their chowing down.

Seemed like a good opportunity to go back to the buffet for those lunch items I'd missed. Shut up.

When, an hour later, Mother and an over-stuffed yours truly arrived home, Sushi was waiting inside the front door with her leash in her mouth. Ever since she got her sight back, I'd been taking the pooch for a walk after each meal as exercise for both of us and a little quiet time for me.

But I'd come to almost dread these once-joyful little jaunts along the neighborhood sidewalks. You see, Sushi had total recall of every spot where she had ever seen a squirrel or rabbit or chipmunk, which made our walks a start and stop, herky-jerky process. Added to that was her need to sniff every blade of grass to determine what other dogs had been by, which turned a ten-minute excursion into half an hour.

So I was a little crabby upon our return when an overly excited Mother jumped into my path like a demented jack-in-the-box.

"Wes wants to see you!" she practically shouted, her eyes frighteningly large behind the lenses. I made a mental note to check her medication.

I frowned. "Isn't he in jail? At least till after the arraignment tomorrow?"

Mother grinned in Christmas-morning glee. "Yes, dear, but Sheriff Rudder has given the okay for you to visit the prisoner."

"Why would he? I'm hardly family, and not exactly a lawyer."

"Do we care? The Sinclairs have pull, dear. Anyway, aren't you anxious to hear what Wes has to say?"

"Not particularly."

She put her hands on her hips and peered down at me like a queen who wished she had a better class of subjects. "I thought Wes was your old and dear *friend*."

"Some friend! He tried to put the old and dear *blame* on me, remember? Telling the police he didn't know anything about the sale of those beer signs! What a creep he turned out to be."

"Maybe he just wants a chance to explain. To get back in your good graces. Brandy, don't let this opportunity pass us . . . that is, *you* . . . by!"

She was getting agitated. And an agitated Mother is never a good thing.

"Oh, *fine*. I'll go. If it'll stop you harping."

"Watch the frown lines, dear! Once carved they are not easily erased."

Soon I was in the Caddy, tooling downtown, before wheeling into the parking lot that the county jail shared with our police station.

Mother had campaigned tirelessly for this new state-of-the-art county jail. After spending several short stints in the crumbling old bug-infested hoosegow, she came to the compassionate conclusion that the prisoners deserved better—especially if that prisoner was Vivian Borne.

From the outside, lacking either wire fence or guardhouse, the two-story octagon-shaped structure might have been a medical center or private business. Only the small, barred windows running along the second floor suggested otherwise.

I went through the glass double front doors and into a large area with white-colored walls and industrial gray carpeting. In the center of the room were two rows of bucket-shaped chairs, back to back, and beyond that, a walk-through metal detector for visitors entering the jail. This could have been any airport waiting area, right down to the vending machines, were it not for the bulletproof window to my right, behind which a male deputy monitored computers.

I approached the window, then spoke into its microphone. "Brandy Borne to see Sheriff Rudder, please."

Not that I didn't believe Mother, but I wanted to hear from the big man himself that Wes really wanted to see me, and that the sheriff truly was fine with that.

The young crew-cut blond deputy, his good looks marred by pockmarks, swivelled toward me. "I'll let him know, Ms. Borne." And he reached for a phone.

I retreated to the row of bucket seats, all empty, as was the rest of the waiting area, taking the one nearest the door next to the bulletproof window. Before too long, the sheriff stepped out.

Tall and burly, oozing confidence, Sheriff Rudder reminded me a little of John Wayne, particularly if I wasn't wearing my contacts. He had that same sideways stride, too, as he came toward me. Or maybe, like Mother, he just had corns.

He looked unhappy to be working. Well, it was Sunday. Of course, he never looked happy to see me and/or Mother.

"You can have five minutes," he growled.

"With you?"

"No! With Mr. Sinclair. In the visitors' booth."

"What does he want?"

"How should I know? Five minutes. I'll get someone to take you through."

Rudder turned abruptly and went back through the side door.

I sat and waited some more, hoping the "someone" would not be Deputy Patty, who hadn't been particularly nice to Mother and me during our thirty-day stint here last year.

The door opened again.

Patty.

In her forties, rather plain, with short dishwater blond hair, the woman had a sullenness that said she got all the crappy assignments. Which at the moment included dealing with me.

I deposited my purse in a wall locker, went through the metal detector—Mother always sets it off, due to her extensive bridgework—then Patty walked me through two sets of locked security doors and into an area consisting of three separate visitors' stations. These small rooms were similar to those used by bank safe-deposit customers.

She ushered me into one, I took a chair in front of the Plexiglas window, and she retreated outside the cubicle, allowing me . . . soon to be "us" . . . some privacy.

The minutes crawled by, and my eyelids were just getting heavy when the door on the other side of the glass opened, and Wes entered, followed by a burly guard in a tan uniform. Unlike Patty, this guard did not relinquish his charge, but did move an unobtrusive distance away.

Wes slid into the chair opposite me. He looked terrible—face ashen, unshaved, eyes red and puffy, hair uncombed. His shirt and slacks were wrinkled, probably the clothes he'd had on when he'd been arrested late last night.

He leaned forward, his manner dejected, speaking through the holes in the glass. "Thanks for coming, Brandy."

I nodded.

He swallowed, reading my displeasure. "I wanted to apologize if anything I said to the police caused you trouble."

"You mean about the beer signs?"

"Yes." He leaned forward even more, his nose almost touching the Plexiglas. "I honestly didn't know Vanessa was selling those things. They're nothing I would ever want to get rid of. I can only assume that she was trying to get back at me for . . . I don't know, *something*."

"Something like seeing you and me together at the swap meet?"

He sighed again. Nodded glumly.

I shrugged. "Guess I kind of figured as much. No apology necessary, Wes. You have enough to worry about."

He shifted in his chair. "That's only part of why I wanted to see you."

I waited. This was his party.

"I understand Wayne Ekhardt is your lawyer. . . ."

"Yes. Mine and Mother's. Why?"

"Well, I'd like to know what you think about having him represent me at the preliminary hearing."

My eyes snapped open wide. "You're not serious."

"I am."

"He's almost *ninety*."

"I know. But he's the most famous criminal lawyer in the Midwest. He got that woman off who outright murdered her husband."

"Well, yeah, fifty years ago. Why, did you outright murder Vanessa?"

"No! No . . ." His head lowered and he covered his eyes with a hand.

"Wes, Mr. Ekhardt is the finest lawyer in Serenity, maybe the state . . . if this were 1975. But today? He's lucky to stay awake in court." Now I leaned forward, saying earnestly, "You must have a fleet of top-notch lawyers you use for your company. Any one of them would be a better choice."

Wes shook his head. "No. They're *corporate* attorneys."

I spread my hands. "So have them help you get the best criminal lawyer in the country—you can afford it. I mean . . . you're being tried for *murder.*"

Wes blinked back tears. "Brandy, I *didn't* kill Vanessa. Do you really think . . . ? I wouldn't . . . I couldn't. Things weren't perfect between us, but I love her. Loved her. Brandy, please. You've *got* to believe me."

I heard myself say, "I do."

He let out a huge relieved sigh. "You don't know how much that means to me."

"What I believe isn't important. What is important is that you get proper representation."

"It's just the preliminary hearing. If it goes to trial, maybe one of my corporate lawyers will have another recommendation."

The guard said, "Time."

As Wes stood, I said, "Please don't use Ekhardt. Even just for that hearing."

"Sorry, Brandy—I've made up my mind. Wayne Ekhardt was my father's lawyer, and I've known him since childhood. I trust him. Age isn't an issue."

"Well, *sure* it is!"

He shook his head. Gave me a sad little smile. "Thanks for coming. Means the world."

I staggered out of there feeling numb and disturbed. I could think of only one person who would be pleased by Wes's choice of counsel.

I lived with her, and I don't mean Sushi.

A Trash 'n' Treasures Tip

To avoid jamming the vendor aisles, use proper walking etiquette at a swap meet—always stick to the right, as if you were driving a car. However, do not, as Mother has been known to do, carry a Harpo-like horn to clear the way.

Chapter Five

A Trick

(Set of four cards played by each player during a hand.)

The day following my visit to the county jail, Wes had his arraignment, where a plea of Not Guilty was entered by Wayne Ekhardt. The preliminary hearing, which was required to take place within a few days, was set for Wednesday morning.

Mother, using her connections at the courthouse, was able to get us seats, with Joe Lange once again pressed into service to run the shop in our absence.

(For those of you who have not learned courtroom procedure from having watched the wonderful old *Perry Mason* TV show, a preliminary hearing determines whether or not the state, or prosecuting attorney, has enough evidence to convince the judge to take the case to trial.)

The hearing was held in a secondary courtroom on the second floor of the Serenity Courthouse, a late nineteenth-century edifice of Grecian grandeur that (in part because of Mother and her historical preservation–leaning pals) had been spared architectural genocide.

Thanks to Vivian Borne's various vehicular infractions, I'd been in this courtroom many times, but that didn't give me a warm fuzzy comfortable feeling. Traffic court had just been let out, and the anxiety of those called to justice still lingered in the air like the smell of drying varnish.

We found two seats in the back row, and felt lucky to have them, the courtroom quickly filling up with the defendant's friends and business associates, along with a gaggle of reporters. Normally such a hearing might at best attract representatives of the local paper and radio station. But the Sinclair name had brought in media from all around the area.

Though the window air conditioner chugged away, doing its best to stave off the rising temperature outside, the room was noticeably warm, thanks to accumulating body heat inside. People spoke in hushed tones, some fidgeting in their uncomfortable wooden pews.

Wayne Ekhardt and District Attorney Jason Nesbit were already present, seated at separate oak tables. I could only see his back, but Ekhardt appeared more frail than ever, his head shaking a little, bony frame sunken into his too-large, navy pinstriped suit, a boy swimming in his father's clothes.

The DA was a young hotshot, slender, with dark hair overly styled with product, glasses with invisible wire frames, and a fashionable two-day stubble on his narrowly handsome face. All this was wrapped up in a light gray number that could not have been purchased locally. He fussed with his papers while Ekhardt's head bowed in slumber.

Seated in the pew behind Nesbit were the prosecutor's two witnesses: Officer Mia Cordona and Gladys Fowler, a neighbor of the Sinclairs. Brian Lawson was also there, and it might not be a stretch to say the interim chief's reputation hinged on the outcome of the hearing.

A side door next to the judge's bench opened and Her Honor swept in, long black robe flapping like Batman's cape. Judge Jones—middle-aged, African American, hair tinged with gray (some of that put there by Mother)—assumed her regal place behind the raised bench.

This judge was the one who had given Mother and me a thirty-day jail sentence last year for breaking and entering (*Antiques Chop*), which annoyed Mother because we had solved a murder case doing so, and made me furious because I gained ten pounds on fattening jailhouse food.

The side door opened again and a burly male bailiff in a tan uniform marched into the room, an army of one, taking a rigid position next to the Stars and Stripes on its sturdy pole. Despite the man and the flag, I somehow managed not to salute.

Ekhardt slumped at the table, a tired student sleeping in class. I shot Mother a concerned look, but she waved a dismissive hand, her confidence in the old warhorse unshakable.

"He's just playing possum, dear," she whispered.

Stern-faced Judge Jones caught the eye of the bailiff, nodded, and the uniformed man stepped back to the side door and opened it.

Wes—the disheveled prisoner of the other day now a well-groomed handsome figure in a black Armani suit—stepped in, accompanied by Deputy Patty. If Wes was disturbed by the sight of his slumbering counsel, he didn't betray it—face calm, he seemed almost serene as he was escorted to his place next to Ekhardt.

Judge Jones banged her gavel. "The court will come to order."

This, of course, woke Mr. Ekhardt, who brought himself up into his suit with a start.

(Mother insists that the court hearing appear here in transcript form for the sake of authenticity.)

Judge: This is a preliminary hearing for the State of Iowa vs. Wesley Sinclair III, case number IA-95121. Would each counsel give his name and appearance for the record?

Nesbit: Jason Nesbit, prosecuting attorney for the state.

Ekhardt: (Unintelligible.)

Judge: I'm sorry, sir. You're going to have to speak up.

Ekhardt: Wayne Ekhardt, counsel for the defendant.

Judge: Call your first witness, Mr. Nesbit.

Nesbit: Mia Cordona to the stand.

(Mia Cordona sworn in.)

Nesbit: You were the first officer on the scene?

Cordona: Yes, well, me and my partner Officer Cassato, but I went inside the house first.

Nesbit: And how long have you been on the force?

Ekhardt: Objection. Irrelevant and immaterial.

Unidentified Voice: Not to mention incompetent!

Judge: Who said that? Bailiff?

Bailiff: Ah . . . a woman in the back. Vivian Borne, I think, Your Honor.

Judge: Who let *her* in?

Vivian Borne (standing): My apologies, Your Eminence—that is, Your Honor. I pledge henceforth to be as quiet as a church mouse.

Judge: See that henceforth you are. Or you'll be out on your (unintelligible).

Court Reporter: Excuse me, Your Honor, did you say "ear" or "rear"? For the record.

Judge: Ah. Ear. Where were we?

Nesbit: I was trying to establish the credibility of Miss Cordona, when Mr. Ekhardt objected.

Judge: Yes, all right. Overruled.

Nesbit: Again, Miss Cordona, how long have you been with the police department?

Cordona: Eight years last month.

Nesbit: Then you've been among the first responders at the scene of other murders.

Cordona: Yes . . . well, a few.

Nesbit: So when you arrived at the home of Vanessa Sinclair, and saw the body, there was no doubt in your mind that the woman had been murdered.

Judge: Mr. Ekhardt? Are you going to object to that? Bailiff . . . I think defense counsel has nodded off. It is warm in here.

Ekhardt: I'm awake, Your Honor. Merely mulling the district attorney's question. Objection. Leading the witness.

Judge: Sustained.

Nesbit: Let me rephrase that. When you saw the body, what was your professional opinion?

Cordona: That Mrs. Sinclair had suffered blunt-force trauma to the head. Fatally.

Nesbit: Which gave you probable cause to search the premises?

Ekhardt: Again, leading the witness.

Judge: I'll overrule that.

Cordona: That is correct.

Nesbit: And what did you find?

Cordona: A man's shirt with bloodstains in the trash can behind the house.

Nesbit: I move for admission of this shirt as evidence number one.

Judge: Objection?

Ekhardt: No.

Nesbit: I further move for admission as evidence number two, the lab report from the DNA sample taken from said shirt showing that the blood was that of Vanessa Sinclair.

Judge: Objection?

Ekhardt: No.

Nesbit: Your witness, Mr. Ekhardt.

Judge: Mr. Ekhardt? Cross-examination?

Ekhardt: Yes.

Judge: Mr. Ekhardt, do you need assistance in approaching the stand? Or would you like to cross-examine from your seat?

Ekhardt: No, Your Honor, I can make it. Just give me a few moments.

(Defense counsel approaches the witness stand.)

Ekhardt: Miss Cordona, have you ever worn a man's shirt?

Nesbit: Objection to relevance!

Judge: Sustained.

Ekhardt: I'll rephrase. Have you ever worn a man's-*style* shirt?

Nesbit: Your Honor, apparently defense counsel didn't hear you.

Judge: Mr. Ekhardt, where are you going with this?

Ekhardt: Where I'm going, Your Honor, is to contend that exhibit number one does *not* belong to my client, which can be easily demonstrated, if he strips to the waist.

Nesbit: Your Honor! I object to this kind of courtroom theatrics!

Judge: Overruled. Mr. Ekhardt, you may proceed. But let's try just holding the shirt up to Mr. Sinclair. Mr. Sinclair, would you rise?

Ekhardt: As you can see, the sleeves are too short, and the width too narrow.

Judge (banging gavel)*:* Silence—if there's another outburst I will clear the courtroom.

Nesbit: Then whose shirt is it?

Ekhardt (to Nesbit)*:* All due respect to the district attorney, but it is not my job to establish the owner, only to show that it could not possibly have been worn by my client.

Nesbit (to Ekhardt)*:* Then why did you let me enter it into evidence?

Ekhardt: Well, it is evidence of a sort.

Judge (banging gavel)*:* That's enough, gentlemen! Mr. Ekhardt, do you have anything further for Miss Cordona?

Ekhardt: No, Your Honor.

Judge: You may step down. The prosecution will call its next witness.

Nesbit: Will Gladys Fowler take the stand?

(Gladys Fowler sworn in.)

Nesbit: You live directly across the street from the Sinclairs?

Fowler: Yes. And you have no idea how much noise and construction I've had to put up with.

Judge: Mrs. Fowler, please confine yourself to directly answering the question. Nothing more.

Fowler: Yes, Your Honor. But it *was* awful—you can't imagine the dust and noise.

Judge: Just the question, Mrs. Fowler.

Fowler: All right.

Nesbit: On the afternoon of the murder, where were you?

Fowler: I was relaxing in my porch swing, reading a book.

Nesbit: For how long?

Fowler: One hour. From three-thirty until four-thirty.

Nesbit: You seem quite sure about the time, is that right?

Fowler: Oh, yes, because I had finished watching "Martha Stewart Bakes" on PBS at three-thirty, and I always start dinner at four-thirty. So that's one hour.

Nesbit: Your porch swing faces the Sinclairs' house?

Judge: Excuse the interruption . . . Mr. Sinclair?

Defendant: Your Honor?

Judge: It is in your best interest to keep Mr. Ekhardt awake. You may need to nudge him.

Defendant: Yes, Your Honor.

Fowler: Could you repeat the question?

Nesbit: I asked if your porch swing faces the Sinclairs' house.

Fowler: Yes, it does, I can see the entire monstrosity plain as day.

Nesbit: And during the hour you spent relaxing and reading, did you notice anyone coming or going from the residence?

Fowler: Yes. I saw Mr. Sinclair go up the drive in that fancy sports car of his.

Nesbit: At what time?

Fowler: I would say, four-fifteen. Give or take.

Nesbit: Which is the coroner's estimation of the time of the murder.

Judge: I'm going to have to object for Mr. Ekhardt. And sustain that objection.

Nesbit: And how did the defendant seem? Angry? In a hurry?

Judge: Again, a sustained objection. Leading the witness.

Nesbit: I'll rephrase. Was there anything unusual about the defendant when he got out of his car?

Fowler: He seemed normal enough. Then.

Nesbit: And how long was the defendant in the house before he came back out?

Fowler: About twenty minutes.

Nesbit: And his demeanor at that time?

Fowler: Oh, quite different. Very different. He looked upset, and drove off in a hurry.

Fowler: I'm through with this witness.

Judge: You may step down. Mr. Ekhardt? Cross-examination? Mr. Ekhardt?

Ekhardt: Yes, Your Honor.

Ekhardt: Hello, Gladys. You're looking most attractive today. Are those new glasses?

Nesbit: Your Honor!

Judge: Mr. Ekhardt, you know such pleasantries are out of order. And we'd all like to go to lunch before it's time for supper. So if you could proceed properly?

Ekhardt: I understand, Your Honor. You know, I'm a little hungry myself. Now Gladys, are the glasses you have on right now the ones you wear for reading?

Fowler: Oh, no. I have a special pair for that.

Ekhardt: And you were wearing that special pair Saturday afternoon?

Fowler: Well, of course. I can't read with the ones I have on now.

Ekhardt: And do you have those reading glasses with you?

Fowler: Yes, in my purse.

Ekhardt: Would you please put them on?

(Witness removes glasses from her purse and puts them on.)

Ekhardt: Thank you, Gladys. Now I'm going to walk to the back of the courtroom.

Nesbit: I object to this line of questioning. It's beyond the scope of what the prosecution presented. It's clear Mr. Ekhardt is going on a fishing expedition.

Judge: Overruled. Bailiff, assist counsel to where he wants to go. Thank you.

(Bailiff assists defense counsel.)

Ekhardt: Now, Mrs. Fowler, are you wearing your reading glasses?

Fowler: Yes.

Ekhardt: The very glasses you had on when the defendant came home that afternoon?

Fowler: I said so, didn't I?

Ekhardt: How many fingers am I holding up?

Fowler: Three?

Vivian Borne: Ha! He isn't holding up any fingers!

Judge (banging gavel): Bailiff! Hold that woman in contempt of court!

Vivian Borne: Couldn't help it, Your Honor. I plead innocent by reason of Tourette syndrome.

Judge: Mrs. Fowler, could you not see Mr. Ekhardt clearly?

Fowler: Well, maybe not as good as with my regular glasses. But the defendant was in a hurry, like he was a guilty man! Why, you should have heard some of the fights that went on over there.

Judge: I've heard quite enough. I'm dismissing this case for lack of evidence. The defendant may be released. (Bangs gavel.) Case dismissed. Mr. Nesbit, I want to see you in my chambers.

End of transcript.

The crowd, clearly on the side of the defendant, burst into applause, and suddenly Wes was surrounded by well-wishers.

My eyes went to Brian, who was standing next to Nesbit; the interim chief spoke a few terse words to the DA, then made a quick exit at the front of the courtroom.

I felt bad for Brian, but was relieved by the hearing's outcome.

Mother and I made our way over to Wes, who was now surrounded by three of his closest friends: Brent Morgan, the tall, dark-haired, good-looking president of the bank; Travis Thompson, a short but broad-shouldered real estate developer with nicely rugged features; and Sean Hartman, a somewhat overweight but impeccably dressed investment broker.

"Wasn't Wayne wonderful?" Mother asked the little congratulatory group, gesturing toward Mr. Ekhardt, who was having a word with Judge Jones.

I figured he was trying to get Mother out of the soup—contempt of court could put her back in the slammer.

Banker Brent, grinning in admiration, was saying, "Wayne Ekhardt is still the best damn lawyer around, at any age."

Mother and I kept our accounts at his bank (the interest was lousy).

Sean was shaking his head, his expression one of half-smiling amazement. "I have to admit I was worried. Especially the times he fell asleep!"

We had some investments with Sean, but so far seemed to be just treading water on his stock market picks.

Travis said, "I tried to talk Wes out of using the old boy . . . but when I'm wrong, I'm wrong. And Wes, buddy, you were right!"

We'd have been better off putting our money with Travis—the land developer seemed to have a Midas touch.

The bailiff came over. "Mrs. Borne, you'll have to come with me."

Apparently Mr. Ekhardt had failed in persuading the judge.

Mother turned to me. "Best you go on home, dear. This may well take a while. Be prepared to pack my kit bag!"

"I can wait."

"No. Wayne will be with me . . . and Judge Jones won't have time for me until she's given the DA a well-deserved dressing down for wasting the taxpayers' money."

The bailiff led Mother through the side door,

with a weary-looking Mr. Ekhardt trailing behind, his day in court not done yet.

Then Brent, Sean, and Travis peeled away from Wes, and I had the freed prisoner to myself.

Wes had a weak smile going, which was about all you could expect from a victory that left him with a wife to bury.

I said, "Looks like I was wrong about Wayne Ekhardt."

He laughed softly. "See, sometimes your mother is worth listening to." Then that small smile turned sideways. "You know, I almost wish this had gone to trial."

"You can't mean that."

"I said 'almost.' But getting the case dismissed for insufficient evidence means there'll be gossip and speculation. It's not the same as 'not guilty.' "

I shrugged. "Since when *weren't* the Sinclairs the topic of gossip and speculation?"

I'd meant that lightly, but he frowned. "What's that supposed to mean?"

"No offense. But in case you haven't noticed, you're Wesley Sinclair. Our quiet little town has always been fascinated by your family—comes with the territory, your wealth and success. That's all I mean."

He was already raising an apologetic hand. "Brandy, I'm sorry. Didn't mean to snap at you or anything. Guess I'm kind of one big raw nerve about now."

"Understandable. Anyway, tongues'll wag for a while, but people have short memories."

I didn't really believe that. Towns like Serenity never forget this kind of thing.

He shrugged. "I just hope these local police are capable of finding whoever . . ." He couldn't finish it. His eyes were moist. "Thanks for being such a good friend, Brandy."

"Even if my jailhouse advice stunk on ice?"

"Even if your jailhouse advice stunk on ice."

He took my hand, squeezed it, then walked out of the courtroom.

Mother was nowhere to be seen, she and Mr. Ekhardt off pleading her case to an unsympathetic judge. If she needed me, she'd call my cell.

The judge had been right about lunchtime, and I was starving, but didn't care to be seen in a public eatery—those wagging tongues again—so I called my BFF, Tina, at home.

"Hey, Teen."

"Brandy! How are you? Wasn't that Sinclair thing this morning?"

"Yup. He walked."

"Is that a good outcome?"

"Very. Got the makings of egg salad sandwiches on hand, by any chance?"

She made the best.

Teen chuckled. "Happens I do. Is somebody looking for a free lunch?"

"Well, the price sounds right, and anyway I'd love to see you . . . and the baby, too."

She laughed once, a kind of grunt. "I see where *we* rate—right after the egg salad."

"Everybody needs their priorities. Can I impose?"

"Sure! Come on over. I was just needing to whip something up anyway. Kevin's here, too."

"Be there in a jiff."

Tina and her husband, Kevin, lived in a white ranch-style house on a bluff overlooking the Mississippi River, a year-round spectacular view. Nothing was more relaxing to me than spending an hour or two on their back patio with a glass of wine, watching the traffic on the water, mostly speedboats but barges as well, hauling cargo downstream as if for my personal entertainment.

As I pulled the Caddy into the driveway, hunky thirtysomething Kevin, his sandy hair now blond from the sun, was in the process of washing their cars (her black Lexus, his silver Mazda). He filled out his white T-shirt and jeans quite nicely.

Hey, the guys get to gawk at the gals, don't they? Turnabout is fair play.

Kevin, spotting me, shut off the hose, then jogged over as I got out of the Caddy.

"Now there's a car I'd love to have," he said with a smile.

"You would till you had to fill the gas tank. Got the day off?"

Kevin used to travel as a sales rep for a drug company, but after the baby arrived, he took a job at a local pharmacy.

"I get Wednesday off when I have to work the weekend," he said. "Go on inside. You won't believe how much B.B. has grown since you saw her last."

B.B. was their nickname for Baby Brandy. If

she grew up to look like Brigitte Bardot that would come in handy. If anybody remembered who that was, when she grew up.

"Yeah," I said, with a sheepish grin, "sorry I've been such a stranger—you coming?"

"In a minute," he said, and went back to the Mazda. He had priorities, too.

I entered the house via the front door, weaving through a tastefully decorated if toy-strewn living room, and on into the kitchen, where Tina was at the sink, peeling boiled eggs.

As usual, she looked beautiful, her features framed by natural blond hair that fell like liquid gold to her shoulders. Of course, I was blond, too. Sorry, no time for further questions.

Tina, trim but shapely in her bleached jeans and yellow top, turned from her work and gave me a smile. "Long time no see."

Was there a tinge of hurt in her words?

I answered in a nervous tumble of words, making a bunch of excuses—the shop, the pilot, the murder, the hearing—ending with, "So— where's the little tyke?"

Tina nodded toward the dining area of the kitchen, where B.B., in a pink sundress, sat on the floor, playing with a doll. She was a living one herself, with her head of yellow curls, blue china eyes, and cupid mouth.

"Put her in the high chair, would you, Brandy?"

"Sure."

I bent, picked the little girl up, and as Tina turned back to the sink, I held the child tightly, smelling her hair, her baby-powder scent, feeling the so-soft skin against my cheek.

I squeezed my eyes shut to keep back the tears. B.B. squirmed, and I put her in the high chair, drawing it up to the table.

Kevin came into the room, crossed over to the sink, and began washing his hands. "Heard on the car radio that Wes got off."

Tina, at the counter, spreading the creamy egg mixture on rye bread, said, "I want a complete play-by-play, Brandy. Since I'm sure you and your mother had ringside seats."

"No problem," I replied. "*After* the egg salad."

Tina smirked. "*After* the egg salad."

I spread my hands. "Hey. It's your fault it's so good."

Tina's Egg Salad

8 hard-boiled eggs, peeled and chopped
3 tbl. mayonnaise
½ tbl. honey mustard
½ tsp. garlic powder
1 tbl. chopped fresh dill
⅓ cp. finely chopped celery
Salt and pepper to taste

Mix all ingredients in a bowl, then spread on fresh rye bread layered with spinach leaves. *Bon appétit!*

Soon we sat around the oak table, munching the sandwiches (okay, in my case wolfing), swishing them down with lemonade, and talking about everything but the hearing, B.B. joining in, in her own special babble. And when the food was gone, and small talk had dwindled, Kevin took a sleepy B.B. away for her nap.

Tina and I moved out onto the patio, where we sat in the shade on padded chairs facing the river, the Mississippi hiding its fabled mud under a deceptive sparkling-diamond sheen.

After I'd filed my report on the hearing, I asked, "Did you know Wes and Vanessa very well?"

"Not really. Kev and I didn't exactly run in their social circle." She took a sip of wine. "But we *almost* did."

"Really? How so?"

Her eyebrows went up and down; her eyes rolled.

"What? Spill!"

"Guess I never told you about something weird that happened to us with Wes and Vanessa. This was a year or so before you came back to town."

I waited.

"Out of the blue, Kevin got this call from Wes—we'd been married, oh, maybe five years. Anyway, Wes wanted to know if we were up for going to Vegas with him and Vanessa and three other couples, and get this—all expenses paid, and we'd fly there in his Learjet."

"Whoa. The one Wes keeps at the municipal airport?"

"Yeah, in the company's name, but for his private use."

I sipped wine. "What other couples?"

"Brent and Megan Morgan, Travis and Emily Thompson, and Sean and Tiffany Hartman."

"His three best buds. They were at the hearing. Go on."

She shrugged. "Anyway, since Wes assured us the invite had nothing to do with selling us time-shares or investments or anything . . . we said yes. But then Kev and I found out *Wes* was going to fly the jet, and that made us wonder."

"Why? Does he have a bad rep as a pilot or something?"

Her eyebrows went up and down again. "No, but when you're invited on a party jet, and the party includes the pilot . . . ? Well, even though we were a little nervous, Kevin and I still went. Turns out Wes was a really good pilot, and didn't partake of the beverage service while he was in the cockpit."

"Must've been a relief."

"Oh yeah. So when we get there, it's really first-class all the way. We have our own suite at the MGM Grand, and everybody has a great time that first day, gambling, seeing shows, eating great food."

"Get to the weird part."

"I'm there. Next night, we all get together in Wes and Vanessa's suite, and, well, everybody drinks a bit too much, and after a while things start to get a touch . . . frisky."

"Frisky how?"

"Wes comes on to me, Vanessa comes on to Kevin."

"Wow. And you never told me about this? What else are you holding back?"

"Brandy!"

"So, what were the other couples doing?"

Tina shook her head. "It's all kind of a haze, but I think there was some . . . mixing and matching, if you know what I mean. All I remember clearly is Kevin pulling me out of there, and us going back to our room."

"*Aaawk*-ward."

"You'd think so, but the next morning, everybody else acted like nothing happened, no embarrassed reactions, or sorries from either Wes or Vanessa. But after that, we were . . . sort of persona non grata for the rest of the trip. Oh, we ate with the group, saw a few more shows, but by midevening, we were on our own. On the flight back, hardly a word was spoken to us. Nobody was rude or anything, we were just . . . wallpaper. We were never so glad to get home after a vacation!"

"What did you make of it?"

Tina shrugged. "Honestly? It was like Kevin and I were being *auditioned* for something—if that makes any sense."

"You mean like . . . everybody drops a room key into a basket kind of deal?"

"Maybe. Docs that kind of thing really go on? And does it go on in *Serenity*?"

"Not on my block it doesn't."

"You sound sure of that."

"I am. Mother would know."

We sat and sipped our wine, both of us digesting what Teen had shared. Finally she spoke again.

"Brandy?"

"Teen?"

"Is there some reason why . . . why you haven't been to see the baby much?"

I sighed. "Teen, I really am sorry—I just wanted to give you and Kevin your space. I won't be a stranger anymore. I promise."

"It's just . . . she's growing fast. I don't want you to miss anything."

I smirked. "*Tell* me about it! Can you believe Jake is thirteen?"

Kevin appeared, settling in another padded chair with an exhausted sigh. "Boy . . . she *finally* went to sleep. They fight hardest when they're tiredest. Did I miss much about the hearing?"

"Just everything," I said. "Teen will fill you in."

I said farewell to my friends—Tina and I made a date for some summer-sale shopping—and I headed out for home. No call from Mother yet. I wondered if Mr. Ekhardt was driving her home. That was the rare situation where we'd be better off with Mother behind the wheel.

Everything was fine as I wound through lovely weather along the scenic river road, until suddenly I had to pull over because I couldn't see through my tears.

Here's the thing.

Baby Brandy was not Kevin's and Tina's, but Kevin's and mine. And before you get all judgmental, let me explain: before Tina's hysterectomy due to cancer, she had some eggs harvested for my surrogate vitro fertilization. And unknown to her—but obviously not Kevin—I had some of my own eggs extracted as a backup. And when Tina's didn't take, mine were used.

Only Kevin and I didn't tell her.

And it came to me in a flash that I was no better than my sister Peggy Sue, who was really my biological mother, a secret kept from me for thirty years.

A Trash 'n' Treasures Tip

It's illegal for vendors to sell counterfeit designer goods. So knock it off with the knockoffs, and don't buy one knowingly just because it's way cheaper. Don't perpetrate a perp's perpetration.

Chapter Six

Nuisance Bid

(Interference bid by a player to upset the game.)

Dearest ones! Vivian Borne with you once again, to provide you with my unique perspective on the events relating to the tragic homicide of Vanessa Sinclair.

But before I begin, I must go on the record to let all and sundry know how very disappointed I am that I have not been given a platform on this subject until now. Sixth chapter, my Aunt Fanny! Why, in *Antiques Disposal* it was *moi* who *began* the book—granted the narrative was whisked away from me after a few pages, but still, I call that progress. In subsequent volumes, however, I've been held off till midway.

This erratic use of my narrative gifts flows from our first book contract being signed by Brandy alone, setting a precedent both unfortunate and limiting. She, and to a lesser degree

our editor, control just how often I am allowed
the microphone, so to speak.

As such, I must call upon you, kind and gentle readers, to double-down on your efforts to
convince our publisher (e-mail, texting, tweet-
ing, and good old-fashioned snail mail) to give
Vivian Borne center stage sooner, and *not* keep
her waiting in the wings. Further, this limitation
of a chapter or two is most unfair. Think of how
entertaining these books would be with me doing more, dare I say, *all* of the writing.

Thank you!

In that regard, I'd like to give a quick shout-
out to Mrs. Felicia Pemberton across the pond
in Bourton-on-the-Water, Glousestershire—a lovely
little village in southwest England right out of
Midsomer Murders—who wrote to say that she has
with no small effort managed to get her local
bookstore to stock our series. Good show, Mrs.
P! (This dedicated reader did intimate that she
had something scandalous on the shop's owner,
and while I don't condone blackmail to get our
books stocked, if a proprietor won't come to his
or her senses, any method is fair dinkum. If you'll
excuse the Australian.)

To that handful of readers (fewer than thirty)
who have written our editor to complain that I
tend to get off the track where the story is concerned, I can only quote my late grandfather:
"If you can't say something nice about somebody, shut your piehole." (Grandpa Ray was, I
would have to admit, not the soul of tact.)

Onward!

During breakfast, Brandy informed me that

she would not be assisting in any further investigation into Vanessa Sinclair's murder.

This proved to be the ex-chief's doing, as I suspected, but she maintained that her Tony was just concerned about us both. That with him on the case, we really didn't need to be. It was a particularly vicious murder and she hoped I'd join her on the sidelines, where it was safe, blah blah blah.

I said I'd respect her decision, but if she interpreted that to mean I would sit next to her on the bench and watch the murder investigation go by, I can only quote the immortal Daffy Duck: "She don't know me very well, do she?"

Anyway, Brandy can sometimes be as much hindrance as help, so I took her news in stride, rather looking forward to not having to justify my actions to, or clear my plans with, the ungrateful child.

I told Brandy that I had some important errands to run today, and asked her to mind the shop, saying I would join her later. Around nine, Brandy left in the Caddy, even though the store didn't open until ten, because we had a box of head vases—including a valuable Marilyn Monroe and an even more rare Jacqueline Kennedy—that needed to be priced and put in a display case.

Sushi remained at home, as the little darling had an upset tummy from getting into a bag of Twizzlers—the red licorice had been unfortunately left on a table within her jumping reach (my bad).

So with Brandy out of my hair, and Sushi napping on the couch, I prepared for a Skype meeting with my thirteen-year-old grandson Jake. Jake lives with his father, Roger, in a suburb of Chicago. We had arranged this confab earlier, when it occurred to me that I could use the young man's computer skills in my investigation.

If you are a grandparent whose well-meaning grandkids insist that you use this newfangled means of visual communication via computer, take heed! While Skype is all well and good for younger people with tight skin, it bodes far less well for those with wrinkles, bags, and sagging jowls (I'm admitting to nothing). Therefore, a little knowledge and preparation may make your experience a more positive one, guaranteed not to scare the little ones (or at least minimize the fear).

DOs AND DON'Ts ON SKYPING FOR THE OVER-FIFTY CROWD
Respectfully submitted by Vivian Borne

1) **DO** position the webcam at eye level so that you won't be looking down, which will give you a double chin. (If you already have a double chin, improper webcam placement will give you a triple.)

2) **DO** place a light source in front of you to soften your features; an overhead will only serve to make you look like Lon Chaney in *The Phantom of the Opera*. (Possible exception: Skyping on Halloween.)

3) **DON'T** lean into the computer screen, which will distort your face, creating a large proboscis. (Jimmy Durante impressions mean nothing to the younger generation. More's the pity.)

4) **DO** make sure a ceiling fan isn't twirling directly over your head, giving the effect of wearing a giant beanie with propeller. (This may come as a shock, but such headgear is now out of style, even on college campuses.)

5) **DO** wear a colorful chin-high scarf to detract from your face. (Suggestion: pile on the bling to dazzle—and distract —the viewer.)

While I'm on the subject of computers, I have a little comment I'd like to make, and it's about the symbol #. We already have two words for #: *number* and *pound key.* Do we really need another, particularly one nicknamed *hashtag?* Especially since said word is a derivative of the word *hashish?* Let's stop messing with the English language! Just say no to hashtags!

I got myself situated in front of my computer at the library table in the music room, and soon Jake popped onto the screen.

The handsome blue-eyed boy, his hair as blond as Brandy's back when she achieved that color naturally, flashed his infectious smile.

"Hi, Grandma. What's up?"

I beamed at him. "*Me,* dear—to mischief!"

"That's no surprise. How are Mom and Sushi doing?"

"Everybody's hunky-dory." I could see by the background that he was seated in his room. "No school today?"

"I'm on a two-week vacation."

Jake attended a year-round private school, getting time off for good behavior every two months.

He was saying, "I wish I could come stay with you guys for a couple of days . . . but you can probably guess that Dad said 'no way' . . . 'cause of what happened the last time."

Jake had become involved in a previous investigation of ours (*Antiques Chop*), which made his father extremely cross with his mother and me.

I said, "Well, I'm on another case, dear, and I could really use your help."

"That woman who got killed that you texted me about."

"Yes indeed."

"Isn't Mom on the case, too?"

"No, she's sitting this one out, my darling. That ex-chiefie boyfriend of hers is turning into as great big a party-pooper as your daddy. Meaning no disrespect to either."

His face brightened. "So I'm your backup man on this caper."

"Yes, dear. My little long-distance Watson. Just don't mention it to your father. Or your mother. Or anyone."

"But *especially* not Dad."

"Especially not."

His father, Roger, and I were oil and water. Exxon-Valdez level.

"So, Grandma, how can I help?"

Unlike his mother, Jake was always game for a good murder mystery.

"I need some information, dear," I said. "The kind only a knowledgeable young person like yourself might know."

"Sure."

"Can a person break into another person's e-mail account?"

He shrugged. "Happens all the time."

"How?"

"Pretty easy. But, Grandma—if you're thinking of trying it yourself, you could get into real trouble."

"Don't you worry about that, sweetheart. It's not likely the murdered woman is going to file a complaint."

His eyebrows went up. "Good point."

"So how do I go about it?"

His eyebrows came down. "Well, have you ever forgotten your password?"

"Why, all the time. Just last week . . . oh! I see! I need to be able to answer Vanessa's 'secret question,' to reset her password."

"You got it, Grandma. But there are other ways. Let me handle it. There's a hacker's site I belong to."

What a sweet, thoughtful, resourceful child!

"Grandma, do you know the murdered lady's e-mail address?"

"Yes, dear. The victim quite fortuitously belonged to New Hope, and it's listed in our church directory. You see how regular church attendance can pay off?"

So many of our young people have fallen away from the church and its teachings. Anyway, having come prepared, I had the directory with me, and gave Jake the information, which he jotted down.

We visited a while longer, but I could sense he had better things to do than jabber with his grandmother. And I was eager to get my day of sleuthing underway.

Since Brandy had taken the Caddy, my mode of transportation would be the traveling trolley, which made a regular stop "on the hour" about a block from our house. The old gas-converted trolley car was provided free by certain merchants to encourage Serenityites to cast their hard-earned bread into the waters of the downtown, instead of out at the mall.

And I was often able—depending upon the driver of the day—to talk him or her into veering off the scheduled route, to take me where I really wanted to go. But today, no wheedling was needed—in true Petula Clark fashion, downtown happened to be my destination.

As regular readers of these nonfiction accounts are well aware, I have a bottomless font (not in the apparel sense!) (or the typesetting one, either) of amusing trolley stories, and here is another one that I'm sure will make you smile if not outright chortle.

One fine day I was riding the trolley while I

was in the midst of rehearsals for a Playhouse production of *Meet Me in St. Louis.* I was playing the Judy Garland part—I did receive some close-minded opposition from the director who felt I was somewhat too mature for the role; but I successfully argued that with the right stage make-up and wig, not a soul would notice, and besides, 99.9 percent of the audience was elderly and afflicted with cataracts.

Where was I? Oh, yes. On the trolley. I was in a euphoric mood that day riding the colorful nostalgic vehicle, this being a beautiful spring morning off my medication, when a sudden, irresistible urge (like the one in *Anatomy of a Murder*) came over me. I rose from my seat and burst into the production's signature number, "The Trolley Song."

(I have been informed by the publisher's legal department that I cannot reprint the lyrics without incurring a considerable fee. Let us leave it at this: they had to do with clanging and dinging and zinging.)

Well, for some reason my spirited vocal rendition startled the driver—true, I *had* been sitting right behind him—and he swerved off the road and hit a telephone pole, which snapped like a toothpick and tipped over on a dry cleaning establishment, whose roof burst into flames. There was reportedly a fire hydrant that the trolley ran over—sending water geysering—but I can't be sure. I was knocked out cold, having been thrown forward and hitting my head on the windshield. Fortunately, no one else on board was the worse for wear.

There was an effort made to ban me from the trolley, but I threatened a lawsuit for my injuries and we came to terms.

Today the trolley was right on time, and I was pleased to see Shawntea Monroe at the helm.

As I climbed aboard, Shawntea—wearing a summery pink blouse and jeans, her lovely black hair cascading in tight curls—gave me a winning smile. "Hello, Ms. Borne. How are you this lovely mornin'?"

"Peachy-keen," I said, adding, "and, dear, we've known each other too long for you to call me anything but Vivian."

I slid into the closest seat opposite her (having learned not to sit directly behind the driver—though I am sure my vocalizing would not have fazed this skilled driver).

Right now the trolley was hauling only a few passengers, this being an off-time for travel, what with people already at work, and the downtown shops not quite open for business.

"And how are Kwamie and Zeffross?" I asked.

Pulling away from the curb, Shawntea afforded me a glance. "Oh, just fine, Ms., uh, Vivian. Kwamie starts kindergarten in the fall, and Zeffross will be in the second grade."

"Delightful. And, tell me, how do you like community college?"

"Girl, I love it! All the teachers are just so *nice*. There's a nursing degree I'm lookin' into."

"Why, dear, you'd do wonderfully in that field."

Shawntea gave me another glance. "Ms. Borne . . . I mean, Vivian. I owe you a lot. I owe you about everything."

"Oh, tish-tosh. I merely gave you a leg up."

She shook her head, curls bouncing along with the bus. "No, I mean it. If you hadn't helped me get a full-time scholarship at the college, I could never have swung it."

"Dear, I did nothing but tell you about funds that were already available—you got that scholarship on your own merits."

I would, however, have been prepared to bring pressure on certain members of the scholarship board if she hadn't received one. Skeletons can always come rattling out of closets, you know.

Shawntea was asking, "Where was it you wanted to be let out, Vivian?"

"Hunter's Hardware, if you please . . . and if you're still on duty later, dear, I might ask for special consideration."

I believe in giving a helping hand to others and seek nothing in return. But a little payback can't hurt.

"You got it," she said. "I may work for the city, but say the word and I'm your chauffeur."

Smiling, I settled back in my seat.

Downtown's Main Street, which ran parallel to the river, amounted to four blocks of restored Victorian buildings housing little shops and boutiques with the occasional bistro. Faux gas lamps, sidewalk benches, and ornate street signs created a quaint turn-of-last-century effect.

Shawntea stopped the trolley in front of Hunter's and I disembarked. Soon a small bell above the ancient door was announcing my tinkling arrival. (Sometimes words with two meanings can create unfortunate misinterpretations.)

Hunter's was a uniquely Midwestern aberration: the front of the elongated store, which hadn't been remodeled since I wore Mary Janes, still retained its original tin ceiling and hardwood floor. This section had everything one might expect of a modern hardware business, but the rear consisted of a small bar area that offered hard liquor to hard-working men who stopped in for hardware.

(No one ever seemed to question this lethal combination of tools and alcohol, the most recent accident occurring after a male customer rose from his barstool, feeling no pain, then bought an electric drill, went home, and made a hole in a board. Then he felt pain, because his hand had been under the board at the time.)

The proprietors were Mary and Junior, the former running the cash register in front, the latter tending bar in back. The middle-aged couple had bought the business some years back with money Mary got after she lost a leg in a freak accident at the Universal Studios theme park in Orlando.

(Since mentioning this in several books, I have received a "cease and desist" letter from Universal, and can no longer report *exactly* what happened to Mary on the *Jaws* ride. Let's just say the mechanical shark short-circuited, and you can take it from there.)

Squat Mary, her brownish-gray hair in a messy bun, was occupied with a customer, so I was spared having to trade small talk with the (frankly) unpleasant woman. No matter how cheerful or complimentary I might be, she was a regular Debbie Downer (make that Mary Morose). Is it my fault that her prosthesis doesn't fit quite right? (You could tell by her uneven gait.) That run-in with a fake shark had made her a genuine crab.

I breezed on by, weaving in and around various floor displays, making my way to the back, where I found Junior polishing glass tumblers behind a scarred bar almost old enough to interest my historical preservation group.

Junior nearly qualified for that himself—a paunchy, rheumy-eyed, mottled-nosed man in his late sixties who all too obviously enjoyed sampling his own liquid wares.

As I slid up on one of the gashed-leather stools, he smiled pleasantly. "Well, hello, Vivian. The usual?"

"That's right. And don't spare the maraschinos."

I had learned the hard way here at the hardware store that the hard stuff (too much?) did not mix well with my medication. Ever since, my drink of choice has been a Shirley Temple. (On really cold days, I might order a hot toddy, hold the toddy.)

Fixing my concoction, Junior said, "Terrible about Mrs. Sinclair. Nasty business. You lookin' into it?"

"I might be."

"Any leads on who mighta whacked her—I mean, since her hubby got let off?"

"Maybe."

He waited for me to continue, and when I didn't, he frowned, shrugged, then set my drink in front of me.

I didn't care if he found me coy. After all, I wasn't here to *give* information, but to *get* it. And certainly not from Junior. He had a terrible memory and always got things mixed up—like telling his customers *I* had been a surrogate mother, not Brandy . . . which I am embarrassed to say I did not hear about until that reporter from the *National Enquirer* called.

What is so newsworthy about the notion of a woman my age giving birth, anyway? And imagine, asking me if it was a bat baby! I straightened out that newshound on that score, and the local gossip mill, too.

I took a dainty sip. Junior might be a buffoon, but he could make a darn good Shirley Temple (including the extra cherries).

"Henry down yet?" I asked.

Henry was Hunter's perennial barfly, who rented a room above the store from Junior. A once prominent surgeon, the hapless Henry lost his license after sneaking a belt of whiskey to steady his hands before performing a gall-bladder operation. The procedure went swimmingly, until a nurse pointed out it was meant to be an appendectomy.

But Henry could be a fountain of information. Seated quietly in his cups, he took in everything anyone around him might say, the way a sponge absorbs a spill. And because he was a regular fixture, no one paid him any heed.

Junior nodded toward the bathrooms.

I leaned forward and whispered, "Everything going according to plan?"

Junior winked back. "Old fella doesn't suspect a thing."

For years we had been trying to get Henry off the sauce, unselfishly so, considering our two vested interests—Junior would lose revenue, and me my top snitch. But we had become concerned about our friend's deteriorating health. Time and again we would manage to get Henry up on the wagon, only to have the old boy fall off again.

Then, as should come as no surprise, I came up with an ingenious plan. We convinced Henry to back off the booze and imbibe strictly beer, which Junior offered to provide free. Henry had no idea the beers Junior would set in front of him were strictly nonalcoholic.

(Since Henry spent all his waking hours at Hunter's, the barfly never had the opportunity to drink the real stuff elsewhere.)

Henry, back from the bathroom, gave me a crooked smile as he took a stool, leaving one between us.

"'lo, Viv—how they hangin'?"

I raised my eyebrows at Junior, as if to say, *Have you been giving him the real thing?* The bartender shook his head.

Which led me to the conclusion that Henry's drunken condition must be a placebo effect. I knew the transition between booze and "beer" had caused Henry some rough days, but he'd weathered them in anticipation of a lifetime of free Budweiser.

"They're hangin' just fine, Henry," I replied, not knowing exactly what of mine were hanging where.

Junior, giving me another wink, set another mug of ersatz suds before the man. Henry took a long gulp, then wiped the foam from his mouth with the back of a hand. "Been thinkin' 'bout that mur . . . mur . . . murder."

My ears perked, like Sushi hearing me open a bag of potato chips (or Twizzlers). "Yes, Henry?"

He hiccuped. "I know who . . . who *done* it." He raised a finger to his lips to indicate to keep this on the down low.

I leaned near. Whispered: "You do?"

He nodded. "One a thaa . . . thaa . . . *them*."

This had been delivered in a dead-on approximation of Foster Brooks (that's what Google's for, children!).

"Them who, dear?"

"*Them!*"

The generally congenial Henry seemed suddenly irritable—a near-beer side effect, perhaps?

"Oh, *them*," I said, nodding in agreement, having no idea what he was talking about but settling him down, at least.

Henry nodded. "Yeah. That . . . that . . . ka . . . ka . . ."

"Ka what, dear? Kaboom?"

"Club."

"And what club would that be?"

"The ay . . . ay . . . *Eight*."

"Eight of what, dear?

"Eight uf . . . uf . . . Clubs! Shuh . . . shuh . . ."

"Shazam?"

"Shuh . . . nan . . . i . . . guns."

"Shenanigans, Henry?"

Henry nodded, eyes half-lidded.

Casually, I asked, "Who belongs to this club?"

"Dunno, dun' care."

I was about to pose another question, but he raised a hand. He had spoken his piece. But what was the Eight of Clubs? And what kind of shenanigans were they mixed up in?

I gulped down my Shirley Temple, then gestured to Junior to follow me to the front of the store, where next to a display of paintbrushes, I asked, "Is he always like that?"

Junior nodded, shrugged, made an *I-don't-get-it* face. "Ever since our little plan went into effect, yeah."

"Maybe you better start giving him the real thing."

He frowned. "What about his health?"

"I'm worried about *my* health. Henry's no good to me in that kind of condition."

Junior shook his head. "Sorry, Vivian. Henry *thinkin'* he's drunk is way better than him picklin' what's left of his liver."

I sighed. "I suppose. But it makes me want to shake him!"

"Why?"

"You *know* I can't abide overacting!"

And I left the store.

Since Henry had largely failed me—*maybe* the Eight of Clubs was a lead—my next move was to connect with the Romeos (Retired Old Men Eating Out), who about now should be having an early lunch at a downtown eatery called Boonie's. The recently opened sports bar was the group's latest hangout, the only place in Serenity where one could get a hamburger cooked rare—and the Romeos liked their cow still mooing, never mind the cholesterol, high blood pressure, and possibility of salmonella. (I wonder—can you get salmonella from eating salmon?)

So I hoofed it over to Iowa Avenue, where Boonie's—named after the owner—was housed on the first floor of another restored Victorian building. But for the original redbrick walls, the inside had been completely remodeled, with modern tables and chairs, colorful sports memorabilia, huge flat screen TVs abounding with baseball, and the usual assortment of games—computer poker, wall darts, retro Ms. Pac Man—found in an upscale sports bar.

I scouted the already busy place, then spotted the boys gathered around a corner table, already hunkered over their lunches.

I say "boys," but really, they were starting to look long in the tooth, and those teeth were mostly not original parts.

Today, only four Romeos were present, affliction and extinction having dwindled their numbers as of late. Those remaining included Harold, ex-army sergeant; Vern, retired chiropractor; Randall, former hog farmer; and Wendell, one-time riverboat captain.

While I enjoyed the company of my gal pals, I

valued the acquaintanceship of these grizzled survivors more. Why? Because 1) men of a certain age knew more about local dirty laundry than any female gossip, 2) they are easily manipulated by one possessing feminine wiles (me), and 3) they can always be counted on to accurately pass along misinformation that I feed them, well-done not rare.

"Hello, fellas," I come-up-and-see-me-some-timed. "Mind if I join you?"

Much as these Viagra snappers might still like the ladies, the female gender was generally not welcome at their gatherings. I, however, had become an exception—like Shirley MacLaine to the Rat Pack. That's what a little charm, some good Danish genes, and a fair supply of tittle-tattle can get you.

My greeting resulted in an affirmative reaction from the boys, though not quite as enthusiastic as usual. *What was that about?*

I slid into an empty chair next to Randall, who might best be described as a less sophisticated Sydney Greenstreet. After all, Sydney Greenstreet had probably never been a hog farmer. Back in the day, I would have never sat near Randall, at least not downwind. But the pork man has had plenty time to air out.

Harold, across the table from me, asked courteously, "How are you, Vivian? You're looking well."

Harold resembled the older Bob Hope, particularly as viewed by me without my glasses. Once upon a time—after his wife passed, and my husband the same—the ex-sergeant had asked me to marry him. But I politely declined, knowing that in addition to being relegated to KP duty, I'd be made Permanent Latrine Orderly.

"Why, I'm fine, Harold," I said.

Interesting that he hadn't mentioned what everyone in town knew: that Brandy and I had recently found a murder victim's body.

"Lots of zip," I went on. "You see . . ." Time to test the waters. ". . . I'm on the case to find Vanessa Sinclair's killer."

This elicited no comments. True, my taking this on would surprise no one. But the men clearly seemed to be avoiding any further eye contact, returning to their remaining lunches. Something was wrong in the state of Boonie's.

The old gents were closing ranks, perhaps suspecting that my questions might lead somewhere embarrassing or troubling. Was this old boys' club trying to protect the members of another club?

The Eight of Clubs maybe?

A waitress, noticing my addition to the group, appeared, and I ordered coffee.

After she left, I looked around at my reluctant hosts as if we were all seated at a poker table. I was about to run a bluff.

"Look, fellas," I said, casual as old shoes, "I know *all about* the Eight of Clubs . . . so there's no reason acting all tight-lipped like this. Do you really imagine you could tell Vivian Borne anything she hasn't discovered already? Especially about their . . ." What was the word Henry had used? ". . . shenanigans?" Unfortunately, I unintentionally slurred it like Henry had.

"*What?*" the men asked in unison.

"Shenanigans," I said sharply. It came out right this time.

Wendell, seated next to Harold, and a dead ringer for Leo Gorcey (Google, kids), asked, "What's the Eight of Clubs?"

He didn't appear to be responding to my bluff with a bluff of his own. A relative newbie to the group, the ex-riverboat captain might not yet be in the complete confidence of the other, in-longer-standing members.

Which was a lucky break for me. And we all know that it's better to be lucky than smart.

"Gentlemen," I said, "perhaps it would be best if one of you filled Wendell in. Not polite to keep a fellow Romeo in the dark."

Vern, on the other side of Wendell, and who reminded me of the older Zachary Scott (who reminded me of the older Clark Gable), leaned toward the newbie, speaking in a whisper. "Couples who get together to play bridge."

Wendell blinked. "So?"

"Well, they do more than deal cards, if you get my drift."

Wendell frowned. "Not really."

Harold grunted at the man's naïveté.

"They trade partners around."

"You do that in bridge sometimes."

"I mean, they're into . . ." Harold looked around, lowered his voice as he said, ". . . spouse swapping, man."

The old newbie's eyebrows climbed his forehead like two gray caterpillars trying to mate. "Who's in this club?"

The others exchanged cautious looks, then Vern spoke sotto voce (but not so sotto that I couldn't hear his voce, despite this darn chronic earwax buildup). "That rich Yuppie bunch— Brent and Megan Morgan, Travis and Emily Thompson, Sean and Tiffany Hartman, and Wes and Vanessa Sinclair."

Harold added, "Started out as a bridge club. That's why they call themselves the Eight of Clubs."

And there it was, out in the open. What Pastor Tutor had merely hinted about with his Biblical references, and the pseudodrunk Henry couldn't quite verbalize.

I had to admit I was shocked. I was no prude, having lived through the Swinging Sixties; but these four couples were pillars of the community, men holding prestigious jobs and wives— minus one, now—much admired. They were churchgoers and members of various community organizations, the kind whose logos decorate WELCOME TO signs at the city limits of small towns.

Like Serenity.

Wendell, his open mouth finally moving, said, "My heavens. I know what *men* are like. But how could the *wives* go along with it? Do you think they were pressured?"

Harold shrugged. "Who knows with that generation? Maybe they all see it as a safe way to fool around. Maybe even the gals *liked* the idea."

I drained the last of my coffee, and set the cup down. "Maybe one of them didn't. The one who's dead."

Mother's Trash 'n' Treasures Tip

At a swap meet, never buy electronics without trying them out first. If this is not possible, get a return guarantee in writing from the seller. By the way, contact us through our website if anyone's out there who knows someone who can fix a Sony Betamax.

Chapter Seven

Squeeze Play

(Forcing the defenders to discard a vital card.)

Morning at the shop was surprisingly busy for a Thursday, and I really could have used Mother's help, but she was off doing some "important errands," the details of which she didn't share and I didn't request.

Over breakfast, I had summoned my intestinal fortitude and informed Mother that I was withdrawing my participation from the hunt for Vanessa Sinclair's killer.

"Oh?" Mother's eyebrows rose high over her round glasses. "That doesn't sound like you, dear."

"Here's a novel idea," I said. "Why can't you let the police handle an investigation for a change?"

"Why?" Mother shot me a sardonic look. "Because, dear, they've proven themselves incompetent a thousand times over. If it hadn't been for me—for *us*—a half-dozen murders in this town might have gone unsolved."

I forked absently at my scrambled eggs. "With Tony back and on the case, they should fare just fine on their own. And anyway, I promised him I'd stay out of it."

Mother frowned. "I thought I detected his fine Italian hand in this! I hope that promise didn't include me."

"No. But I wish you could see how any further meddling in police affairs could hurt his chances of becoming chief again."

"Poppycock. He *needs* our help." She placed her napkin on the table with purpose. "Tell me— has the killer been found?"

I poked the eggs some more, shrugged.

"That's not an answer, dear."

She was actually going to make me say it! "No. They haven't."

"Case closed. Or anyway it *will* be, after I'm finished." And she sat back with a satisfied smile.

I set the fork down. "Mother, this is a particularly vicious murder. Tony is just thinking of us, our safety. I think we're better off on the sidelines this time around."

Mother had a wounded look. "All right, dear—if that's the way you want it."

"I do."

And that's how we'd left it.

Even though I'd been occupied at the shop with a steady stream of customers, I was distracted by the sinking feeling that I'd let Mother down. I didn't really think she was going to consign herself to the sidelines. Those "errands" she was running almost certainly represented her going off poking around and checking with her "snitches."

Adding irritation to my discomfort was the sale of several I ♥ VIVIAN T-shirts this morning, and not a single I ♥ BRANDY. So I removed two of mine from the stack, hid them in the back of the bottom counter drawer, and put my own money in the till to cover the secret transaction.

I had no choice in the matter—if Mother won the T-shirt war, she would be even more insufferable.

Around noon, foot traffic subsided, and I was eating a brown-bagged turkey sandwich at the checkout counter, Sushi patiently waiting for scraps, when the bell above the front door tinkled.

I suppressed a groan as Dumpster Dan came in, in another rumpled shirt and slacks, his sparse white hair windblown, the dirty cloth bag dangling from one thin arm, bulging with his latest find.

I mustered some semblance of a friendly greeting as he shuffled toward the counter.

"I think you'll *really* be interested in *this*," Dan said excitedly, tiny eyes behind the thick lenses shining like bright new pennies. Which was about how much his latest discovery would likely rate.

Reaching into the bag, he withdrew the item and placed it on the counter. "It's a cast-iron toy truck," the man said proudly. "These are really collectible."

I picked up the toy. "Well, it *is* a truck," I granted. "Only it's not cast-iron."

His new-penny eyes faded with sudden wear. "No? How can you tell? That's metal, right?"

"Right, but not iron. You can tell by the weight."

"Oh. Didn't know that."

"Plus, this is a cheap reproduction, and we have a policy of not taking that kind of thing." I handed the truck back. "How about a little free advice?"

"I'd appreciate that."

"There's a reason things end up in Dumpsters—usually the stuff's either broken or just plain worthless."

"But sometimes I find things," he replied, spirit undampened. "Your store, it's called Trash 'n' Treasures. So I don't have to tell *you* that a treasure can wind up in the trash."

"Yes. It can. And people win the lottery, sometimes. If you could do a little research on what you find—the library has computers you can use—you might spare yourself from being disappointed."

And wasting my time, I thought, but hoped my smile didn't show it.

After Dan shuffled out, I hoped I hadn't seemed too curt; I supposed I should have given him a couple of bucks, if not for his trouble, for getting that fake out of circulation.

Still, I felt like I'd let him (and myself) down,

and I got out from behind the counter, and went outside to call him back. But Dumpster Dan had disappeared.

And that's when I noticed that something else had disappeared—specifically, the New Jersey godfather's black Cadillac.

The Caddy had been parked at the curb, and now I stood gaping at its empty spot, as if staring long and hard enough might make it magically reappear. I even blinked like Barbara Eden on *I Dream of Jeannie.* No magic.

My first thought was that someone had stolen the Caddy—maybe that guy at the swap meet who'd wanted to buy it—but then I noticed something written on the sidewalk that hadn't been there when I arrived, and went to investigate.

Scrawled in what appeared to be lipstick, like a serial killer's plea for help, was: NEEDED THE WHEELS.

In Mother's favorite shade—Red Door.

I closed my eyes, opened them, and just as the Caddy had refused to reappear, this lipstick missive refused to disappear.

Panicking, I ran back into the shop and tried to reach Mother on her cell. But my call got forwarded to an already-full mailbox, which wasn't surprising—Mother never wanted to be bothered when she was out sleuthing. So I tried the landline at home. No answer there either, but I did leave a message on the machine (which can't be repeated here, if we ever hope to get these books into Walmart).

There wasn't anything else I could do. I certainly couldn't call the police without getting Mother into the hottest water ever, since not only did she have no valid driver's license, this would be her umpteenth vehicular offense. Mr. Ekhardt had been able to get her out of that courtroom contempt charge with a hundred-dollar fine, but this? Did the county jail have solitary confinement, I wondered?

And I most assuredly couldn't call Tony, and ask for his help on the q.t., without seeming to have let him down on my promise to keep us out of this one.

So I returned my attention to the shop, keeping myself busy by dusting the merchandise, and waiting on customers, while I ran around inside my head like somebody trying to flee a burning building.

Around four the phone on the counter rang; I was in the living room area and, thinking it was Mother, made a sprint for it.

"Brandy? It's Wes."

"Oh. Wes. Hi."

"Everything all right?" he asked. "You sound out of breath."

"Everything's fine," I said. "Expecting a call, that's all. Uh, what's up?"

"I can really use a favor."

"Sure, I'll try to help. What is it?"

"Would you mind going with me to see Gladys Fowler?"

I couldn't imagine why on earth he'd want to see that awful woman, after she'd testified for the DA, and I told him so.

"I know," he said with a sigh. "But she called me just now, at the office, and said she had information about who really killed Vanessa, but refused to tell me over the phone."

"I don't trust her. You should call Brian Lawson or Tony Cassato about this."

"I don't trust her, either. But I don't really care to interact with the local police unless I have to. And I've just got to find out if there's something to it. Plus, the woman sounded, well . . . weird."

"Weird how?"

"I don't know—anxious? Even . . . scared."

"Whoa."

"Listen, if I'm going to deal with this woman, on any level, about anything, I need a witness."

"Okay. But why me?"

"All my male friends are tied up at their own jobs. And I guess you're about the only . . . female friend I have, right now."

"All right. I'll go with you. I can lock up here."

He sighed. "Look, Brandy, before you say yes . . . there's something else about this that you should know—something I didn't even mention to Wayne Ekhardt."

"Okay."

"Just before the hearing, the Fowler woman called me at home, and tried to . . . well, there's no other word for it. She tried to blackmail me."

"Holy . . . what *about?*"

"She said if I paid her ten thousand dollars, she'd withdraw what she told the police—you know, that garbage about me coming home the afternoon of the murder."

"What did you say to her?"

"What do you think? I told her to stick it. Anyway, I wasn't afraid of her telling the truth."

"Maybe, Wes, but it's a good thing Mr. Ekhardt was able to discredit her testimony."

"He really is the best, awake or asleep. But now I'm wondering . . . did that woman *really* see somebody at my house?"

"And maybe," I said, thinking aloud, "didn't see who it was because of her glasses? And just guessed it was you?"

"Or something. And maybe now has figured out who it *really* was. Anyway, are you up for this?"

"I am."

"Can you come over to my office now? I'm just finishing up for the day. You don't mind closing up a little early?"

"That's okay. Never much business in the last hour. See you in a few minutes."

And I hung up.

In my mind, I saw Tony, looking at me. Frowning. Come on, I wouldn't really be investigating. I'd be helping out a friend. Right? This time my Jeannie blink worked, and Tony's image went away.

I closed up the shop but did not set the alarm, since I was leaving Sushi behind with some water, kibble, and newspapers. I'd come back for her and close up more completely later.

Then I made the two-block jaunt over to Sinclair Consolidated, a striking new addition to the downtown, a three-story building of stone and glass, a rare modern building among Victorian neighbors.

Wes had moved his corporate offices to these new digs just two years ago, one of his first major decisions after the death of his father. I assume that the relocation was to get away from the stench and smoke of the Sinclair grain processing plant south of town.

I entered the gleaming, opulent lobby and checked in with an attractive young female receptionist (was that an Albert Nipon suit?), who sent me up to the third floor, where I checked in with an older, no-nonsense secretary (but just as expensively attired). By phone she let Wes know I was there, then replaced the receiver and sent me to take a seat in the waiting area.

Interesting. Sinclair Consolidated put a lovely face in its lobby, and a strict grade-school teacher's puss outside the CEO's office. Made sense, I guessed.

Less than a minute later, Wes stepped out of his office, looking sharp in a tailored navy suit, yellow shirt, and light blue silk tie.

He approached me saying, "Brandy, I'm just wrapping up in here. One more phone call to make. Can you wait? Won't be more than ten or fifteen minutes."

I shrugged. "No problem."

"Joyce can get you some coffee."

"That'd be great."

The secretary, hearing her name, looked up, suddenly pleasant.

"Cream or sugar?" she asked.

"Just cream, thanks."

Wes disappeared back into his office.

If I had to cool my heels anywhere, it might as well be in the fanciest corporate offices in Serenity. This reception area looked like a high-end furniture showroom with its abstract-pattern plush rug, comfy leather couch, black leather chairs, flat screen TV (business channel, natch), and unlit gas fireplace. Even the magazines on the mahogany coffee table were current.

Joyce returned with my coffee—no oil-slick surface here—and I settled back with *Entertainment Weekly*. There was an article about pending TV pilots for next season, and we had rated a mention. Our pilot really leading to a series was something I half-dreaded, half-dreamed of.

I tried Mother again. Mailbox still full. No answer at home. No answer at the shop.

The coffee was magnificent, but the caffeine was probably not helping my anxiety over Mother. Still, I was about to ask Joyce for a second cup when Wes's office door opened and he came out, unbuttoning his collar. He blew air out his mouth, and his forehead was lightly beaded.

"Joyce," he said, "would you call someone about the air conditioning in my office? Could be the sun coming in all those windows . . . but I'd like it checked out just the same."

"Yes, Mr. Sinclair."

"Either that, or I need to deal with an easier-going distributor." He smiled boyishly and the middle-aged secretary returned it warmly. "I'll be gone for the rest of the afternoon. But you can reach me on my cell."

Then he turned to me with a smile and asked, "Ready?"

I said yes, and followed him back into his office, unexpectedly decorated with Asian-style furnishings, then through a door leading to a small elevator that took us down to street level. In the back parking lot, a reserved spot was home to a silver Jaguar.

"That is one nice ride," I said.

"Vanessa wanted me to drive something, uh . . . suitable for my position." He shrugged. "But I'm a Midwestern boy. Would've been fine with a pickup truck. A Sierra, maybe."

"She was right," I said. "Wrong image entirely."

He gave me a smirk. "Even for a guy who sells grain for a living?"

"Why not split the difference? Surely Jaguar makes a pickup."

That got a laugh out of him. "Get in, you goof." And he opened my car door for me. Then, as he shut me in, he said seriously, "Thanks for this."

I gave him a nod and a smile.

After a few blocks, he turned onto Mulberry Street, a main artery leading out of the downtown area. We rode in silence for a few minutes.

Then Wes said, "There's something I'd like to come clean about."

"Clean is good."

We had stopped for a light. "You may have heard rumors . . ."

"Green."

"What?"

"Green light."

We moved through the intersection.

I said, "You mean about wife-swapping?"

Wes pulled the Jag over to the curb. Twisted to face me. "You've heard about that?"

"Tina and Kevin are good friends. So I know that it's more than just a rumor."

He sighed a laugh. "Yeah . . . was *that* trip a debacle . . ."

I raised both hands as if in surrender. "Hey, what consenting adults do behind closed doors is no business of mine. Anyway, I'm no angel. Maybe you've heard why my husband divorced me. Not a pretty story."

He was interested. "I *haven't* heard anything about that, really, but . . . wasn't he a lot older? I always figured it was an age thing."

"Well, there was *that* . . . but I had a one-night stand with an old boyfriend at my ten-year high school reunion. So I can hardly sit in judgment of the, uh . . . peccadilloes of others." I paused, then added, "A bottle of cheap champagne may have had something to do with it."

Smiling sadly, Wes nodded. "That's pretty much what happened to us. One evening, three other couples we were playing bridge with got bored with the game, and the drinking got a little out of hand, and well, with no inhibitions to stop us, one thing led to another, as they say."

"Where would bad judgment be without alcohol to help it along?"

"Exactly." Another sigh. "Then, after we sobered up, instead of being ashamed, we found we'd all . . . rather enjoyed it. We were frat brothers, the other guys and me, and the wives all sorority sisters, and a fairly wild, sophisticated group. And this is Serenity, so . . . any fooling around was better off handled sort of . . . in house. I mean, isn't that better than—"

"A one-night stand with an old flame?"

"I wasn't going there, Brandy. Really."

"Wes, you don't have to justify yourself to me. Like I said, you were all consenting adults."

Or were they? Vanessa had to have been unhappy about something.

Wes put a hand on my knee. "I knew you'd be understanding."

Suddenly uncomfortable, I lifted the hand off my knee and gave it back to him. "Emphasis on the consenting, okay? I'm just here to be a witness this afternoon."

"I'm sorry, Brandy. I didn't mean . . . you know I've always liked you."

"And I've always liked you. Now, let's get going."

Gladys Fowler's house was what they used to call a bungalow—a one-story brick affair with a wide wooden porch and low-slung roof typically built in the 1920s for a middle-income family.

Wes parked the Jag in the driveway, and we got out.

He stood for a moment, looking across the street at his own home, which seemed to exist on some other planet than the Fowler one.

"I'm going to sell that monstrosity," he said quietly. "It's just too . . . too damn hard, living there anymore."

"Give it some time. You might change your mind."

He shook his head. "I've already talked to Travis about putting it on the market."

That sounded to me like a bereaved widower making a bad decision.

"But who in Serenity could afford to buy it?" I asked. "You'll never get your money out of it."

"I know I'll take a loss—Vanessa went crazy over-improving the property. But at this point I just don't care."

Must be nice, having enough money not to care.

"Well, try not to do anything too rash," I said. "Come on—let's go see what the ever delightful Gladys Fowler has to say for herself."

We walked to the front steps, went up, then crossed the wide porch where a wooden swing, hanging by chains from the porch's ceiling, swayed in the breeze, as if a ghost were rocking there.

The doorbell brought no response—no surprise, with the television blaring inside—but a pounding on the door failed to summon the mistress of the house, either.

I went over to a picture window and peered in.

An old *Match Game* rerun was playing on a console tube television facing me, Gladys seated in an easy chair, just the top of her head and one arm visible.

"She's in there," I said. "Try the door—maybe it's unlocked."

It was, and Wes went in first, me following. The small entryway opened into a dreary living room of well-worn green carpeting, faded floral wallpaper, and dated furniture, with an abundance of lowbrow knickknacks.

As Wes approached the back of the chair, he called out over the loud TV. "Mrs. Fowler? It's Wes Sinclair. Sorry to intrude, but the door was open. . . ."

As he rounded the chair, he visibly stiffened.

I moved toward him. "What . . . ?"

Eyes wide with alarm, he held up a *stop* hand. "*Do not* come over here."

But his warning had come too late.

Gladys Fowler had obviously been strangled, a red raw line rimming her neck, face blueish-purple, eyes bulging and bloodshot, mouth open in a silent scream.

I stumbled backward, and fled outside, where I threw myself shaking into the porch swing, eyes closed tightly, trying to erase the terrible image of the dead woman's face, knowing that I couldn't. That the image would be replayed in my mind again and again in days, weeks, years to come.

Then Wes was standing next to the swing. "I've called the police. Used my cell. Didn't touch her phone."

I nodded numbly.

"Damnit," he said.

I looked up at him.

"What did she want to *tell* me?"

I shook my head. Swallowed.

"Did whatever it was get her *killed?*"

A siren sounded in the distance.

"Are you all right, Brandy?" he asked, risking a hand on my shoulder. "You look awfully pale."

When I didn't answer, couldn't answer, he shivered and said, "I'm pretty shook up myself. What a horrible thing."

The siren grew louder.

Wes squeezed my shoulder gently, then let it go. "I'll handle this."

He walked across the porch, down the steps, and out to the driveway, to meet the police car that had just pulled in, coming to an abrupt stop behind his Jaguar.

Numbness gave way to anxiety, as I saw Tony behind the wheel.

Alone, the tall uniformed officer exited the squad car and faced Wes, who gestured to the house as he spoke.

When Tony saw me in the swing, his face turned to stone. He walked briskly in my direction, yet instead of coming over to me, he went into the house—but not before giving me a disapproving, disappointed look.

For the next hour, Wes joined me in a ghastly ritual that had become much too normal in my life of late, as we watched the all too familiar parade of paramedics, coroner, and forensic team.

Finally Tony exited the house and came over, planting himself in front of us.

Looking down at me blankly, he asked, "Ms. Borne, would you please explain what you're doing here?"

I opened my mouth, but Wes preempted me.

"I asked her to come with me, Officer Cassato. Mrs. Fowler called me at the office and said she had information regarding Vanessa's murder, and I asked Brandy to come with me as a witness."

Tony's voice remained cold. "Is that so, Brandy?"

"Yes. The door was unlocked and we went in and found her."

His bullet-hard eyes returned to Wes. "What time did Mrs. Fowler call you?"

"A little before four. But I had some work to finish, so I called Brandy and she walked over to my office. She and I didn't arrive here until about fifteen minutes ago."

Tony's gaze at Wes was unforgiving. "And why, when Mrs. Fowler called you about your wife's murder, did you not call *us* about it?"

"I know I should have. But my relations over the past few days with the Serenity PD have been less than . . . stellar. And meaning no respect to the dead woman, but Mrs. Fowler struck me as a kind of crank."

"Really."

"Really. She tried to blackmail me just before the trial. Said if I didn't pay her, she'd say she saw me come home the afternoon of my wife's murder. Which of course is exactly what she did say."

"And you didn't come to us with that, either?"

"How would you have responded to that claim, under the circumstances, Cassato?"

I couldn't take any more of this, and said, "I'd like to go home, please."

Besides feeling like I was underwater, all I could think of was that Mother was out there being Mother while a murderer was out committing vicious murders.

Tony shook his head. "I have more questions for both of you . . ."

Wes said sharply, "Can't you see she's in shock, man? Let me drive her home, and I'll come back here and we'll deal with this. Or would you rather I call my attorney?"

Tony shifted his stance, sighed. "All right," he said gruffly. "Go."

As Wes escorted me to his Jag, I could feel Tony's eyes on my back.

After maneuvering around the other vehicles, Wes got his car into the street.

"Thanks for getting me out of there," I said.

"No problem. I needed a breather myself, even for a short time."

I knew Wes was thinking about the afternoon Vanessa had been killed, as was I.

Eyes on the road, he said, "I know you're dating that guy, but if you don't mind my saying, he seemed pretty insensitive toward you."

I had to agree, but said lamely, "Tony was just doing his job."

"Yeah, well, I wouldn't have treated you that way."

"I need you to stop by my shop. I need to pick up my dog and lock up better."

And see if Mother is back.

"Sure," he said.

We did that, but Mother was still nowhere to be seen. Now Sushi rode on my lap, sniffing at the Jag's unfamiliar, new-car scent.

We fell silent until Wes pulled up in front of our house, where, to my great relief, the Caddy was parked in the drive.

His expression was warm but troubled. "Let me walk you up."

"No. Thanks, but I'll be fine. Mother's home, I see, and she was off . . . gallivanting. So that's a relief."

"You will be careful? This killer isn't kidding around."

"I will. You, too."

I got out of the Jag, and Wes pulled away.

Walking up the drive, with Sushi trotting along beside me, I couldn't help but think that nothing Mother had done today could top what happened to me.

I was approaching the rear of the Caddy when I noticed a dark shape on the cement, between the rider's side and the hedge. As I drew closer, and Sushi began to bark, that shape became a body.

A body in the clothes Mother had been wearing this morning, lying now in a pool of blood.

A Trash 'n' Treasures Tip

Never buy a pet at a swap meet. In addition to the possibility of the animal carrying a disease, the sellers usually don't have paperwork on the animal's origin. A friend learned that the hard way when the puppy she thought was a Welsh Corgi grew into an Irish Wolfhound.

Chapter Eight

Attacking Lead

(Lead that instigates an active defense.)

Vivian here—(everybody sing!) *back in the saddle again!*

And before you ask, no, I don't know why Brandy insists on breaking up my chapters by inserting one of her own in between, which completely discombobulates my forward momentum. (Isn't that a wonderful word, *discombobulate?*) Furthermore, it further chips away at my precious word count (editorially enforced) by the need to remind you, dear reader, where we were when last we were together.

As a matter of fact, I can't remember where that was myself!

Oh, yes. I had just had a most interesting and informative lunch with the Romeos, where I was able to confirm persistent rumors that the Eight of Clubs was, in fact, not a bridge club but a . . . shall we say . . . swing set. (Clever, no?)

(*Note from Brandy to Mother*: Clever no.)

(*Note from Mother to Brandy*: Clever yes!)

(*Note from Editor: Ladies* . . .)

Even though the afternoon stretched out before me in seeming infinity, I had plenty of places to go, things to do, and people to see. Which meant I needed to get cracking and seek transportation.

And with my extensive lists of stops, I could hardly impose on Shawntea for so many trolley route deviations. That meant my only other option was the Cadillac. While I consider my lack of a driver's license a mere technicality, normally I would have called upon Brandy for chauffeuring services. But since she had removed herself from the investigation, I felt justified in taking this liberty.

And the Caddy.

Unbeknownst to Brandy, I was carrying our extra set of car keys in my purse—she had hidden them from me (top kitchen cupboard—such a lack of imagination!) after catching me coming back from a midnight convenience-store run. What can I say, sometimes a girl has a chocolate-mint ice-cream Jones!

Anyhoo, quicker than Tinker to Evers to Chance (an ancient baseball reference for you really devoted Cubbies fans), I hoofed it over to our shop where the Caddy was parked out front at the curb.

But there I took pause.

What if the excitable girl noticed the vehicle was gone, assumed it stolen, and called the constabulary? The spoilsport authorities did *not* view my lack of a license as a technicality, and I would be in (as Nero Wolfe would say) a pickle!

I decided to write my ex-sleuthing partner a quick note on the sidewalk. Unfortunately, the only thing I had in my purse was my favorite Elizabeth Arden lipstick, in her signature shade Red Door, and consequently in leaving my message, wore the stick down to the nub (thankfully I buy it in bulk).

Did you know that Miss Arden built her entire cosmetic empire on that single tube of red lipstick? (Brandy insists the plucky entrepreneur began with cold cream, but I'm almost certain she's got it wrong. Wikipedia no help on this one!)

Word count!

(By the way, those who insist I use exclamation points with too much frequency clearly need to put a little more zing into their lives, and snazzy punctuation into their writing.)

Thank goodness the Caddy's muffler was sound (or I should say soundless), otherwise Brandy might well have heard the car pull away from the curb, and come running out to stop me, like an armed guard after a bank robber.

Making haste, I maneuvered over to Cedar Street, a main artery leading out of the downtown and connecting to the Bypass. I was on my way to an exclusive housing addition where the other three couples of the Eight of Clubs resided—

Brent and Megan Morgan, Travis and Emily Thompson, and Sean and Tiffany Hartman. My strategy was to talk to the wives while their husbands were at work.

Soon I was veering off the Bypass onto a secondary road and, before too long, a stone monument announced my destination as if in welcome: Mark Twain Estates.

Interesting sidebar. Mark Twain—Samuel Clemens, that is—briefly lived in Serenity when he was nineteen and worked at the *Serenity Sentinel* as a typesetter. There's a very amusing story I'd like to tell you about the great orator being fired after only a few months for insubordination, but I can't due to my restricted word count. I really do apologize, and my only advice is for you to write my editor at the publisher and request that my word count be expanded. Thank you.

A winding blacktop took me along gently rolling hills reminiscent of a Grant Wood painting, and when the blacktop leveled out, those green hills remained a soothing backdrop for million-dollar homes sitting on spacious lawns dotted with oak and maple trees.

Every quarter mile or so, an offshoot street would appear, street signs marked with Twain-cutesy names—Tom Sawyer Road, Aunt Polly Lane, Becky Thatcher Drive. I wheeled the Caddy onto Samuel Clemens Court, where Travis and Emily Thompson resided in the grandest of all these homes—no surprise, since Travis had been the addition's developer.

After spotting the multi-gabled three-story tan-brick edifice—a monstrosity I wouldn't live in if you paid me (depending on the offer)—I pulled up the wide cement drive to a four-car garage, shut the engine off, and stepped out, feeling about as welcome as Injun Joe. (Fault Mr. Twain/Clemens for the political incorrectness of *that* one!)

A curved stone walkway conveyed me by well-tended flowerbeds bursting with color, then to a recessed front door buttressed on one side by the garage and on the other an extended living room.

Here I will risk word count accountability to complain about the fad of recessed front doors, so prevalent in new homes nowadays. Besides having no porch on which to while away the hours, one can't just stick his (or her) head out to see what the weather is like. He/she has to walk all the way out! (Which I wouldn't care to do in my pajamas.) And what if it's a salesman, or an unwanted religious proselytizer? Why put a mini-roof over *their* heads? (Meaning no offense to religious proselytizers.)

(To those who think I am using too many parentheses, I refer you to my earlier comment on exclamation points.)

I ascended the three narrow stoop steps, then rang the doorbell, its chime mimicking Big Ben. Suddenly I wondered if the light suggestion of an English accent that I sometimes used might not be appropriate, when calling on so much money.

Still mulling that, I was about to ring again, when Emily Thompson opened the door.

She looked perhaps unintentionally patriotic in a crisp white cotton blouse with red belt and navy slacks, her bare feet sporting red-painted toenails. A dainty creature, barely over five foot, the thirtyish wife of the creator of Mark Twain Estates had curly shoulder-length strawberry-blond hair, translucent skin, and delicate facial features enhanced by minimal makeup. (Young ladies often wear too much makeup these days. Girls, try a little powder and Red Door lipstick!)

The few times I'd had an opportunity to observe Emily Thompson (at country club do's), she had seemed quiet and even reserved alongside the gregarious Travis. But some of my Red-Hatted League gal pals (nosy Norma, in particular) claimed the little woman had a big temper, and you know what they say about still waters running deep.

(For you cliché spotters, never forget that clichés got to be that way because they reflect a basic, often uncomfortable truth.)

Emily seemed a little rattled by the sight of me, but I was fairly accustomed to that reaction, and didn't read much into it.

I smiled sweetly. "I *do* hope I've not arrived at an inopportune time, dear. I realize I should have called first, but I was out and about, and the impulse just hit me!"

"Uh . . . well . . . well, certainly. Mrs. Borne, isn't it?"

"Yes, dear. I'm sure you've seen me perform

at the Playhouse. You and your husband are Golden Ticket subscribers, and we're very grateful."

"Well, Mrs. Borne, if you're collecting for that, I'm afraid Travis handles all—"

"Oh, no, no! You misunderstand, dear. This is a *social* call."

I waited for Emily to invite me in, and when she didn't, I turned to a familiar page out of my ploy book.

Hand to forehead, I swooned. "My, it's gotten so very *hot* out here—unseasonably so, don't you think? I feel . . . I feel . . . I feel a little *faint*."

Afraid I shifted from Great Britain to Tennessee Williams, there.

I went on: "Would it be poor etiquette for me to ask to come in? Perhaps sit down? Perhaps impose upon you . . . for some . . . some water?"

About halfway through that, concern had replaced her guarded expression. "Oh, of course! Certainly, Mrs. Borne."

And she moved aside.

I stepped into a vast entryway with an elaborate parquet floor beneath my feet and enormous chandelier above my head (not that either would be anywhere else). An antique grandfather clock stood like an expensive sentinel to my left, while to my right was an elaborately carved coat rack with mirror, also an antique. Perfect for the shop!

Emily escorted me farther into the cavernous entryway, then into a formal sitting room with an Asian sensibility: oriental rug, room-divider screen with cherry blossom design, and framed wall pictures of Mount Fuji and ocean waves, which I recognized as the work of the Japanese artist Hokusai.

Only the floral chintz couch, where she seated me, and various chairs were modern; but their muted colors fit in aesthetically with the rest of the room. Everybody feng shui tonight! (It was afternoon, actually.)

Emily asked, "Can I get you a glass of water?"

"Yes, most generous. So terribly thoughtful." The British accent was creeping back in. That was all right—even a fancy place like this could use some classing up.

As soon as she disappeared, I jumped up from the couch as if sitting on a tack and crossed to an oriental writing desk with a dragon motif, and began rifling through a drawer. But nothing among the contents seemed significant.

Due to my unfortunate hereditary earwax buildup, I nearly didn't hear Emily's footsteps in the parquet hallway, and as such, was not able to straighten the drawer's contents before closing it, let alone make it back to the couch. I had to reclose it, because at first the drawer caught a fancy blue silk bookmark ribbon.

"My dear," I said as she entered with a water glass in hand, "this piece is extraordinary! I simply *had* to come over for a look."

Emily approached and handed me the glass. "That desk once belonged to Emperor Hirohito."

My jaw dropped, no acting required. "How

ever did you come by it?" Some shady means, no doubt.

She shrugged. "It was smuggled out after World War II. How Travis acquired it, I never asked."

"I do hope it's properly insured."

"Oh, it is. Travis has also found some wonderful pieces for Wes, for his corporate office."

The petite beauty gestured to the couch I'd vacated. We sat, the center cushion between us.

She said, "Now, how can I help you, Mrs. Borne?"

"Do call me Vivian, dear. As I say, it's a social call. Long overdue."

"Vivian. I'm a little pressed for time—I have to pick Jennifer up from ballet class."

"Such a lovely child—ten, is she?"

"Eleven. The reason for your visit? It's not really purely social."

I took a sip of water. "Well, dear, as you may know, the Sinclairs are members of New Hope Church—that is, *Wes* is . . . and Vanessa *was*." Another sip of water. "We are a small congregation, and as such, aren't able to give her the kind of memoriam that she so rightly deserves. Therefore, I am out seeking additional donations."

Emily frowned. "I thought you said you weren't out collecting donations."

"For the Playhouse, yes, or that is, no. This is a memoriam for your late friend—for Vanessa."

Still frowning, she asked, "What *kind* of memoriam do you have in mind?"

I took another sip of water, stalling—I admit I

hadn't quite thought this memoriam angle through. Without Brandy as a sounding board, I was pretty much winging it. It wasn't easy, not having a flagpole to run things up.

"Well, dear," I said, calling upon my improv training, "we were thinking a new stained glass window in the church sanctuary might be appropriate . . . dedicated to Vanessa's memory. So labeled."

Her cold lack of interest almost gave me goose pimples. "I told you already, Mrs. Borne. Travis handles that kind of thing. Anyway, why don't you just ask Wes for the money?"

Her tone said, *He's the rich one.* You could have fooled me, based on this palace.

I touched my bosom with my free hand. "Why, it would be simply gauche to approach the bereaved husband to foot the bill, don't you think?"

"I suppose," she replied, unconvinced. She shrugged. "I guess I could call Travis at the office, and maybe write you a check."

She began to get up.

"Oh, no money *now,* dear!" I replied quickly, thinking of the disturbed drawer. "We don't know the precise cost just yet. Our committee is taking quotes. I'm merely out soliciting interest among potential supporters, and since you and your husband run in the same circle as the Sinclairs, this seemed a natural first stop."

She seemed not at all moved by the notion of a memorial window for her late friend. But she said, "Okay, then. You can count on us. Now, if there's nothing else, as I said, I have to pick my daughter up."

Those were obviously my walking papers, so a direct approach was my only remaining option.

"Uh, there is something else, dear . . . just briefly? I wondered if perhaps you had an idea of who may have wanted Vanessa dead?"

I expected her to duck my query, but the woman said, "I thought so. I've heard about your amateur sleuthing."

Of course she had! Everybody in Serenity had.

She was saying, matter of fact, "I thought Wes killed her, originally."

"My! Why was that, dear?"

A facial shrug. "Because of an argument he and Vanessa had at the swap meet. Wasn't your daughter the instigator?"

"Oh, I'm afraid I didn't witness the altercation. Were you there, dear?"

A nod. "I'd taken Jennifer and one of her friends down to the riverfront for it. They wanted to go on the rides, and I get a kick out of wandering around the tents."

"Do you know what the argument was about? Was it simply about my daughter and Wes running into each other . . . ?"

She shrugged. "I was too far away to hear what Vanessa and Wes were saying. But I can tell you this—it got *ugly.*"

"Was your husband with you?"

"No, Travis was out playing golf with Brent and Sean."

That select circle again. I made a mental note to examine the clubhouse registry, to find out how long the three men were actually out on the course.

Emily was saying, "*That* could have been what the argument was about. Wes wanted to play golf with the guys, but Vanessa insisted he go to the swap meet. Anyway, that's what my husband said, later."

I said, "Doesn't seem like anything to kill a person over."

"It wasn't merely that," Emily offered. "Those two hadn't been getting along for some time."

As the judge used to say to Hamilton Burger on *Perry Mason,* she had opened the door.

I asked, "Was their discord over Vanessa not being able to conceive?"

My knowledge of this clearly shocked her. "Why, yes."

"Well, then, dear, you should know that Vanessa told Brandy . . . the very afternoon of the murder . . . that there were still options open to her, in that area."

The woman laughed once. "Well, I don't know what those would be."

"Then should she and Wes have divorced, she'd have received nothing. Because of their prenuptial agreement." I beamed at her surprised expression. "Oh yes, dear, I know all about that, too."

Emily narrowed her eyes to slits. "Mrs. Borne, I think Vanessa had something up her sleeve that would land her some of that Sinclair money, prenup or no prenup."

"Oh?"

Suddenly my somewhat reluctant hostess seemed uncomfortable. "Sorry, Mrs. Borne. I'm afraid I've already said too much." She waved away our entire conversation. "As far as I'm concerned, we should move on. Wes has been cleared. Let's go on with our lives."

"But, dear—Vanessa's murderer is still out there."

"Why do you care? Anyway, I really must go to get my daughter."

I rose. "Thank you for the glass of water, Mrs. Thompson. I'll be in touch when I know the exact cost of the church window."

I bid the woman adieu, pleased that she had corroborated intel provided by my gal pals Frannie and Cora, but disappointed that I hadn't been able to find out more about whatever it was that Mrs. Wes Sinclair had had "up her sleeve." Had that sleeve's-worth been enough to cost Vanessa her life?

My next stop was the home of Brent and Megan Morgan on Captain Bixby Way (named for a steamboat captain friend of Twain's). The president of the Serenity Bank, his homemaker wife, and their two small boys lived in a sprawling one-story ranch-style house.

Getting no answer at the front door, I followed high-pitched laughter and water splashing to the pool in back.

Megan was seated beneath an umbrella at a glass-topped table, reading a book. A trifle on the plump side—by yesterday's standards "curvaceous," by today's euphemisms "curvy"—she wore a navy-and-white striped bathing suit, her chestnut hair pulled back in a ponytail. The woman exuded a wholesome, girl-next-door quality sharply at odds with the notion that she might be involved in extramarital hanky-panky.

"Hel . . . *lo* . . . oh!" I called out, peering from over a locked wooden fence—natural wood, no Tom Sawyer paintbrush trickery here.

Megan looked up from her book, which I am sorry to say was not one of ours (it *was* a mystery novel, but never mind what—the other writers can do their own promotion!).

"It's Vivian Borne, dear. Might I have a word?"

She put the novel face down, open to her place (rough on the spine!) (the book's, not the reader's). "Yes, all right, Mrs. Borne. Just reach over and undo the lock."

I did so, then made my way to the table, skirting various pool toys.

"What is it you want?" she asked, neither unfriendly nor welcoming.

"Do you mind if I sit? These old knees just aren't what they used to be!"

My knees were fine—just another ploy. (It was my hips that had been replaced.)

She gestured unenthusiastically. "Have a seat."

Settling into the chair next to her, I began, "I dropped by because—"

I paused as the woman's attention went to her two towheaded boys in the shallow end of the pool, where they were hitting each other with rubber mallets.

"Tommy! Jimmy! *Stop* that! I'll take those away from you."

The boys ceased their roughhousing, giggling at each other.

Megan's eyes returned to me. "Sorry . . . you were saying?"

I went into my stained-glass window spiel again, after which my bored hostess said, "Brent and I have already given a substantial contribution to a charity in Vanessa's name."

I tisk-tisked. "Oh, that *is* too bad."

"I *will* discuss it with Brent, though," she said. "How has the support been?" This seemed more out of politeness than interest, her eyes back on the two boys.

"Very good, actually," I replied. "As a matter of fact, I've just come from calling on a friend of yours, I believe—Emily Thompson?"

Now she was interested. "Oh? Is Emily contributing?"

"Yes."

A wry smile. "Emily always has been a soft touch."

"Well, the support of the Thompsons is most appreciated. And I hope to find Tiffany Hartman receptive as well."

A smile turned smirky. "Good luck getting anything out of *her.*"

"You seem to know both Emily and Tiffany well. You three girls must be *so* close—like sisters, I would think."

Megan's eyes narrowed. "And *why* would you think that?"

I gestured expansively. "Because you're all

about the same age, and all live out here at
Mark Twain—such a lovely place, by the way. So
picturesque, so peaceful."

She nodded. "It is nice."

"Emily mentioned you girls knew each other
from college."

Actually this was a lie—the info had come from
the Romeos.

Megan shifted in her chair. "We all went to
Columbia, yes."

"And you were sorority sisters?"

"Well, only in the sense we were all in sororities. We didn't know each other well, not like
the guys did."

"Your husbands went to Columbia as well?"

"Yes. Brent, Travis, Sean and Wes all belonged to the same frat."

"Delta Sigma."

She registered surprise. "How did you know?"

I shrugged. "Just stands to reason—it's widely
known as the most desirable fraternity." I had
fumbled the ball, but hoped my recovery had
been adequate.

Megan was saying, "It wasn't until the last se-
mester that I got to know the other girls—Emily,
Tiffany, and Vanessa. We'd met at general Greek
events. But mostly it was because we all started
dating the guys. And they were tight."

I nodded. "It's obvious why Wesley came back
to Serenity—to run the family business. But how
is it that everyone else wound up here, too?"

"Well, it's fairly simple. Wes said he could get
his friends, our husbands, good jobs—positions
that otherwise might've taken them years to at-

tain." A shrug. "He said he had a lot of influence."

He hadn't been lying—I had no doubt that Brent, Sean, and Travis owed Wes their careers, or at least the fast ascent of them.

Megan was saying, "Another reason we all live here is that the guys didn't want to split up 'a winning combination.' They *are* like brothers."

I beamed at her. She was sitting down, but was about to get her shapely bottom kissed, anyway. "And weren't they all fortunate to find such wonderful wives on the Columbia campus. It's almost like a fairy tale!"

Dollars to doughnuts, those four young men went coldly, calculatingly wife-hunting among the best sororities—a chauvinistic attitude not at odds with their eventual wife-swapping.

I asked pleasantly, "What did you major in, dear?"

"Elementary education."

"Have you had a chance to do anything in that field?"

She shook her head, ponytail swishing. "Brent prefers I not work, and anyway, raising two boys is a full-time job."

"If you don't mind my saying so, dear, in your tax bracket, hiring a nanny would hardly be out of the reach."

"Oh, we could afford that, all right. But Brent thinks, in a small town like Serenity? Better I be a stay-at-home mother, active in PTA and other local affairs—activities more befitting a bank president's wife."

Try as I might, I could not find resentment in

her words. But I sensed their presence nonetheless.

Megan went on with forced cheerfulness, "And let me tell you—these two boys are a handful. But rewarding? *So* rewarding . . ."

I laughed politely. "I'm sure they are." The little hooligans were hitting each other with the rubber bats again. "Perhaps when they're grown and off to college, you can make use of that degree. Mothers have as much right to seek fulfillment outside of marriage as the next guy."

She seemed to like my little homily, so I ventured on: "It must have been hard on you, dear, when you heard about Vanessa's terrible passing."

For a moment she stared out at the water, at the waves her boys were making. "I keep thinking . . ." She blinked. "I keep thinking about what *I* was doing the afternoon she was killed."

I waited.

"I had gone to the grocery store around three. By four I was home." Megan's eyes met mine. "Wasn't she *killed* between four and five? I was putting the food away, then cooking dinner. Doing something so . . . so mundane."

"Dear, that's the way of these things," I said gently. "The mundane is our solace, the source of our sanity." Then I asked, "How *did* you receive the news?"

"Brent told me. When he came home, around six. He heard about it in the clubhouse after a round of golf with Travis and Sean."

Apparently the three men *were* together that

afternoon —unless their wives had been given a story to keep straight.

I asked, "Who do *you* think killed Vanessa?"

She looked surprised I'd even raise the issue. "Oh, a burglar, of course. Who would want Vanessa dead?"

Who indeed.

I had saved Tiffany Hartman for last. She lived on Huckleberry Finn Drive with her investment broker husband, Sean (no children), in a two-story cement and glass house that looked like a modern fortress, its exterior as uninviting as the woman herself could be, according to my gal pals, anyway.

My finger hadn't yet touched the doorbell when the front door opened, and Tiffany stepped out, tall, willowy, with ice-blond long hair, and features that could have graced the cover of any fashion magazine. Her attire was crisply fashionable, too—white silk blouse with blue silk scarf, white jeans.

"Look," she said crossly, "Sean and I aren't interested in contributing to any damn stained-glass window."

Emily had called her, or maybe Megan.

"Oh, that is too bad," I said disappointedly. "I'm sure Vanessa would have appreciated your gift."

"And I'm sure she *wouldn't*."

I frowned. "Why is that, dear?"

Her face wasn't nearly so lovely when she sneered. "Because Vanessa only went to church for appearance sake. She didn't believe in anything but herself."

"Oh, I'm *sure* you must be wrong. And even so, isn't it better to be charitable to the recently departed?"

A smirk did even less for her looks. "Listen, lady—I think I knew Vanessa Sinclair just a little bit better than you."

I switched tactics. "So, then, you *were* good friends. The rumors *aren't* true."

"What rumors?"

"That the two of you hated each other."

Nor did a frown do anything for her beauty. "That's utterly ridiculous."

"Is it? Then I would imagine you have an alibi for the afternoon of her murder."

"You're just an old busybody of a snoop. Why should I tell you a damn thing?"

I smiled sweetly, but I was burning. "Because, dear, if you have a cast-iron alibi, as we say in the trade, I can put an end to all that nasty gossip."

She studied me, eyes condescending and insolent. "How's this for ironclad? I was in Chicago on a shopping trip that Saturday, and didn't get back until Sunday."

"You *and* your husband were away?"

"No—Sean stayed home to play golf with Brent and Travis . . . as I'm sure you already know, Miss Marple. Now, I want you *out* of here! Or do I call the police?"

"On my way, dear, on my way. Oh! Would you mind just one teensy-eensy last question . . . and I promise you it's not about Vanessa or the murder."

"What is it?" she snapped.

"Well, I understand you and your friends have a bridge club—the Eight of Clubs?"

"Yes. So what?"

"I used to be a whiz at it, years ago, and have taken it back up lately, and find myself simply floundering."

"How sad."

"Maybe you could tell me—if a declarer were to open one spade, what would the next person's bid have to be?"

For a brief moment, Tiffany's eyes glazed, then the cold patronizing gaze returned.

"Unless I'm actually playing," she replied, "it's difficult for me to say. Sorry I couldn't answer your question."

"Oh, but you did, dear," I said with a sweet smile and an attitude at least as condescending as her own.

She didn't understand the game.

(Answer: one no trump or two of clubs.)

I bid her a cheerful good-bye.

It was with some trepidation that I arrived home, late afternoon, knowing that Brandy would be perturbed about me taking the Caddy.

I got out of the car, then went around the front to retrieve my purse on the rider's side floor, when I caught just the barest glimpse of someone darting out of the hedges that bordered the driveway.

Pain exploded into a starry sky inside my skull, Vincent van Gogh coming back to do one last painting.

And that's the last thing I remember.

Mother's Trash 'n' Treasures Tip

Clothing bought at a swap meet cannot be returned, so if the vendor doesn't have a makeshift dressing room—or won't allow you to try the item on in a nearby bathroom—don't buy it. Can you imagine how frustrating it would be to have a pair of jodhpurs you can't get into?

Chapter Nine

Knockout

*(In tourney, winning teams advance
to next round.)*

In the emergency room at Serenity General Hospital, an unconscious Mother lay pale and still while a female nurse in green scrubs, nametag NANCY, checked her vitals. The paramedics who responded to my 911 call had already applied a head bandage to stem the bleeding, along with a neck brace.

I was waiting for the doctor working tonight's shift to finish with another emergency down in another ER room—according to Nurse Nancy, a young man who'd been in a motorcycle accident—and the fifteen minutes or so that had already passed might have been an hour.

I could only stand next to the examining table, feeling helpless, holding Mother's limp hand, stroking it gently.

What if she died?

Or what if she never regained consciousness?

"Dear," Mother once joshed, "if I should ever become a vegetable, please don't pull the plug till I'm down to a size eight."

At the time, that had made me laugh.

At the time.

The doctor finally appeared, a distinguished if mildly harried-looking middle-aged man with silver metal-frame glasses, hair gray at the temples, and a bit of a paunch beneath his white lab jacket. Nametag: DR. WARNER.

"Status," he said to Nurse Nancy.

"Head trauma—unconscious, but breathing on her own."

The nurse filled his extended hand with her clipboard. He studied the white sheet on top. Looked up at me. "Did you see what happened, Ms. Borne?"

I shook my head. "I found Mother on the driveway near our car."

Dr. Warner leaned over his patient, unwrapped the head dressing, then carefully examined the wound.

Straightening, he asked, "You found her on her stomach?"

"Yes."

He lifted an eyebrow, set it back down. "This wound wasn't caused by a fall. With blunt-force trauma like this, someone must have hit your mother a severe blow on the back of the head. Would take that to knock her out." He paused. "She'll require stitches—we'll have to shave off a fair-sized patch of her hair. Then we'll run a CT scan to look for bleeding within the brain, and excess pressure."

I posed the question he'd been asked so many times: "Will she be all right?"

"I'll let you know as soon as I can," he replied, an answer he'd given so many times. "Make yourself comfortable in the waiting room, please."

I nodded, then leaned over and kissed Mother's cheek, finding it reassuringly warm.

If there is a hell, there's a good chance it will be an ER waiting room, where the coffee is bitter and cold, the magazines ancient and dog-eared, the wall hangings purposely mundane, and your only company other anxious folks, each lost in their own terrible thoughts.

And that's where I was now.

Why did I leave Mother to her own devices? Why didn't I try harder to check up on her? When was the last time I told her how much I loved her?

Detaching a little, I wondered how many deals with the Man Upstairs had been made in this room—and how many had been kept, from either side of the bargain.

Letting Mother out without the leash I usually provided was a big mistake. She was a bright, energetic woman, but she was, let's face it, on bipolar medication. She needed supervision. For the most part, my participation in her sleuthing had been to keep her out of (or at least limit the extent of) trouble.

Out of harm's way.

This time, under a little pressure from a man

I cared about, I'd abandoned her to the fates. If she didn't make it, how would *I* be able to?

I was seated near the door to the ER. The loved ones of the motorcycle victim—a young wife or girlfriend, an older couple who were either his or her parents—had taken seats at the far end of the room. When Dr. Warner came through the ER door, we all stood, eyes filled with hope and dread.

His expression unreadable, the doctor moved by me to the others, spoke softly, and the trio began to sob and hold on to each other.

I quickly left through a second door that led into the hospital lobby. Mostly I did this to give the bereaved their privacy, but some weak part of me didn't want their bad luck to rub off on me.

I used my cell to call Wes but got sent to voice mail. I left a quick report about what had happened to Mother, saying it was probably a robbery, but that if he needed me for anything, I'd be at the hospital through the morning, most likely.

Finding a vending machine, I got myself a bottled water, then returned to the waiting room, where the bereaved had been ushered away, off to sign insurance papers, or make funeral arrangements, or whatever happened when a loved one didn't make it in the ER. I was fuzzy about that.

I hoped that it wouldn't soon be coming into focus.

Seated again, I was relieved to see Tony, in uniform, come in through the ER door. His smile was small and sad and supportive, as he came toward me.

Sitting beside me, shoulders hunched, hands loosely clasped between his legs, he looked over at me sideways and asked gently, "How is she doing?"

"Still unconscious. Breathing on her own."

He sighed. "I left Mrs. Fowler's as soon as I could."

"Thank you for coming."

"Do you know what happened to Vivian exactly?"

"Not exactly, no. Just that somebody hit her on the head when she got home from doing . . . what she does. I found her purse on the ground, but the wallet was missing . . . so it may have been a robbery."

"May have." He could hardly have sounded less convinced—not that I'd sounded terribly convinced, myself.

I said, "A thief *might* have thought Mother was carrying a lot of money—you know, because we made that pilot show? Been a lot of publicity. Somebody waiting for her in the bushes by the house?"

He shrugged. "Possible."

"But not probable, in your opinion."

"Is it in yours?"

My turn to sigh. "No. I think this happened because of something she did today. Poking around Serenity."

"Do you know where she went?"

I shook my head. "She was none too happy

about me telling her I was 'off the case.' So she shared none of her plans, and frankly I didn't ask her to."

I told him about Mother taking the Caddy.

His dark eyes widened momentarily. "I'll pretend I didn't hear that. . . ."

"Usually, when she goes off investigating, Mother confines herself to her downtown haunts . . . but with a car? She could have gone anywhere and seen anybody."

He shook his head once, eyes hooded with concern. "And we won't know where and who till she wakes up."

"*If* she wakes up . . ." I blinked through tears. "And it's . . . it's all *my* fault."

He put a hand on my arm. "How is it your fault?"

I pulled in a breath and let it out, trying to control my emotions, but not doing a great job of it. "I told Mother I wouldn't help her this time, but she went off anyway—unchecked. I knew she would, but still didn't try to stop her, much less go with her."

His smile was a rumpled thing. "Would I be out of line thinking you blame me for that?"

"I blame myself for agreeing to what you asked. From where you sit, it was a reasonable request—understandable, logical, responsible. But Tony, I share a house, and a life, with Vivian Borne, and she's none of those things."

He half-smiled in acknowledgment of the truth of that.

I went on: "But I'm officially breaking my

promise. Who was it said, 'This time it's personal?' Somebody tried to kill Mother. And I'm going to do everything I can to help find out who."

Tony nodded, still wearing a supportive little smile, though it was edged with weary resignation. "All right, Brandy. Since I can't stop you, I might as well aid and abet."

I looked sharply at him. "You *know* something?"

"Yes, and I'll share it with you . . . but there's a condition. If you're out there doing this amateur detective thing of yours, you have to promise to keep me apprised of what you're up to. I can't be at your side—I have my own duties—but I want it understood: we're in this together."

Now I smiled—first time that evening. "That's a promise I *can* keep."

"Okay," he said, and his smile went away. Businesslike, he said, "Pathologist found blue silk threads imbedded in the skin of Mrs. Fowler's neck."

"From a woman's scarf, maybe?"

"Yes, or possibly a man's tie. And a recent bank statement I turned up at Mrs. Fowler's house showed a ten-thousand dollar *cash* deposit that was made into her checking account."

Not so easy to trace.

I said, "You heard what Wes said about the Fowler woman offering to change her testimony for that exact amount . . . but he sent her packing. She must have blackmailed someone else. The *real* killer."

He nodded. "That does make sense. And whoever he or she is, the murderer decided just to get rid of her."

Dr. Warner came through the ER door, his expression again unreadable.

But as he neared us, the doctor did give us a barely perceptible smile.

I was on my feet. Tony, too.

The doctor said, "The results from the CT scan look good. No internal cranial bleeding or excess buildup of pressure."

I sighed in relief, then asked, "Is she still unconscious?"

"Yes. But I'm optimistic that your mother will come around—possibly tonight, maybe tomorrow, or anyway in a few days. Of course, each case is different."

Left unsaid was the possibility that Mother might never regain consciousness.

Tony said, "Doctor, I'll be investigating the assault. When Mrs. Borne comes around, what are the chances she'll remember what happened, after a blow to the skull like this?"

His head went slightly to one side. "Hard to say, Chief."

The doctor was clearly local, because everybody in Serenity still called Tony "Chief"—except for Brian Lawson, of course.

The doctor went on: "Often with a head trauma, the person will have short-term memory loss that they may never regain. This frequently happens in the case of a car accident, as you probably know, Chief."

The doctor's eyes moved from Tony to me. "Ms. Borne, I'd like to put your mother in a private room on the third floor."

This alarmed me. "Wouldn't she be better off in Intensive Care? Wouldn't it be safer?"

Dr. Warner frowned and looked back at Tony. "Is she still in some danger from her assailant?"

Tony said, "This may not have been a mugging. It could have been an attempt on her life relating to an ongoing murder investigation."

Tony didn't clarify whether he meant the department's investigation or Mother's.

"I see," Dr. Warner said, punctuating that with a nod. "Still, I recommend a private room. Situated across from the nurses' station, Mrs. Borne should be well positioned for both safety and care." His eyes returned to me. "You would be able to stay with her, if you like . . . whereas, in the I.C., that wouldn't be possible."

I wanted to be with Mother when she came to, so I agreed to the private room.

Dr. Warner nodded again. "I'll make the arrangements. Ms. Borne. Chief."

And he was off to deal with other patients and families. How men like that held up, I would never know.

Tony took my hand. "I'm off-duty now, sweetheart. I could stick around. If you wanted a nap, I'd be there in case of any trouble."

I shook my head. "I'll be all right—couldn't sleep now, anyway. And if whoever hit Mother comes around, I'll hit him in the head with a bedpan. Repeatedly."

Tony ignored that and squeezed my hand. "Call me if you need me."

"You know I will."

In spite of my good intentions, I did fall asleep in the chair next to Mother, where she lay hooked up to various monitors, her partly hairless head bandaged.

I was having a dream where I was being chased but could not run, with some unknown figure bearing down on me. Then, before the figure could jump me, I was startled awake by someone singing, "*Praise the Lord and Pass the Ammunition.*"

Mother!

I jumped out of my chair. Sun was streaming in the windows—morning already. I went to her bedside.

"You're awake! You've come out of it."

She turned her bandaged head to look at me curiously. "But of course. Do you suppose I sing in my sleep?"

I leaned over her. Despite her half-scalped head, she looked normal. Using that term loosely.

I asked, "Do you know who I am?

She squinted. "You *do* look familiar."

I put her glasses on her, but she still didn't seem to know me.

I asked, "Do you know who *you* are?"

"Haven't the foggiest." Her expression turned serious. "How's the war going?"

I frowned. "In Afghanistan?"

"*Where?* No, no, no, I'm talking the Pacific

Theater. European Theater. Double-you double-you two! By the by, where am I exactly?"

"In the hospital."

"Well, I *know* that! But *what* hospital? *Where?* Paris, is it?"

"Oh . . . Serenity General. In Serenity."

"Never heard of it. *Sérénité* General, you say?"

"Take it easy. You've had a concussion."

One hand went to the bandaged head. "Ah . . . from an incoming shell, no doubt. I'm lucky to be alive!"

"Do you remember anything about how it happened?"

"Last thing I remember is the USO tour, standing onstage, and tooting 'Boogie Woogie Bugle Boy of Company B' on my trusty, never-rusty cornet."

I raised a finger. "Will you excuse me a minute? I'm going to let the doctor know you're awake."

"As charming as these French doctors admittedly are," she said, "could you please try to find me one who speaks English?"

Then, as I headed out, she launched into song again, this time: "There's a Star-Spangled Banner Waving Somewhere." Not available on iTunes.

At the nurses' station, I informed the woman at the counter that Mother was awake, and asked her to see if Dr. Warner was still in the ER, and if so, could he come ASAP?

Then I returned to the room where Mother continued serenading me with more war songs:

"Over There" (from another war entirely) and "Pistol Packin' Mama," even borrowing a few numbers from the British, like "The White Cliffs of Dover," and "It's a Long Way to Tipperary."

Where was Tipperary, anyway? I mean, other than being a long way.

And why did Mother think she was on a USO tour in the Second World War? She would have been a kid then! She didn't seem to know me, and I'd avoided calling her "Mother," not wanting to do the wrong thing and traumatize her in some fashion.

Anyway, it was a great relief when Dr. Warner walked in, in a rare lull between songs. (Mother has performed in musical theater countless times, but truth be told she can barely carry a tune.)

Dr. Warner approached the bed. "And how is Mrs. Borne?" he asked her.

Mother rolled her eyes. "I don't know who or how *Mrs. Borne* is, but *I'm* just tickety boo!"

I said, "She seems to be stuck in World War Two—on a USO tour."

That raised the doctor's eyebrows. He checked her pulse, then used a little flashlight to look in her eyes, asking her to follow one finger as he moved it back and forth.

Finally, he turned to me. "It's not unusual for your Mother's memory to be fuzzy at first. But I'll schedule an MRI now that's she awake. And we can remove some of the monitors to make her more comfortable."

To Mother, he said, "I want you to eat, all right?"

She scrunched up her nose. "Well, it better not be K-rations! I've had my fill."

"No, it's food from our kitchen here at the hospital."

"Well, that's wonderful news! I do love French cuisine. And, *docteur,* might I compliment you on your splendid English? Why, I can barely detect your accent."

Dr. Warner gestured for me to follow him out into the hall.

"If the MRI report comes back good," he said, "I'm going to recommend that your mother be released."

I couldn't believe what I was hearing. "But . . . her memory's all screwed up! She thinks she's Dinah Shore or something, pulling stuff from movies and radio in her childhood."

"I *do* understand," he said patiently, "but she'll recover faster at home, surrounded by familiar things. If you need help taking care of her, I can recommend several private home-care nursing services. And I'll also give you a referral to a good neurologist specializing in head trauma."

These hospitals sure didn't waste any time getting rid of patients, did they? Maybe that's why so many of those patients wound up back in the emergency room, costing insurance companies and taxpayers even more.

Dr. Warner, possibly reading my expression, flipped a hand. "I'm sorry, Ms. Borne, but if the MRI result is good, your mother won't meet the criteria for hospitalization."

I returned to the room unhappily, bracing

myself for even more off-key singing—geesh, how many war songs were there, anyway?

A knock at the doorjamb made me jump.

Wes leaned in and asked, "May I come in?"

In an expensive pale silver-gray suit, peach-colored shirt, and narrow patterned tie, Mother's first visitor (not counting me) held a bouquet of flowers in a glass vase.

"Please do," I said, happy to have the distraction.

He came in and handed me the flowers. "Thought Vivian might like these."

"Really nice of you."

"No biggie." He shrugged, smiled shyly. "Picked them up in the gift shop downstairs. How's the patient?"

Mother said, "Peachy keen, young man. Should be back on the USO tour before very long. You look awfully fit not to be in uniform—4-F? Nothing to be ashamed of—there are other ways to serve. I do hope you're not out on a Section Eight!"

Wes swivelled to me with a wide-eyed look. "Ah . . . no, ma'am, I, uh, already served."

Mother beamed. "That's a relief—everyone should do their patriotic duty. Me? I'm with Bob and Bing on the Foxhole Circuit." She laughed. "Bing calls it the Cow Pasture Circuit—ain't he a card?"

"Mother," I said, "I'd like to talk to Wes alone."

"Mother?" She frowned. "You're my *daughter,* then?"

"That's right."

She already seemed over the shock of that. "Well, if I left this room, the MPs would surely come. You two will have to take it out into the hall."

"That's what I meant," I said to her.

I motioned to Wes.

Out in the corridor, he said, "Wow. Didn't know your mother was old enough to be part of the Greatest Generation."

"She isn't. Depending on how you spell *great.*" I laughed. "If she hadn't taken such a serious blow, it would almost be funny."

He was gazing at me with the same kind of small sad smile Tony had worn. "Hey, you look beat. Have you slept at all?"

"A little. But I'm not tired. I would, on the other hand, *kill* for a hot shower."

He put a hand on my shoulder. "Look, Brandy—I can stay with your mother while you go home for a while. Don't you have a dog that probably needs letting out?"

I grinned. "Oh yeah—or a heck of a mess to clean up. But don't you have to go to work?"

He gestured with a thumb to his chest. "Haven't you heard? I'm the boss man. And I don't have any pressing engagements this morning. I'll just tell my secretary I'll be a little late. What? An hour?"

"That should do it. And Wes? You won't leave her? There could be another attempt on her life."

He frowned. "I thought you said she was robbed."

"Now I'm not so sure. You see . . . Mother was looking into Vanessa's murder."

Wes grunted a humorless laugh, nodded. "I shouldn't be surprised. That's what she does, right?"

"Right."

"No worries, Brandy. I won't leave her side."

"Thanks. Be back soon." I gave him a quick kiss on the cheek.

A very excited Sushi was happy to see me, and I was pleased to see no little gifts had been left anywhere, at least not on first glance. I gave the sweet little pooch some attention, then fed her, and administered her insulin shot. Upstairs, I took a lingering shower, then changed my clothes, putting on a fresh pair of jeans and a new blouse.

In the kitchen I sat on the 1950s red stool and ate a bowl of cereal (Mini-Wheats), after which I called Joe Lange to tell him what had happened to Mother, and ask him if he could run the shop for a few days. His answer was affirmative. I mean, it really *was:* "Affirmative."

Then I placed a call to my son in Chicago, figuring he might be awake by now. But Jake sounded a little groggy when he answered.

"Grandma's had a little accident," I told him.

"Oh no. What kind of accident?"

"Well . . . the kind where somebody hit her on the head."

His concern jumped from the phone. "She all right?"

"Just a little confused, but she should be fine in a day or two." No need to worry him.

"She see who did it, Mom?"

"Apparently not. Came up from behind."

"Was what happened 'cause of that woman who got murdered?"

"How did you know about that?"

"Well . . . I don't want to get Grandma in trouble."

"You won't. I promise." Not any more than she was already.

He said carefully, "Grandma wanted my help in getting into the dead lady's e-mail account."

Mother *never* would have involved Jake that way if I hadn't bowed out! My bad. My very, very bad . . .

Jake was saying, "Anyway, I reset that lady's password and got into her account, easy peasy."

"Anything of interest?"

"Well, I didn't have much time, 'cause after a minute, the account got shut down. But I did open the last e-mail she sent. But it didn't make any sense, at least not to me."

"What did it say, Jake?"

"Something about . . . using some club to get lots of money."

The Eight of Clubs?

"Jake, can you remember the e-mail address it was sent to?"

"No, sorry. But the letter started with 'Hey Tif.' If that helps."

Tiffany Hartman?

And what exactly did the e-mail mean?

"Mom, is it okay if I call Grandma at the hospital?"

"Call her here, in a few days, okay?"

"Okay. Bye. Love you guys."

"Love you back."

On my way out the door, I grabbed a book to read, and returned to the hospital in less than the promised hour.

Wes looked relieved to see me as I entered Mother's room; she was asleep, snoring softly.

"How'd it go?" I whispered.

He stood, whispered back, "Apparently it's a long way to Tipperary."

"Yeah, a very long way. Hey, thanks for staying with her. I feel almost human again."

"Glad to do it. Let me know how she does."

After Wes left, I settled into the chair with my book.

Late in the morning, a nurse I'd seen working the floor came in and took Mother away for the MRI.

I used my alone time to call Tony and give him an update on Mother, and tell him that he wouldn't have much luck conducting an interview with her right now, not with her memory as it was.

I called Tina, too, not wanting her to learn about this secondhand. Thought about calling my sister Peggy Sue in D.C., but no need to worry her—she was unlikely to hear about this.

Mother came back from her MRI, and lunch arrived. She had just wolfed it down—apparently satisfied that it wasn't K-rations—when Dr. Warner appeared.

"I've seen the results from the MRI," he told us, "and I'm pleased—no cranial bleeding, pressure is fine."

"No shrapnel?" Mother asked.

"No shrapnel at all, Mrs. Borne. You're going home."

Mother pulled herself up in the bed. "Home? You mean I'm leaving the tour? Bob and Bing will be heartbroken. They'll have to replace me with ZaSu Pitts!"

Dr. Warner gestured to me with a crooking finger. "A word, Ms. Borne?"

Again I found myself out in the hallway facing the doctor.

"Besides running an MRI," he said, "I also had a thermal imaging test done on the head wound—it picks up heat from the effected area."

". . . okay."

"Made for an interesting outline."

I wasn't following him.

He gestured with a hand. "When I'm not here, Ms. Borne, or with my family? You can usually find me out on the links."

Now I *really* wasn't following him.

"So," he went on, "that means I'm familiar with all kinds of golf clubs."

Now I was following.

"Mother was hit with a golf club," I said softly.

He nodded. "Yes she was. A putter. And in a way we should be grateful."

"Why is that?"

"A larger club might have made a . . ."

"Hole in one?" I asked.

A Trash 'n' Treasures Tip

Jewelry is often for sale at swap meets. But never buy fine pieces such as gold, precious and semiprecious stones from anyone other than a legitimate jeweler. Not unless you want to risk having your neck turn green, as mine did thanks to a "gold" necklace I once purchased.

Chapter Ten

Sacrifice

(Deliberately bid over an opponent's bid.)

In spite of my pleas for Dr. Warner to keep Mother in the hospital a day or two longer, the Dream Girl of the USO was released in midafternoon; she was pushed in a wheelchair by Nurse Nancy to the curb where I waited in the Caddy.

"Is that a hearse?" Mother blurted, in apparent alarm. "I don't require a hearse just yet, I'll have you know!"

Nurse Nancy assured Mother that the Caddy was not a hearse, merely her daughter picking her up.

After that—back in the clothes she'd worn when brought to the ER, her partly shaved head bandaged—Mother sat quietly in the passenger's seat on the drive home, lost in thought. Or was that confusion? Either way, I was grateful for the silence, my head swirling with notions about how I might best take care of my amnesiac mother once we got home.

In our driveway, where the rust-colored stain from her blood remained visible, I helped Mother out of the car and—because she was unsteady on her feet—assisted her along the walk, then up the porch steps. This was a rare instance of awareness on my part that Mother was getting older, and it shook me some—she was so vital, so full of energy . . . to think that she'd *ever* be infirm. . . .

Inside, a waiting Sushi jumped with joy, beside herself that Mother was back, and our little family was once again complete, if somewhat the worse for wear. Soosh couldn't keep from piddling in delight on the wood floor, but at least she avoided the Oriental carpet, which made the cleanup easier.

I settled Mother on the Queen Anne couch with a needlepoint pillow behind her back, and the doggie curled up in her lap.

"Hello, Sushi," Mother said, petting her.

My mouth dropped like a trapdoor. "You *remember* her!"

"Of course, dear," she said, matter of fact. "I remember everything."

My eyes narrowed. "What do you mean by 'everything'?"

"Why, everything that's happened, dear."

"You mean, going on the USO tour with Bing and Bob?"

She regarded me with mild disgust. "Heavens no! How old do you think I *am,* anyway? I was merely playing possum, as a means of protecting myself from further danger."

I could have given her a lump on the other side of her head.

"Why didn't you *tell* me?"

Mother, continuing to stroke an appreciative Sushi, replied, "Because you wouldn't have been able to keep it to yourself. You have many wonderful qualities, dear, but acting skills are not among them—apparently talent of that kind is *not* in the DNA. Why else do you think I keep you backstage in all of my productions?"

I let the comment about my acting abilities slide, opting to pick my battles elsewhere. Besides, she was right.

Next to her on the couch now, I almost snarled as I said, "How could you put me *through* that! I wouldn't have had any trouble keeping your real condition to myself."

Lightly she said, "Couldn't take that chance, dear. It was vitally important that word get around I was out of my mind."

"No comment," I said.

She frowned at me. "Dear, 'no comment' is a comment in itself."

No comment.

She continued on, rather grandly, in full Cecil B. Director mode. "Because *I* was so convincing in my depiction of addled memory loss, *you* were convincing in your concern." She patted my knee. "Now, dear, don't you think we'd be better off spending our time more productively? For example, by bringing each other up to speed on what each of us knows?"

Grudgingly, I filled her in on the following: Wes and me finding the strangled Mrs. Fowler; Tony's information about the silk blue fibers found in the blackmailing woman's neck; Dr. Warner's theory that Mother had been hit with a golf putter; and the e-mail Jake had uncovered that Vanessa had sent to Tiffany.

"For an uninterested party who removed herself from further investigation," she said, arching an eyebrow, "you've done remarkably well. Actually, better than I have."

"I'm back on the case. I told Tony and he accepts it."

"Goody goody!" she said, but thankfully did not go into the song and put Johnny Mercer to the trouble of spinning in his grave.

"Now you," I said.

Mother informed me of her confirmation (by way of her regular network of snitches) of the four couples who comprised the apparently spouse-swapping Eight of Clubs, as well as her interesting visits with the three remaining wives.

Then she said, "Dear, it's time. Get the incident board!"

This last was delivered in full "*To the Batpole, Robin!*" style.

Dutifully I rose, with considerably less enthusiasm than Burt Ward would have mustered, and went into the library/music room to roll out the old blackboard, positioning it in front of her on the couch.

"Write!" she commanded.

"Not so fast," I said, holding up a crossing-guard palm. "Not till after we clear up a few things."

She frowned. "Such as?"

"Such as you stealing the Cadillac."

"First of all, dear, I did *not* steal it. As an investigator, I merely commandeered it. In the second place, I fail to see how one can steal a car that belongs to one in the first place."

"Don't give that 'first' and 'second' routine. *You* know what I mean—driving with a suspended license. No, 'suspended' doesn't cover it. Driving with an *exploded* license!"

"Frown lines frequently leave permanent traces on a young woman's forehead, dear. Anyway, it wouldn't have happened if you'd hidden the spare keys better."

"So it's my fault?"

She shrugged facially.

"You make this sound like a game!"

"Well, isn't it? And the game's afoot!"

"Afoot my backside! What about involving Jake? Do you think that was appropriate? I'm just getting back on a nearly even keel with his father after the *last* time we got Jake mixed up in one of our investigations."

"First . . ."

"Grrrr," I grrrred.

". . . I am pleased to hear you refer to it as 'our investigation.' Second, if I remember correctly, you had refused to help me and I was left to my own devices."

"Devices like car theft?"

"We've covered that, dear."

"So it's my fault again?"

Another facial shrug.

I put my hands on my hips, after managing not to put them on her throat. "I'm not writing *anything* on this blackboard until you admit you were wrong on both those accounts."

"I prefer to refer to it as the incident board, but if that's what it will take to proceed, dear, then all right . . . I freely admit I was wrong."

"I don't think you mean it."

Mother gestured impatiently. "Dear . . . my sincerity or lack of same is hardly the issue. A killer has now struck twice, and nearly added me to the list. We're wasting precious time with this falderal."

She did have a point, and a good one. Since no further admission of her culpability was likely to be forthcoming, I picked up a piece of white chalk from the board's lip, and began to write as instructed.

When I had finished, the blackboard looked like this:

SUSPECT	MURDER #1	MURDER #2	ATTEMPTED MURDER
Opportunity	Vanessa	Mrs. Fowler	Vivian
EMILY T.	swap meet	?	?
MEGAN M.	grocery store	?	?
TIFFANY H.	Chicago	?	?
TRAVIS T.	golf course	?	?
BRENT M.	golf course	?	?
SEAN H.	golf course	?	?
WES S.	office	w/Brandy	w/Brandy

Mother was saying, "I think it's fair to assume that all seven suspects had motive, so let's not concern ourselves with that."

"You mean, because of Vanessa's e-mail."

"Yes. I believe *that* was the catalyst in this little drama of death, and sufficient reason for us to focus our attention on the Eight of Clubs."

"We haven't looked into any other aspect of Vanessa's life," I pointed out.

"True, but this tight-knit group of friends, largely because of their, uh, sophisticated hobby . . . shall we politely call it . . . seem to exist in a little private world of their own."

"But, Mother, surely Vanessa had *other* friends, other interests . . ."

"Well, dear, let's leave *something* for the local police to run around in circles chasing."

I nodded. "Anyway, all roads do seem to lead back to the Eight of Clubs. Vanessa wanted a divorce, but without a child, she'd get nada. Her only leverage in obtaining a settlement was by threatening to expose the Eight of Clubs, and she e-mailed Tiffany her intentions to that effect."

Mother raised a finger. "While Wes, as the husband, remains a viable suspect in Vanessa's murder, he was with you when the Fowler woman was killed, and when I was bonked."

"True," I said. "But *anybody* in the Eight of Clubs would feel threatened by Vanessa's exposure."

"And," Mother said, "Tiffany surely shared that e-mail with *her* husband, Sean . . . and he, most likely, with the other men, who probably would have told *their* wives."

I nodded. "Suddenly everyone felt the real possibility of embarrassment and ruin." I gestured to the board. "But we don't have much to go on. The only information gathered so far is on Vanessa's murder—given to you by the wives, and there's no guarantee they were forthcoming. One or more could have been lying."

Behind her huge lenses, Mother widened cartoon eyes. "Perhaps *everyone* did it! The entire Eight of Clubs! Well, seven of them anyway. Just like . . . spoiler alert! . . . *Murder on the Orient Express!*"

"Mother, please. For one thing, everybody has an alibi for Vanessa's murder. And it doesn't take seven people to strike one blow."

"Then the four *men* could have done it! Or anyway, the three supposedly on the golf course."

"Didn't you check with the country club on that?"

"Well. Yes."

"What did the country club say?"

"The three were on the course golfing. But they could have sneaked off!"

Maybe that putter did jar something loose.

"Mother, can we settle down, please? And take this a step at a time?"

"Yes, dear."

"Let's start with what I said about everybody having an alibi for Vanessa's murder—that deserves some skeptical examination."

"Examine away, dear! I adore skepticism."

I put the tip of the chalk to Emily's name. "*She* could have left the swap meet earlier than the time she told you, taken her daughter and friend home, then gone to see Vanessa." The chalk moved to Megan. "*She* could have visited Vanessa in between getting groceries and going home to cook dinner." The chalk moved to Tiffany. "And *she* could have driven back from Chicago, killed Vanessa, then returned to Chicago."

"That ploy was done in a *Perry Mason*," Mother admitted. "Good episode!"

"And what of the three husbands? Even if the country club registry book shows they *had* been on the course all that afternoon, who's to say one of them *couldn't* have snuck away—with or without the others' knowledge. With all seven Eight of Clubs members threatened, the possibilities of accomplices is strong . . . if not likely to reach *Orient Express* levels."

Mother was nodding rather more vigorously than a concussion patient ought. "Thick as thieves, this group. But are any two or more of them thick as murderers?"

I shrugged. "Could be. If one falls, they all fall. That's why they're willing to lie and cover for each other."

Mother put a finger to her cheek. "But would they be willing to *kill* for each other?"

"It is possible."

"Do we think it's safe to assume that whoever killed Vanessa also killed Mrs. Fowler?"

"It is—not ruling out a conspiracy."

"And that the same perpetrator or perpetrators bonked *moi*?"

"That's a reasonable assumption, yes." Not that there weren't other people in town who would gladly bonk Mother.

Mother sighed. "This *is* a quandary! And unless I reveal to one and all that my memory has returned, my hands are tied!"

"But mine aren't," I said with a smile.

"Dear?"

"There's really only one way to get at the truth here."

I made her ask.

And then I answered: "I'll just have to infiltrate the Eight of Clubs. They're short a member, after all."

The following evening, I had dinner with Tony at the Serenity Country Club. The two-story cream brick-and-stone structure with wide pillared portico was located on the outskirts of town, on a prime patch of real estate almost certainly brokered by Travis Thompson.

Tony didn't belong to the club—even when he was chief, his police salary couldn't cut that—but Mother and I had a limited membership not including golf (neither of us knew how to play anyway). But it gave bridge-playing privileges to Mother, allowing her access to the local hoity-toities, a key source of gossip (or "intel" as she called it). Me, I could make use of the pool, a real blessing on hot summer days (and a challenge to keep my figure in swimsuit shape). Both of us could dine at the club's restaurant, which served the only food in town that you could classify as "cuisine."

Tonight was prime rib, and the expansive linen-and-fine-china dining room was at capacity. I was lucky to have landed a last-minute reservation, since just about anybody who was anybody in our little burg was present: bankers and businesspeople, politicians and physicians, many with their families.

As Tony and I were escorted to our table, I noticed the Eight of Clubs (now seven) seated at their usual round table by the window overlooking the Olympic-size swimming pool. Emily, Megan, and Tiffany were dressed to the nines, with Travis, Brent, Sean, and Wes in sharp, tailored attire. Nothing the group wore could be purchased in Serenity.

Maybe our apparel paled in comparison, but Tony and I didn't look too shabby—he was in a nice navy Men's Warehouse suit with light blue shirt and yellow tie, and I had on a Kate Spade black cocktail dress with jeweled accents around the neck, a pair of her pink patent-leather pumps, carrying a clutch purse that looked like a transistor radio—all bought at a nearby outlet center for forty percent off, and another thirty percent off because it had been Presidents' Day.

Tony ordered the prime rib and I opted for the filet of sole—not being much of a red meat eater.

And my date was not much of a talker, tonight certainly no exception.

"Don't care for it?" I finally asked, after watching Tony pushing the rare beef around his plate.

"It's fine. Just not very hungry."

Half of my delicious fish was gone already.

"Brandy." He paused, choosing his words. "I wish you'd rethink this . . . I know I said that I'd—"

"No. Trust me. It'll work."

He sighed, then nodded. "All right then—go ahead."

I raised my voice a little. "Really? Do I need your permission? Maybe I'm getting tired of you telling me what I can and can't do!"

"I wouldn't have to," he shot back, almost booming at me, "if you had the common sense God gave a goldfish."

My eyes flared at him. "Are you calling me . . . *stupid?*"

"No, Brandy. You're bright, all right. It's your judgment that's dim."

I threw my napkin down. "That's all! That's plenty! Don't call me, don't text me, don't come by the house."

"Got it," he said coldly, and returned to his food.

I huffed at him, got no response, stood abruptly, and stalked out, feeling eyes on me all around the dining room. I went into the adjacent, more intimate bar, where I took a seat at the counter, ordering a Scotch on the rocks from the bartender.

I was on my second drink when Wes slid onto the stool beside me. He was wearing a light gray suit, black shirt open at the collar, and his cologne smelled good. Good and expensive.

"Little lovers' quarrel?" he asked, with a tiny smile.

I stirred my drink with a swizzle stick. "More than a little, I'm afraid." I sighed. "But it's been a long time coming."

Wes caught the attention of the bartender, gestured to my drink and said, "The same." Then to me: "I never could quite see you two together."

"Right now? I can't either."

"What is he? Ten years older?"

"Twelve. Maybe I was looking for a father figure."

"Sounds a little kinky."

"More like needy." I sighed. "He *knows* my mother is a handful. That I have to . . . spend a lot of time just keeping track of her. He can't seem to handle that."

"Family is important. He should know that."

I shrugged. "Well, I admit she gets into his business. She has this ridiculous *Murder She Wrote* hobby, which means I really have to keep on top of things with her. She's bipolar, you know."

"I *heard* she was . . ."

"Nuts?"

". . . eccentric."

I laughed a little, took a sip from my tumbler, then asked, "Won't your friends miss you?"

He shrugged. "We were done with dinner. They'll be along for a nightcap . . . here they are now."

Travis and Emily Thompson came in, followed by Brent and Megan Morgan, then Sean and Tiffany Hartman, in a brittle cloud of laughter and conversation. If there were better-looking couples in town, I hadn't seen them.

As the group congregated at the bar, Wes asked me, "You know everyone, don't you, Brandy?"

"Sure . . . hi."

Brent Morgan, looking good in a navy pin-stripe suit, came over and put a hand on my shoulder in a way that might have been appropriate if we'd known each other better. The tall, dark-haired, chiseled-featured president of Serenity Bank asked with practiced concern, "How is your mother? I heard she was in the hospital."

"She's home now, but just very confused."

Brent's wife Megan leaned in, frowning sympathetically. She wore a chiffon pastel floral dress, her brown hair pulled up into a French twist.

"What happened, anyway?" Megan asked. "Word around town is she was mugged!"

Brent said lightly but not flippantly, "Doesn't sound much like Serenity."

I said, "Apparently it *was* a mugging. Everybody thinks we're rich since we made that TV pilot. We wish."

Travis Thompson joined the group gathering around me. The real estate developer was apparently comfortable enough with his rugged looks—and station in life—to dress down a little. His navy sports jacket and tan slacks probably only cost a grand.

He asked me, also at least feigning concern, "Don't know what this town is coming to. Was anything taken?"

"Yes," I said, nodding. "Her wallet was stolen."

"Identity theft is the *real* worry," Emily Thompson said, "in a sad situation like this." She was in tight green silk slacks with a matching sleeveless blouse that complemented her loosely waved strawberry-blond hair.

Sean Hartman, compensating for his heft and lackluster looks with a killer black suit and gold Rolex, asked, "Did your mother get a look at this mugger?"

I shook my head. "She doesn't even remember getting hit on the head. She's had short-term memory loss and is *really* addled. The doctor who treated her thinks she may never remember."

A *what a terrible thing* look passed between Sean and his wife Tiffany, but if there was any subtext, I couldn't discern it.

Tiffany, in a strapless pink dress, her white-blond long hair worn straight, remarked cryptically, "Perhaps it's a blessing. Sometimes memories can be too traumatic to handle."

"You might be right," I admitted.

Wes said, "You should really take her to the University Hospital, to a specialist."

"We'll see how she does the next few days."

"Shouldn't mess around with that, Brandy."

Megan shivered. "Why do they keep it so damn *freezing* in here? . . . Let's have our drinks over by the fireplace."

The group moved in that direction.

At first I wasn't sure if I was included in the invitation, but then Wes took my elbow, easing me off the stool, escorting me over to join the others in a corner of the bar where several couches and overstuffed chairs formed a semi-circle in front of an unlighted gas fireplace.

The shivering Megan flipped a switch on the wall and flames sprang to life behind the glass, then joined Emily and Tiffany, who had claimed one of the couches.

Brent, Travis, and Sean took the other couch, leaving Wes and me side by side in overstuffed chairs. The otherwise boys-together/girls-together arrangement said something about this group. Maybe it was just me, but I couldn't help but feel the wives were an adjunct to these frat brothers, interchangeable parts where the husbands remained as one.

The bartender came over and took drink orders, Wes putting everything on his tab. I already felt tipsy from the Scotch—I am *not* a world-class drinker—so I ordered a diet cola.

The three women immediately settled in to a huddled conversation, making me feel the outsider. Perhaps that was why Brent leaned my way, friendly.

"Say, Brandy." From his manner you'd think we socialized all the time. "When will you know if that TV show of yours is a go?"

"By the end of the summer, they say."

Travis asked, "What about your mother? I have a hunch her personality has a lot to do with how that show came to be. What kind of curveball will it throw, after what's happened? I mean, if her memory's not better."

I shrugged. "Who knows? Maybe she'll be even more entertaining."

"How's that?" Sean asked with a half smile.

I launched into a spirited account of Mother in the hospital, how she thought she was in the USO over in France entertaining the troops with Bob and Bing. This prompted Wes to share the hour he had spent with her, in which she had regaled him with backstage stories of her experiences behind the lines with Jane Russell and the Andrews Sisters.

Between the two of us, we had everybody howling with laughter. Mother may have disparaged my acting skills, but tonight I was a hit. Thanks to a little Scotch, anyway.

Then, wanting to leave on a high note, I announced that I had to leave, having been away from Mother for too long.

"Caregiver and all that," I said with a smile and a shrug.

Everybody gave me warm good-byes, then Wes walked me out.

At the Caddy, I was about to get in when he drew me close. I was expecting this, and had already formulated how to handle his kiss. Not too passionate, not too tepid. Just promising enough.

When we parted, he asked, "How would you like to go to a party tomorrow night?"

"What kind of party?"

Wes gave me a wink. "Let's call it a . . . swinging affair."

"Hummm . . ." I smiled, hiding the combined glee and dread that were jumping up and down within me like naughty twin children. "Sounds interesting. But with Mother in her current state . . . could I meet you there?"

"Sure."

He gave me the details.

In the Caddy, I dialed a familiar number on my cell.

"Well?" Tony asked.

"I'm in," I said.

A Trash 'n' Treasures Tip

Most swap meet vendors start shutting down their tables midafternoon, so go early in the day. But stick around for last-minute bargains from sellers who don't want to cart their unsold wares back home. Their aching backs may put a smile on your face.

Chapter Eleven

Danger Hand

(Opponent who can damage the declarer's prospects.)

After dinner next evening, I was seated at the Art Deco dressing table in my bedroom, putting the finishing touches on my makeup, when Mother came in and sat on the foot of the bed, leaning forward, hands folded. I could see her behind me, in the huge round mirror, gazing at me somewhat oddly.

Part of that oddness might be explained by her hair, a chin-length red bob with bangs, one of a variety of wigs a fellow thespian had dropped off after plundering the Playhouse wardrobe for means to disguise Mother's half-shaved head. With her big round glasses, she looked like an older version of Scooby-Doo's pal Velma, another amateur sleuth with a dog in her life.

"Dear," Mother said, brow furrowed, "I simply

must express my qualms about this evening. Do you have even the remotest idea exactly what kind of sybaritic bacchanal you may be attending?"

"No. I don't even know exactly what either of those two words mean. Probably not potluck dinner."

Her eyebrows went up over the big lenses of her glasses. "Actually, you're rather *close.* . . ."

I was to meet Wes at eight o'clock at the Grand Queen Hotel on the river front, specifically on the top floor near the ballroom.

"I'll be fine," I said. "Nothing will be behind closed doors. I'm a newbie, after all. Anyway, I assume Wes is taking me to the VIP Club."

The VIP Club was an exclusive key-card bar on the same floor as the ballroom, frequented by the likes of Wes and other well-off Serenity citizens.

Mother said, "I can live with it, as long as you don't wind up rendering unto Caesar in the Roman Spa."

She was referring to an ancient Rome–themed suite with a Jacuzzi that probably didn't date back quite as far as Cleopatra. A decade ago, the Grand Queen Hotel had been slated for demolition, but the wealthy publisher of the *Serenity Sentinel* stepped up to save the Victorian edifice, which got a much-needed three-million-dollar face-lift. Now people came from all around the state to stay in one of the Grand Queen's many "theme rooms," like the aforementioned many-columned playground, a way-out moon room complete with space-capsule bed, and a

King Arthur Suite with suits of armor and an even more unlikely hot tub.

(Originally there had been a Tarzan Suite with a bed in a tree, until a honeymooning couple fell out, breaking various limbs—the tree's mostly, but one each of the bride and groom's. The room has since been remodeled into a Valentine's Suite.)

Mother was asking, "So, dear—what's your plan? Your investigative agenda?"

I looked at her in the dressing table mirror; she so hated that she was not coming along. Me taking the lead was driving her batty. Battier.

I said, "I'm hoping the other members of the Eight of Clubs will be there, and, well, we'll just see how it plays out."

"See how it plays out," she said.

"Yes. How it plays out. Like, maybe someone will let something slip while in his or her cups."

"That *is* a plan of sorts."

"Thank you."

"A plan for catastrophe. A recipe for disaster."

"Mother. I . . . will . . . be . . . *fine.*"

She took in a sharp breath. "You must stay on top of your game. You dasn't drink too much."

"I 'dasn't,' huh? You know I'm not much of a drinker . . ."

"Yes, and keep that in mind! In this group, who knows what some miscreant might drop in your drink! And then, after your defilement, word will get around and everywhere you go, they'll be calling, 'Hey there! Orgy Girl!' "

I closed my eyes. "Mother, no one is going to slip me a roofie."

"You don't know that!"

Drinking, date-rape drugs . . . was I back in college?

"Stop worrying," I said. "If I get uncomfortable, I'll just book it, okay? I'm a big girl, all right? I'll have the car."

Her sigh started at her toes. "Very well, dear. But I'd feel better if you took along my Taser."

"Won't fit into my evening bag."

"Mace?"

"It's a tiny purse."

"What about using one of my surveillance gizmos?"

She got those by the dozen from spy sites on the Internet.

"For instance?" I asked.

"My voice-recorder pen."

"What, and sit and doodle on a napkin? And hope people come around and just casually spill their guts? No."

"The camera necklace?"

I shook my head. "Clashes with my outfit."

She raised a finger, a gleam in her eyes. "How about my new self-sticking, motion-activated, clothes-hook hidden camera?"

"Only if you can say that three times, very very fast."

Mother stuck her tongue out and made a *nah* sound. I had reduced her to that, and it felt pretty good.

But I also felt a little bad for her, so I pretended to be seriously considering these ridiculous suggestions, asking, "So if I take your clothes-hook camera—suppose someone actually hangs a coat on the hook, blocking it?"

"A definite drawback," she admitted, frowning. "I *do* wish I could find a use for my hook-cam—it was terribly expensive. But now that you mention it, there are design flaws. . . ."

My makeup complete, I turned and looked directly at her. "Mother, I'll have my cell. Stop worrying."

She frowned. She looked disturbingly cute in the red wig.

"You say your boyfriend, our esteemed ex-chief, has approved your participation in my investigation of these murders."

"Yes. But of *my* investigation. You are on the bench, lady. Sidelined with injuries."

"Be that as it may," she said, brushing the air with dismissive fingers, "let me ask you—have you cleared tonight's exploratory incursion with your Tony?"

I shook my head. "No. Just isn't necessary yet. He knows I'm infiltrating, but . . ."

"Not that you have a date with Wes Sinclair."

"No," I admitted.

Her sigh was on a grand scale, her hands on her knees, her Velma wig shimmering under the overhead light.

"I have a suggestion," she said.

Rut-ro.

"A suggestion that I admit pains me to make. You simply must call Tony Cassato and tell him what you intend. See what he thinks. If he clears it, I will clear it."

I got up, smiled politely, and said, "I don't need permission from either of you. I'm a—"

"Big girl, yes." Her expression was glum. "But a foolish one."

At sunset I pulled the Caddy into the hotel's packed parking lot, the sky awash with color, a blaze of pinks and purples, as if the bold strokes of a master water-colorist.

I got out, entered the hotel via the back lobby, and took the elevator up, stepping off the eighth floor. There a sign on a metal stand greeted me, white letters on black.

WELCOME SWINGERS!

Welcome swingers?

What had Serenity come to? What had America, what had the *world*, come to? A swingers' convention in the ballroom of the Grand Queen Hotel—in our little burg? How had I not heard about this? Not that I would have been interested, other than to bemoan the state of affairs. So to speak.

Then I remembered. We had dropped the *Sentinel* after it gave Mother a scathing review for her version of Whoopi Goldberg's one-woman Broadway show. The theater critic (also the head sports writer and the obit guy) had found Mother's performance "wildly inappropriate." He had a point, but it had been pretty entertaining, and for what it's worth, the African Americans in the audience laughed their heads off.

Still, I couldn't believe I was looking at a bold

public announcement of a swingers' party like this. Nor could I imagine Serenity's conservative Christian mayor not putting a kibosh on this affront to those family values he was always going on about.

This thought had just crossed my mind when His Honor and his honorable missus, both beaming, stepped out of the elevator on its return trip, and walked past me arm in arm. They went cheerfully through the ballroom doors just as two of Mother's gal pals—Alice Hetzler and Cora Van Camp—emerged, faces flushed with excitement, giggling like high school girls during a sock hop.

If my mouth had been open any wider, somebody would have put a hook in it.

I felt like the lead in a *Twilight Zone* episode who, just before Rod Serling came on for a final word, realized the quiet little town he was visiting was full of vampires.

As Alice and Cora entered the ladies' room, an elderly man came out the adjacent men's, adjusting his trousers. Then I recognized him as a Romeo named Harold, the ex-army sergeant who had once asked Mother to marry him.

Spotting me frozen by the elevator, Harold came over.

"Man, what a gay old time *this* is!" he said, the forehead beneath the white crew cut beaded with sweat.

That I refused to even think about.

He was saying, "Too bad Vivian couldn't make it."

"Well . . . she's recuperating."

"Yeah, everybody says she got herself clobbered. Damn shame. But hey, little girl—maybe you and me could go partners."

My mouth was open, but nothing was coming out. I wasn't even breathing.

Harold went on, "But, then, what the hey—I bet you'll be wantin' somebody *younger* to hook up with." He gave me a wink, then hurried back to the ballroom, change in his pockets jingling.

I shivered. Was I in some alternate universe?

Wes was nowhere to be seen, but my curiosity had the best of me—time to check the wild party out for myself. . . .

Inside the ballroom, I stood near the back wall, surveying the boisterous crowd of several hundred, mostly senior citizens but a scattering of younger and even much younger, too, many standing with drinks in hand, others seated at a dozen or so round cloth-covered tables placed on the periphery of the dance floor.

Suddenly music blared from a DJ's speakers, and couples young and old flooded the dance area to boogie to Louis Prima's "Jump, Jive an' Wail."

Oh!

That kind of swing party.

I laughed at myself, sensing someone coming up alongside me.

"Brandy?"

Wes, looking sharp in a black sharkskin suit, white shirt, and skinny black tie, took my hand and pulled me out onto the floor, where the jitterbug steps Mother had taught me came in handy, him twirling me every once in a while, me wishing I'd worn Mother's old poodle skirt.

A young couple next to us had come in full array—he in a zoot suit, she in '40s-style dress with shoulder pads—and they really knew how to go truckin'.

The song ended, and a slow number began.

Wes held me close, though not terribly close, and asked with a smile, "Mad at me?"

"What for?"

"Playing this little joke on you. I know you're nervous about our group, and I thought a little swingers' joke might help."

I smiled back. "You don't want to know what I was thinking, when I saw the mayor and his wife heading in here."

He chuckled, and held me closer, as we swayed to Cole Porter's "Night and Day" sung by Sinatra back when he was still Frankie.

Later, as the Voice's voice faded away, Wes whispered in my ear, "Let's get out of here, shall we? Leave the swinging to the old folks and the kids."

He took my hand and led me winding through the crowd, which dispersed onto the dance floor for "Boogie Woogie Bugle Boy." Couldn't get away from Mother even when she wasn't around. . . .

Outside the ballroom, I asked, "Where to? VIP Club? I've never actually been in there."

"Naw, we'll do that some other time. We've booked the Executive Suite—the rest of the gang's already there."

No doubt meaning Brent and Megan Morgan, Travis and Emily Thompson, and Sean and Tiffany Hartman.

"Great," I said, relieved we weren't heading to the Roman Spa for a sybaritic bacchanal.

One floor down, the Executive Suite was essentially a luxurious apartment—large sunken living area, full kitchen, dining room, and two bedrooms, each with a bath. I had been here before, just once, when Senator Edward Clark, my biological father, threw a party last summer for local campaign volunteers. (I apologize for not mentioning him earlier, but he has no function in this story. Or my life as of late, for that matter.)

Wes entered using a keycard. On a table in the entryway was a glass bowl with cell phones in it. Had cell phones replaced house or car keys as the new way of picking a partner? This might not be Rome, but a sybaritic bacchanal still seemed possible. . . .

"You don't mind, do you?" he asked, putting his cell in with the others. "They can be such a nuisance when you're trying to have a good time."

"Ah . . . no," I said, adding mine to the mix.

But now if I did need Mother, *or Tony, I had no life line. . . .*

Wes led the way to the anonymously modern living room, its lighting subdued. The couples, dressed casually if expensively, were in little groups of three. Brent and Travis were talking to Tiffany over by a big window with a magnificent view of the Mississippi. Just down from them, where the window ended, Megan and Emily were chatting with Sean. Everyone had a drink in hand, and several were smoking.

I said, "Hi, everybody," and waved, and everybody but Tiffany returned my greeting. She seemed unsteady, and a little bleary, as if her drinking today had begun long before the party.

Wes and I lounged in the sunken area on soft leather seating that rimmed the inner part of the square. A low table sat in the center with an assortment of liquor and wine bottles, glasses, and an ice bucket.

"Care for something?" Wes asked me.

"White wine would be nice."

He poured pale liquid from a bottle into a wineglass and got himself a tumbler of whiskey.

"So," I said, "I've been wondering . . . what's kept you and your fraternity brothers so tight, when usually school friendships are sort of, you know . . . temporary."

He shrugged. "We just got along. And then I was in a position to help the guys out, really get them started on their individual paths."

"They really owe you a lot."

The boyish features broke out in a smile. "Ah, I owe them. Bank president for a best friend, how can a guy in business beat that? I was able to get Trav started in the real estate game, and that helps me land housing for new employees . . . especially important for executives. And Sean just needed a little start-up capital, and me guiding certain folks his way for investing. What wouldn't a guy do for his best friend?"

How many best friends did Wes have, anyway? I guess I knew the answer: three.

Wes excused himself to use "the little boys' room" and I was alone, but not for long. The well-stocked table near me was the watering hole where glasses were filled and refilled, and beefy Travis came over to refresh a tumbler with bourbon. He did that sitting next to me.

"So," he said, a smile splitting his nicely rugged features, "you're thinking about joining our merry band."

"Well, I haven't been officially invited. But it looks like a friendly bunch."

"Oh, yeah, it is. Great people. You don't need to worry."

"I don't?"

"No, nobody has to do anything they don't want to."

"Not even play bridge?"

He laughed. "Not even play bridge." Then he became more serious. "How's your mom doing?"

"Better. I think the police think that what happened to her had something to do with Vanessa's murder, and that Fowler woman's."

He sighed. "Yeah, they questioned all of us. That ex-chief, and the current one, too. Wanted to know where we all were when Mrs. Fowler was killed."

"Ah. Just like TV—everybody needs an alibi, huh?"

He raised and dropped his eyebrows, then sipped bourbon. "Apparently. No problem for me—I was at a real-estate closing with my attorney."

"Hope Sean and Brent are in the clear. It's not like innocent people *know* they're going to need an alibi."

"True that! No, Sean was home with Tiff by midafternoon."

Had he been? Mother made no mention of seeing him there. Of course, Tiffany hadn't invited Mother in. . . .

"And," Travis was saying, "Brent was still at the bank. Works right up to six. That old notion of banker's hours doesn't hold anymore, at least not for him." He sipped more bourbon, shook his head. "Murders. What kind of way is that to live?"

Then he and his drink were gone.

Wes, on his way back from the restroom, had fallen into conversation with the Megan/Emily/Sean group. Maybe a minute later, Sean peeled away and came down into my sunken world where I was apparently guarding the liquor.

"You look like a little girl lost," he said, sitting too close for my liking as he poured himself more Scotch. "But don't worry."

Nobody wanted me to worry tonight.

He was saying, "This is strictly a consenting-adults type association. And very discreet."

"I suppose you all must be a little nervous," I said, making a girlish face, "having the murder of Wes's wife looked into."

He gave me a sharp, possibly alarmed look. "Why would we be?"

I shrugged. "Well, you know how small towns are. And you're all kind of royalty around here.

People always like to take people like you down a notch."

He shrugged. "I don't know if that's true anymore. Who really cares what other people do behind closed doors?"

"Conservative small-town people," I said. "The kind who do business with banks and brokerages and real estate offices."

"What are you getting at?"

"Nothing. Just making conversation. Anyway, Travis said you were all cleared by the police."

Sean shrugged, swirled his drink. "Well, they talked to us. About where we were when that woman across from Wes got killed. And when your mother got mugged. How is she, by the way?"

"Getting there. No memory of how it happened, though."

"Shame."

I shifted in my seat. "So I suppose the police talked to you guys about the golf club."

He frowned in confusion. "You mean the country club?"

"No. Not exactly. I mean the golf club Mother was hit with. A putter."

Blood drained from his face. "Is *that* what she was hit with?"

"Yeah. I supposed the police would've talked to you about that, considering that you guys are all golfers. They have tests they can make. If there's blood on a putter, they'd find it."

He shrugged noncommittally. "Well, I guess they would. If you'll excuse me, this isn't my choice of cocktail conversation."

I gave him an embarrassed little grin. "Sorry. Won't happen again."

He was barely gone when Brent showed up for more wine. He noticed my glass was half full and topped it up, gentleman that he was.

He put a hand on my shoulder. Normally, I'd have plucked it off. But I was undercover, and— even if I would never be under the covers—I left it there.

"You need a better escort than Wes," the banker said. He was a hunk, all right, those chiseled features, that dark hair. I wondered if he touched it up.

"I do?"

"Guy brings a newcomer into the group and then abandons her to her own devices."

"I'm not sure I have any."

"Any what?"

"Devices."

He smiled, sipped wine, and asked how my mother was. I said she was doing better.

"Listen," I said, "I heard something interesting."

"What about?"

"These murders. Isn't that what's on everybody's mind?"

"Well, not tonight!"

I scooched closer to him. "Come on. I just have one question."

"We'll see if I have an answer."

"You're a banker."

"Well . . . yes. I kind of like to think that, in Serenity, I'm *the* banker."

"You certainly are. My apologies. Anyway, that

terrible Fowler woman . . . sorry to speak ill of the dead . . . but she tried to blackmail Wes. Did you know that?"

He nodded. "Sure. Wes told us. Horrible woman. Sorry she's dead, hate to see that kind of thing happen to anybody, but . . . horrible old gal."

"No argument," I said. "But I heard she deposited ten thousand dollars in cash at the bank. Your bank. That means, or at least it *could* mean, that somebody else *did* pay her off."

He was frowning in thought. "You mean . . . whoever really killed Vanessa."

"Right. So my question is, I know it's cash, but could that transaction be looked into?"

"Not really."

"But if the police found a cash withdrawal at the bank in that amount, couldn't that point to the killer? Well, I guess they've already tried that."

He stood and moved away from me, frowning. "Here comes Wes. Look, he's had a rough time of it. None of this murder talk, okay? Give the guy a break."

Wes came down into my sunken lair and sat next to me. "Sorry. Didn't mean to leave you in the lurch or anything. But I'm kind of the host."

"No problem."

Now he was the one sitting close, and he slipped an arm around my shoulders. "Look. This is just a kind of . . . meet and greet. You're not getting yourself into anything."

"I'm not?"

"No. We'd be . . . months away from that, if you're interested."

"Okay . . ."

"You see, we need to get to know each other better, before anybody else gets into the act."

Then he was nuzzling my neck.

Now what the heck was I going to do? How do you tell a guy in a swingers' group—who knows that you know full well what kind of party it is— that you think he's being fresh?

And did anybody even *use* the word *fresh* that way, anymore?

Everybody else came down into the sunken area to join us. Maybe they all got thirsty at the same time. Maybe it was almost time to pick a cell phone out of the glass bowl. . . .

Shortly after everybody had settled in, a knock came at the suite's door, a muffled female voice calling out, "Room service!"

Wes drew away from me. "Somebody order food?"

"Me," Sean admitted, then nodded toward his tipsy wife. "Tiff needs something in her tummy besides booze."

"Says you," she said.

He got up and went to the door and opened it.

A tallish woman in a man's formal shirt with bow tie and black slacks wheeled in a food cart. She had long blond Veronica Lake–style peeka-boo hair.

"Where would you like this, honey?"

"This way," Sean said.

The woman followed him with the cart over to the edge of the sunken area.

"Please sign," she said, handing him the bill and a pen.

Sean gave her back the bill and pen, and she looked past him at me, drew back the hair to reveal her features, and winked. *Peekaboo!*

Mother!

"Where would you like the food?" Mother asked in a whispery seductive voice, fake hair back in place.

Sean descended the steps into the sunken area and gestured to the central table. "Here would be fine."

Mother picked up the tray of hors d'ouevres, balanced it with one hand, following Sean, but missed the last step —she wasn't wearing her glasses—and fell, her wig coming off, the tray going up in the air, then down on Sean.

Sean, covered in shrimp sauce and guacamole, snarled, "*You!*"

His wife was laughing. She was very drunk.

Drunk enough to squeal, "You should have hit the witch *harder,* Sean!"

"Thank you, dear," Mother said to Tiffany with a self-satisfied smile.

There was a mass effort to clean up the mess, but I took Mother by the arm and escorted her out, looking back at a stunned Wes to say, "I am *so* sorry about this! I need to get her home. . . ."

We moved fast and soon were on the elevator where I was so thrown by both Vivian Borne's disguised arrival and Mrs. Sean Hartman's incriminating blurt, that I didn't know whether to hug Mother or throttle her.

She had only one thing to say on the ride down: "And that, my dear, is why you need a plan!"

Finally I found a question to ask: "Was that pratfall on purpose? Or are you just blind?"

"A true artiste does not reveal her secrets."

Then we were in the parking lot, but as I headed toward the Caddy, Mother yanked me toward another car—a Toyota with Tony sitting in the front seat.

He leaned out the window. "How did we do?" he asked.

Addressing Mother!

"Home run, dear," she said, and handed him her recorder pen. "Sean Hartman's wife has something very interesting to tell you."

A Trash 'n' Treasures Tip

If someone else is looking at an item you want, good etiquette dictates that you wait until they have put it back down. Once, to get a potential buyer to set a Fire-King bowl back down, Mother kindly told him that his car was being towed, which it wasn't. And that's not good etiquette, it's good strategy.

Chapter Twelve

False Card

(Card played with the intention of deceiving an opponent.)

A day had passed since Sean Hartman's arrest on suspicion of assault and battery.

Tiffany Hartman's blurted confession of her knowledge of her husband's actions—caught on Mother's spy pen—had allowed Tony to obtain a warrant to search the Hartman home and vehicles. Mother's wallet was found at the curb in a garbage can in front of the Hartman home, and in the trunk of Sean's BMW was a bag of golf clubs whose putter was confiscated for blood and hair analysis.

While awaiting the test results, Mother and I were back taking care of business at the shop, behind the counter going over an inventory spreadsheet.

I paused in the work. Some questions about

last evening were finally making their way to the front of my brain.

"Mother—how did you know you could find me in that Executive Suite?"

Mother—now in a more age-appropriate chestnut wig reminiscent of no celebrity in particular, except perhaps Mr. Ed—replied, "Elementary, my dear Brandy . . . at least, it is when you have a snitch working at the hotel's front desk."

"But however did you know Sean had called for room service?"

Mother shrugged regally. "Afraid I must plead sheer luck, dear. I found myself riding the elevator up with the young woman who was bringing the cart." She chuckled. "You know, these college students are likely to do all kinds of things for a little extra mazuma."

"You mean, like allow you to take her place—even switching clothes?"

"For fifty dollars, yes. . . . She and I were about the same size, which was more luck, and the wig was my own, of course."

The little bell above the front door announced a uniformed Tony, coming in with a businesslike smile.

"How's everyone today?" he asked.

"Fine so far," I replied. "Any word back on that hair and blood analysis?"

Sushi, who'd been asleep near our feet in her bed, uncurled herself and trotted around to greet her favorite man, pawing at his pants legs, eager for his attention. (We had that in common.)

"Not yet," he said, leaning down to scratch Sushi's neck, "but we won't be needing it."

"Why ever not?" Mother demanded.

He rose, shrugged. "Sean Hartman has confessed to assault and battery."

"*I have been avenged!*" Mother said, smiling like
a pirate holding up the head of a rival.

Tony exchanged smirks with me.

Mother was saying, "Fancy a cuppa, kind sir?"

She had gone zero-to-sixty into the fake Brit
accent she affected when in the mood to impress. Or serve tea.

"Why not," he said.

Mother went to the nearby cart where an antique silver tea set was in use. We'd given up on
selling it—who wants to polish silver anymore?

"So," I said, "are you saying the case is closed?"

"Just the attack on Vivian," Tony said, pulling
a stool up to the other side of the counter.

Mother came back to pour steaming tea into
dainty china cups—nobody wants to wash china
anymore, either—giving Tony his usual single
sugar.

Tony stirred tea with a silver spoon. "Hartman denies having killed either Vanessa Sinclair
or Gladys Fowler."

Mother, Brit accent suddenly M.I.A., asked,
"You've checked his whereabouts for both murders, of course?"

Tony nodded. "Yes, and both alibis seem to
hold. He *was* playing golf at the time of the Sinclair killing, and was in conference with an in-
vestor when the Fowler woman was strangled."

Mother's latest sip of tea might have been bitter, considering her expression. "How conve-
nient for him, and how inconvenient for us."

I asked, "What about Brent Morgan and Travis Thompson?"

"Their alibis for both murders check out, too."

Frowning, Mother asked, "How about the little women?"

She meant the wives, not characters created by Louisa May Alcott.

Tony shrugged. "In the clear, I'm afraid. Starting to look like the Eight of Clubs is an eight-way dead end."

"Eight-way something," I muttered.

"So," Tony continued wearily, "it looks like we're back at that square one you hear so much about." He drained his cup, set it on the counter. "Thanks for the, uh, 'cuppa,' Vivian."

She beamed. "It's my pleasure, working with our once and future chief. And may I say, as to last night, I hope you've learned that cooperating with me in my investigative efforts is far preferable to opposing me at every turn."

"That was a one-off, Vivian," he said, staring her down. "And should we need to use that recording you made last night, keep in mind I knew nothing of that."

"But, Tony dear, that's not—"

"I knew *nothing* of it. Right?"

She looked for a moment like he'd cold-cocked her. Then she smiled and nodded and gave him a thumb's up and winked and drew a thumb and forefinger across her lips, in the *zipped* gesture. I was grateful there were no semaphore flags around.

He closed his eyes, sighed, then summoned a smile for me. "Guess I'd better get back to it."

"Dinner tonight?" I asked. "At the cabin, maybe?"

Tony was back living in his cabin in a beautiful woodsy area north on River Road.

Nodding, he said, "I'll buy the groceries and we'll do the cooking together."

I smiled. "Sounds like my kind of aiding and abetting."

He nodded and winked (but did not give me a thumbs up and *zipped* gesture) and went out.

After Tony left, I said, "I'm glad your attacker's behind bars. But otherwise, where the two murders are concerned? We really haven't accomplished much. I could even make a case that we were indirectly responsible for the ruination of a respectable man now charged with assault."

Mother stiffened. "Don't be silly, dear—that 'respectable man' could have killed me!"

I sighed, nodded. "Sorry. You're right. Nothing 'respectable' about what he did. You came around asking questions and Sean panicked and . . . now you're wearing a hideous wig."

"Yes, dear, I do think the Veronica Lake is much more flattering. But I got guacamole on it, I'm afraid."

The bell tinkled again as the front door opened and Dumpster Dan trudged in, sporting the familiar wrinkled clothes and carrying the usual soiled canvas tote.

Mother assembled a smile. "Well, hello there, Daniel."

The man shuffled over, but his eyes were bright.

"I have something *really* special today," he said,

reaching into the bag, then drawing out the item, placing it on the counter.

The heavy pewter beer stein with a woodland motif of grazing boars seemed at once a surprising example of something decent that Dan had come up with, and vaguely familiar . . . *where had I seen it?* Or anyway, one like it?

Then it came to me: *on the fireplace mantel in Wes Sinclair's man cave.*

"Where did you get this?" I asked excitedly.

"In a Dumpster downtown."

"Which *one?*"

"Why?" His eyes said he thought perhaps he'd done something wrong. "Does that matter?"

"This time it does."

He swallowed thickly, and his eyes traveled to the ceiling for help. Finally he found the answer there. "Ah . . . behind the bank."

"When?"

My pointed interrogation suddenly rattled poor Dan, and Mother had come to attention, too, like Sushi at a hydrant.

"I . . . I didn't steal it," he answered defensively. "Anything in a Dumpster is fair game! Taking trash is legal . . . it's not stealing."

Mother—sensing that my keen interest in the beer stein had nothing to do with antiques—said soothingly, "*Of course* you didn't steal it, Dan. But we do like to know the provenance of anything we buy."

"The providence of what?"

"Its *history*, dear."

"Oh. Well, sure." He took a breath and let it

out. "I found the beer stein a little over a week ago, and kept it for myself. I mean, it *is* cool. But now my rent is due, and I need some money. And it looks valuable, so . . ."

I asked, "How much do you want for the beer stein?"

He swallowed again. "Is . . . twenty-five dollars too much?"

I would have paid a lot more for what was very likely the weapon that killed Vanessa Sinclair.

Dan was saying, "It was all dirty and crusty, so I cleaned it up. Not a single chip or dent! It's mint, ladies."

So much for any forensic evidence.

I gave Dan fifty dollars from the till, and he went out, giddy with triumph and delight.

When the shop door closed behind him, Mother asked, "Dear, what made you pay twice what that little man asked . . . for a beer stein?"

"I've seen this thing before."

"Would *I* have seen it?"

"Only in a photo."

I moved down the counter to the computer, then opened the file containing the shots I'd taken of Wes's beer-sign collection the afternoon Vanessa was killed. Scrolling through, I found an angle that had captured the fireplace mantel with its proudly displayed array of beer steins. As Mother looked over my shoulder, I enlarged the photo, then isolated one in particular . . .

. . . the beer stein, which now sat on our counter.

"Great Caesar's Ghost," Mother said, quoting Perry White. "We're out of the woods and back in the game!"

I raised a cautionary finger. "But we have to be sure it's the *same* beer stein."

"As Dan pointed out, there are no chips or dents on this one. And the photo betrays none, either. Still, like any collectible, there *are* identical ones out there . . ."

"If it was used as the murder weapon," I said, "and the killer disposed of it right *after* the murder, then . . ."

Mother snapped her fingers. "Then it will be absent in the crime scene photos!"

I nodded. "If it isn't in them, then that . . ." I pointed to our new acquisition. ". . . is the blunt instrument that killed Vanessa Sinclair."

I called Tony on his cell, explained to him what we had, then e-mailed him the picture. With uncharacteristic urgency in his voice, he said he'd get right back to me.

Mother was practically doing a Riverdance jig (just imagine if she'd been Harold's partner at the swingers' affair). "You know what *this* means, don't you, dear?"

"What does it mean?"

"That Wes was the murderer all along!"

I held up a *not so fast* finger. "That beer stein could have been used to implicate him."

"He *did* have alibis for both murders," she granted. "He was at his office when the police came to tell him about Vanessa, and you were with him when Mrs. Fowler was found." She frowned. "Who else *could* it be?"

"A stranger, maybe? Some drifter lowlife who took advantage of an open garage door?"

"Unsatisfactory," Mother growled in her Nero Wolfe voice.

"Well, *somebody* who isn't on our suspect list."

Mother sighed. "Too bad Dan didn't provide us with the second murder weapon—the blue silk scarf, or tie."

I smirked at her. "Yes, darn thoughtless of him." Then I frowned.

". . . Dear? Something? You have a strange look on your face. Stranger than usual, I mean."

"Mother, Wes was wearing a blue tie the day I went with him to see Mrs. Fowler. That is, he *had* one on . . . then didn't have it on."

Her eyes narrowed. "Elaborate."

"When I first saw him, he came out of his office wearing the tie. Then fifteen or twenty minutes later—after I'd waited in the outer area, as he supposedly made a business call—Wes came out *not* wearing the tie."

She squinted at me, as if trying to get me in focus. "But he was there with you at his office!"

A hundred pinpricks prickled my skin. "No— he wasn't with me . . . he was in his office. Behind a closed door. Later, we went out a back way, using his private elevator. *That's* how he did it. He left, used his tie to strangle Mrs. Fowler, then returned to the office. He came out sweating, complaining about the air-conditioning!" My stomach churned, nauseated. "And all the while I was sitting there, drinking designer coffee."

"Well, he did need an alibi, dear. And who better than you?"

My face burned with anger. "Mother, he manipulated me. *Used* me."

She batted that away. "Yes, dear, that's how sociopaths operate. Let's not waste time there." She touched her chin with a forefinger. "We must now assume Wes also murdered his wife."

I was nodding. "Because Vanessa wanted a divorce and a hefty settlement. And, childless, she needed to get around the prenup . . . so she threatened to expose the Eight of Clubs."

Mother was nodding, too. "His M.O. for the first murder was the same—go to the office, slip out the back, do his foul deed, return the same way to his closed-door office, where he'd be waiting for word from the police."

"What was his motive for killing Mrs. Fowler?"

Mother grinned like the Joker. Well, maybe a little crazier. "Ah . . . that one is *easy!*"

"Really?"

"Let's assume Gladys was telling the truth at the preliminary hearing, when she said she saw Wes come home, then leave again . . ."

"Assume away."

". . . and let's further assume *Wes* was telling the truth when he told you that Gladys tried to blackmail him by offering to change her testimony for cash."

"Still with you."

Her eyes danced. "So why didn't he pay her off *then,* before the hearing?"

I shrugged. "No idea."

"Because, dear, he *wanted* Gladys Fowler to testify against him."

"*What?* Why?"

Mother had that *cat that ate the canary* smile going. "So that there would be sufficient evidence for him to be bound over for trial."

"Why on earth would Wes *want* to go to trial?"

"So he could beat the rap. One cannot be tried twice for the same murder. The double-jeopardy rule."

I put a hand to my forehead, as if taking my own temperature. "Whoa . . . *I* get it. Before the trial, Gladys would have either been paid off, or found dead in her bungalow."

"I knew you could think it through, dear, given half a chance. It's not like you're dense."

"Thanks a lot."

She raised a forefinger. "But our esteemed attorney Wayne Ekhardt tripped up Mr. Wesley Sinclair, by discrediting Gladys Fowler at the preliminary hearing."

"Wes hadn't figured on the old warhorse coming through in the race," I agreed. "He figured Mr. Ekhardt was past his prime, and *that's* why he picked him. When the time came for the trial, he'd have brought in a top out-of-town gun."

Mother gestured with open hands. "After the preliminary hearing, Gladys undoubtedly approached Wes again for money, and this time he *did* pay her off. In cash."

"And who was it that said blackmailers always want more?"

"Probably Erle Stanley Gardner, dear. But after

reflection, possibly spurred by my investigation, the time came not only to pay Mrs. Fowler off, but to get rid of her once and for all."

"And I became his alibi."

"Yes, dear. You did."

We fell silent for a moment. Then Mother picked up the beer stein. "If Wes used this to kill Vanessa, he most certainly will want it back."

I shook my head. "Not if there isn't any forensic evidence, he won't."

Mother smiled slyly. "Why, were you planning to tell him there isn't? Because, dear, it's not very likely he knows."

My cell rang and it was Tony with just the news we'd been waiting for: the beer stein in our possession indeed was absent from any of the crime scene photos.

"We have him," Mother said. "Or at least, we will, very soon."

Just past the witching hour, huddled in the dark behind the shop counter, were Mother, Tony, and I, sitting Indian-style on the floor, waiting for someone to break in.

For once, Sushi was absent—her barking at an intruder would not be desirable here.

Tony was leaning back against the wall, and I was leaning next to him. He was in uniform, having come from work to pick me up at the shop. I'd had a surprise for him.

He said in my ear, "When you asked if I wanted to spend the night, you forgot to mention it'd be *here*, with Vivian in the mix."

I whispered back, "Sorry. Couldn't be sure you'd go along with our little scheme."

He grunted. "Not sure I should be."

"Well, if it works, you might be chief again."

"If it doesn't, I might be a security guard somewhere."

"Not at Sinclair Consolidated, you won't."

"Good point."

Around noon, I had called Wes on his cell.

"What is it, Brandy?" he'd asked icily.

In the background I could hear restaurant chatter and clatter.

"Wes," I said, "I'm *really* sorry about last night." Referring, of course, to the Eight of Clubs gathering in the Executive Suite. "But it did lead to Sean confessing he attacked Mother, and you can understand why that's a good thing from our point of view."

"And you can understand why I don't share your point of view," he snapped. "Look I'm in the middle of lunch with Travis. Maybe—"

"This is something that doesn't have anything to do with what's been going on. Will you listen for a second?"

". . . All right."

I explained about the fancy beer stein Dumpster Dan had found over a week ago, and that we had just bought it for our shop.

"I know you have a really incredible collection of beer steins," I said, "and hoped you might be willing to tell us what we should ask for it."

"What's it look like?"

"Pewter, about six inches high, running boars. I can e-mail you a photo."

"Ah . . . yeah. Sounds interesting. Do that. I can access it on my phone."

He called right back, his tone far friendlier now.

"Brandy, that beer stein goes for two hundred dollars and up. The market's a little soft right now, but I'll gladly give you three."

"Really?"

"Sure. It'll make a super addition to my collection."

"That'd be great. Oh, but Mother promised a regular customer a first looky-loo tomorrow morning. But if we price it at the three hundred you've offered, he might pass. And if he doesn't want it, it's yours."

"Kind of you, Brandy."

"Consider it an olive branch."

"Do you have the stein there at the shop?"

"Yes. You want to come by for a better look?"

"No, I've got meetings all afternoon. Just let me know tomorrow, if your customer passes."

"You got it," I replied, and ended the call.

Now we three were waiting in the dark, our trap baited with the beer stein positioned prominently on the counter, easily visible through the two front windows.

Mother and I felt reasonably sure that Wes would come in through the front, the house being set back from the residential street, its low porch overhang providing dark cover. In back, an alley-pole light directly behind the structure shone brightly. Still, the rear door was a possibility, so we would stay alert. Either way, we were tucked behind the counter out of sight.

"I'm not sure he'll show at all," Tony said softly.

"Oh, he'll be along," Mother said.

"I don't know. He's a businessman, isn't he? He'll figure the shop will have a security system."

Mother shook her head. "But we didn't set it."

Tony goggled at her. "And he's to know that how?"

"Tish-tosh. Even with a security system, he'll look through that window, see the beer stein on the counter, break in, grab it, and make his getaway, long before anyone can react to an alarm, silent or otherwise."

"Vivian . . ." Tony began, irritably.

But I said, "Quiet, you two. Do you want to talk over the break-in?"

As the hours began to pass, Mother's optimism seemed to wane, and she fell asleep, her snoring thankfully subdued in her sitting position. I rested my head on Tony's shoulder and soon was visiting the Land of Nod myself.

Suddenly Tony nudged me awake.

I nudged Mother, who snorted to alertness.

The beam of a flashlight light-sabered through a front window, moving slowly across the room, scanning the area, then settling on the beer stein on the counter just above us.

At the sound of breaking glass, Tony moved into a crouch, getting his gun out. Then the revolver was in one hand and mag light in the other.

Fear spiked through me, and Mother looked electrified, eyes wide and glistening behind large lenses, waiting eagerly for what would happen next.

The door opened. Footsteps broached the short distance to the counter. A black-gloved hand reached for the beer stein, then picked it up, and that's when Tony stood.

"Right there is fine."

I heard a startled yelp, then two *clunks,* which must have been the beer stein and Wes's flashlight hitting the floor.

Mother, disobeying Tony's orders to remain hidden till an arrest had been made, Jack-in-the-boxed up.

"Well, heavens to Murgatroyd!" she exclaimed. "It's Travis Thompson!"

I stood, too, surprised to see that the intruder caught in Tony's mag-light beam was in fact the real estate developer, his rugged features catching noir-ish shadows in the harsh illumination.

"Hands on the counter," Tony said, gun trained on the guy.

Travis complied, as Tony moved around to pat him down.

Mother crossed to a wall switch, turning on the overhead light.

Tony—his search bringing forth no weapons, the intruder's pockets empty—put an annoyed-looking, vaguely embarrassed Travis in handcuffs, then stepped back and read him his rights.

Then Tony said, "Of course, Mr. Thompson, if you'd like to explain yourself, we're glad to listen."

Travis shook his head scowlingly, eyes on the floor. "Not saying a word without my lawyer."

"Your privilege. You can call him from the station." Tony looked my way. "Leave everything as is. I'll send someone over to take photos of the broken window and the beer stein."

The latter was on the floor, looking none the worse for the trip.

He gave us a small, tight smile. "Looks like we have our killer."

Tony escorted Travis out, and Mother and I followed, watching from the porch in frowning confusion as he put the real estate developer in the backseat of his unmarked car at the curb.

As Tony drove off with his charge, I asked, "So were we *wrong* about Wes?"

"Apparently so. But we did catch the killer."

"*Did* we?"

She turned my way, still frowning. "What troubles you, dear?"

"Probably the same things that're troubling you, if you'll admit it. Let's start with Travis's reaction. Shouldn't he have been scared?"

Mother shrugged. "He *was* scared. He yelped."

"Sure, in surprise. But I mean, *after* that. It was more like he was . . . mad."

"What perpetrator *wouldn't* be, falling into a clever trap like the one we set? Anything else, dear? Let's not kick victory in the teeth."

"Why wasn't Travis carrying any car keys?"

She had to think about that for a few seconds. Then: "Likely because he left them in the ignition, for a fast getaway."

"With the car doors unlocked? And risk it

being stolen? And do you see a car out there with its motor running?"

Mother's eyes popped. "I've got it! He didn't have keys because—"

"*Somebody drove him.* Right."

I trotted down the porch steps and out to the front walk, where I looked up and down the street.

The houses were dark and quiet, owners snug in their wee little beds, oblivious to the dramatic doings that had just taken place in our shop.

The cars on the street were parked nearly bumper to bumper, silently slumbering like metallic beasts.

But then one of those beasts awoke, a particularly sleek one, its dash and headlights snapping on, the vehicle pulling away from the curb, engine roaring as it sped past.

I called back to Mother. "That was Wes's *Jaguar! He* brought Travis! To do *his* bidding!"

Mother was at my side in an eye blink. "It's just like that scoundrel to let one of his pals do his dirty work for him."

"Actually, this is the first time. He really *did* kill his wife and Mrs. Fowler."

"I believe you're right, dear . . . but tonight he sensed the possibility of a trap . . . and sent a stalking horse in to cover that contingency!"

My cell call to Tony went straight to voice mail, so I called the dispatcher to get word to him.

Mother was saying, "We mustn't let Wes get away! He saw Travis being taken to the station. And as we Brits say, he'll do a runner."

No time to remind Mother she wasn't a Brit.

I said, "He must be heading to the airport."

"To the Batmobile, dear!"

Suddenly I was Burt Ward again.

"What about the shop? Lock it up?"

"Never mind—the photographer will be here presently. Now chivvy along, dear!"

Maybe she was British at that. Have to take a closer look at the Danish family tree. . . .

The Caddy was parked a few blocks up the hill on a quiet side street, the classic ride's convertible top up, to (as Mother put it) "prevent mischief from thieves and vandals." It took a few minutes to get there because Mother wasn't moving as fast as once she had—not since her double hip replacement.

Then I was behind the wheel, Mother riding shotgun, heading toward the riverfront, then barreling south on River Road.

Even with pedal to the metal, getting to the Municipal Airport would take ten minutes, anyway. And Wes might well be long gone. Still, we had to try. . . .

We were singularly quiet as we sped along, the rolling bluffs turning to flat farmland, headlights cutting through the night like lasers.

Then there it was, off to the right: Serenity Municipal Airport.

For years it had been only a Quonset-hut main building with a single hangar, plus one landing strip with wind sock, a facility used only by small-plane aficionados. But after Wes Sinclair bought his Learjet, a modern brick main building suddenly replaced the Quonset hut, several other hangars were added, and the runway was extended. But the wind sock remained.

I wheeled the Caddy into the small parking lot near the main building, and Mother and I got quickly out.

Everything was dark and quiet, buildings locked up, runway lights off.

I said, "Guess maybe we were wrong about Wes coming out here."

"It would appear so," Mother admitted. "But that private jet of his is the logical way for him to make his escape."

We were about to get back in the car when the landing strip's lights popped on, bright as daylight. After hours, this could only be directed from a pilot coming in . . .

. . . or taking off.

"Mother—hear that?"

The high-pitched whine of a jet engine.

"Yes, dear, that cuts through even my ear-wax buildup!" She pointed. "Over there—that hangar door is open."

Excitement ran through me like chills. "What should we do?"

"I don't know, dear—*something*. The fiend'll get away otherwise. Some foreign land, and with his money—"

"Get in the car," I said.

We got in the Caddy and I tooled it out of the parking lot and along an access road leading to the hangars, with the main runway looming beyond.

The Learjet had exited its hangar, making its way to the strip. I caught up with the plane, then zoomed ahead of it, continuing on out to the runway.

Mother said, "If you're about to do what I think you might, I am quite in agreement. It's a bold move and I'm proud of your reckless abandon!"

"Thank you." Her praise in that regard meant a lot to me. Who knew more about reckless abandon than Vivian Borne?

Halfway down the lighted strip, I slowed the car, then swung it sideways with a screech of tires so that the Caddy was blocking the runway.

We got out and stood by the car in a sort of two-woman challenge to the man who thought so little of our sex that he used and swapped and killed them.

The Learjet was poised for takeoff.

Would Wes attempt it anyway?

The answer came quickly as the high-pitched engine noise increased, and the jet rolled toward us, picking up speed.

"Run, Mother!" I yelled. *"Run!"*

I grabbed her hand and we sprinted to the adjacent field, dropping down to the ground, twisting our necks around to see the jet, engines screaming, bear down on the Caddy.

A second before impact, the jet's nose jerked upward, its front wheel clearing the car. Wes was making a break for it and there was nothing to be done, our best effort, however reckless, a failure. . . .

Then a back wheel caught the underside of the Caddy's cloth-and-metal-frame convertible top, lifting the car off the ground. Then the top snapped off, the Caddy dropping back to the runway, roughly, as did the jet ahead of it, off-balance and out of control now, careening down the remainder of the runway and coming to an abrupt halt, its nose shoved in the dirt like a bullied child.

Sirens screamed, distant at first but quickly upon us, and more lights cut across the runway, headlights, as a trio of police cars sped toward us.

Helping Mother to her feet, I said, "I'm afraid the godfather's car's a goner, Mother."

Mother adjusted her brown wig which had gone askew, and—smiling through misting eyes—replied, "A sacrifice worth making, dear. A sacrifice worth making. . . . I wonder if we're insured in case of aircraft collision?"

The rest was anticlimactic—Tony emerging from a police car, gun in hand, as a slump-shouldered Wes Sinclair came down out of his plane without incident, hands up, his face a slack-jawed mask of defeat. As Tony led him to a vehicle flashing red and blue, Wes didn't even glance our way. We were unimportant now, Mother and I, just two women who, like all women, didn't matter to him at all.

A Trash 'n' Treasures Tip

Smart shoppers haggle. The amount listed on a price tag should be the starting point for negotiating a better deal. And if you have the ability—as does Vivian Borne—to really wear down a seller, a world of bargains awaits you.

Chapter Thirteen

Late Play

*(Hand that is played after the event
has finished.)*

When thoughts become actions, those actions can have consequences—sometimes good, sometimes bad.

It was August now, and two months had passed since Wes Sinclair was pulled out of his bunged-up Learjet, to be charged with the murders of his wife Vanessa and of blackmailer Gladys Fowler.

This time around, Wes didn't do so well at the preliminary hearing—turned out there *was* usable forensic evidence on the beer stein (maybe Mother and I should start watching *CSI*), and a silk blue tie found beneath the front seat of Wes's Jaguar matched microscopic fibers imbedded in Mrs. Fowler's neck.

So Wes, now with a very expensive out-of-town lawyer at his side, got his original wish—he *would* be going to trial, this time facing two first-degree murder charges.

Sean Hartman got six months for assaulting Mother—a relatively light charge, taking into consideration that this was the broker's first offense. But his real punishment would be disgrace and a ruined business.

Travis Thompson received an even lighter sentence for his breaking and entering, the district attorney unable to substantiate that the real estate developer had prior knowledge of either murder, or that the beer stein he was dispatched to retrieve was evidence. Travis stuck to his story that he was doing an ill-advised favor for a friend without knowing the reason behind that favor.

I know—lame. But Travis's real estate partners forced him out, while wife Emily sued him for divorce, moving with her daughter into a condo. Tiffany Hartman filed for a divorce, as well, packing up a U-haul and heading back east, to wait for her share of community property.

After his, yes, sybaritic lifestyle came to light, Brent Morgan—at the urging of the board of the bank's directors—resigned as president of the Serenity First National. He alone of the Eight of Clubs men landed on his feet, however, relocating to the Chicago area at another bank, his wife Megan sticking by him. But somehow I thought the only swing set Megan might endorse at this point would be in their backyard for their two boys.

As for the Borne girls, we did not emerge from the experience unscathed, although Mother's hair was growing back nicely (she was still alternating various Playhouse wigs). Our involvement in bringing down the Eight of Clubs came with a surprising backlash: a number of folks were irked with us. As it happened, some Serenityites had long despised *both* Vanessa Sinclair *and* Gladys Fowler, and while no one said in public that those two women got what they deserved, the general feeling was that our meddling had ruined the lives of three prominent couples and disrupted the local economy along the way.

Mother took this in stride. "No good deed goes unpunished, dear! What's important is that the *bad* deeds of Mr. Wesley Sinclair are not going *un*punished."

On this hot August morning, I was heading to the police station in our new blue Ford C-Max hybrid. Yes, our new car!

Remember the swap-meet/car-show guy who wanted to buy the Caddy? Well, he still wanted to, even though it had been dragged by a Learjet. Of course we did have to come down on the price quite a bit, and did not get anything out of our insurance claim except giving the adjuster a big laugh.

The C-Max took some getting used to. For one thing, I had trouble remembering the order in which to do things to start the thing. For an-

other, every time I stopped at a light, I thought
the engine had stalled, and tried to restart it.
But it's good for the environment, so if you
wreck your car on a landing strip when a Learjet
tears its roof off, I can recommend the C-Max.

And despite not being used to the vehicle, I
managed to make it to the police station with
both it and myself in one piece (I guess that
would be two pieces).

For once I was not stopping at the station to
bail Mother out of a holding cell or otherwise
deal with some aspect of an investigation of hers
(ours). Not that this was any more pleasant: I
was here to see Brian, who was leaving the department tomorrow, having taken a job in the
Chicago area, after losing the top cop slot to Tony.

Things had gotten ugly when Brian accused
Tony of dereliction of duty by running an "un-
official investigation with Vivian and Brandy
Borne." It hadn't gotten him anywhere, since
the district attorney was in the local camp that
was glad we'd brought Wes, Travis, and Sean to
justice.

Still, Brian and I had meant something to
each other once, not so long ago, and despite
his carping about Tony helping us, Brian too
had been helpful to Mother and me in several
of our prior murder inquiries. So I very much
wanted to say good-bye.

And very much didn't want to.

Inside the station, I walked over to the Plexiglas and asked dispatcher Heather to tell Brian I
was here, and would like to see him. As per
usual, the redhead with red eyeglass frames told

me to take a seat in the waiting area, and also per usual I obeyed, sitting next to the ever-neglected rubber tree plant.

Too quickly, Heather called me back over.

"I'm afraid he's busy," she said.

"Meaning," I said, mostly to myself, "he doesn't want to see me."

The dispatcher shrugged apologetically.

"Get him back on the line, would you?"

"Well . . . I don't know what good it would—"

"Tell Brian I have a picture of him in Superman undies that's going viral if he doesn't give me two minutes."

The dispatcher smiled, turned away, spoke into a phone, nodded, then faced me. "What do you know? Now you can go through."

When the steel door buzzed, I entered the inner police sanctum and followed the beige hallway with its framed vintage police photos all the way down to the last office on the left, where I paused in the doorway.

Brian, in a blue short-sleeve shirt, yellow tie, and navy slacks, was standing behind the desk, packing personal belongings into a cardboard box.

"Sorry I had to play the undies card," I said. "But I wanted to say good-bye."

Brian looked over with those puppy-dog brown eyes of his, his brown hair slightly tousled—like it was after I used to run my fingers through it.

But the boyish smile I remembered fondly was not in evidence.

"Good-bye," he said flatly, resuming his packing.

"And I wanted to wish you the best in your new job."

Could that sound more awkward? More stilted?

"Well," he said, "now you can check that off your to-do list."

What had I expected? A warm embrace, one last kiss?

"Well . . . just don't unfriend me," I said, wounded nonetheless. "*That* I don't think I could take."

I'd given it a shot.

I turned away.

". . . Brandy."

He came out from behind the desk and crossed over to me, eyes softening. "Sorry. Pouting isn't becoming on a guy, is it?"

"Not that great on a female, either."

"I do appreciate you stopping by."

I nodded, smiling weakly. "Look, I know you were disappointed about not being selected chief. But I heard you're going to be chief somewhere else, right?"

He laughed softly. "What did I expect? Tony has credentials way beyond mine. And it's my own damn fault, too, the way I jumped the gun on Sinclair's first preliminary hearing."

Consequences.

I asked, "So where are you going to be chief now?"

"Naperville. And I'm not chief, exactly. Deputy chief. It's a big town. Bigger than Serenity, anyway."

"And part of the Chicago Metro area and everything. Maybe I mentioned that Jake lives there with his dad."

He gave me a wry smile. "Please tell me your son's not a crimestopper like you."

I gave him one back. "Well, he's already helped out a few times. But if Mother and I come to visit, I promise we won't look into any homicides."

"I wonder if I'll have to hold you to that? But will you promise to look me up?"

"Absolutely." I touched his arm. "I just know you'll be happy."

He shrugged. "I think I will. I'll be close to where my daughter lives, and my ex was almost friendly the last time I visited." He cocked his head. "Now, about that *picture* . . ."

"Do you really think I'd let any other woman on the planet see how cute you *really* are?"

And I kissed him on the cheek and got out of there. Whether I had to dry my eyes in the parking lot is not really any of your business, is it?

Next on today's to-do list was to deal with a consequence of my own, but one that I shared with my best friend's husband. The time had come: Kevin and I needed to tell Tina about Baby Brandy.

As I drove the C-Max up the drive of the white ranch-style home, Kevin came out from working in the garage to meet me. We had planned this confession together, so for once there was none of our usual banter.

"Ready?" I asked him.

His eyebrows flicked up and down; his anxiety was obvious. "As I could ever be."

I followed Kevin through the garage to the back door that led into the kitchen, where Tina was chopping vegetables at the island counter.

Teen looked up.

"Brandy! Nice surprise!" But her smile faded as she took note of my solemn expression. "What's wrong, honey? Please don't say your mother's had another relapse?"

"No. She's fine. Happily medicated." I glanced around. "Where's Baby Brandy?"

Tina wiped her hands on a kitchen towel. "Down for a nap." She frowned, eyes going from me to Kevin, then back to me. "Okay. What's going on? If this is an intervention, I promise I haven't touched chocolate in days."

I took the lead—after all, using one of my eggs as a backup to Tina's had been my idea.

"Kevin and I have something to tell you." I looked at him, then gave my BFF a smile that must have been ghastly. "Maybe this should be done away from sharp knives. . . ."

Bad nervous joke.

Tina moved to the kitchen table, then sank down in a chair. Again she looked from him to me, me to him. The blood drained from her face. "Are you . . . are you two having an affair?"

"No!" I blurted. "Oh my, no. I'm so *sorry* that I am so *lousy* at this. . . ."

"At what?" Tina asked, looking a little relieved, getting her color back, but still clearly concerned.

Kevin pulled another chair around, sat down and took his wife's hand. "Teen, it's about the baby. . . ."

I said quickly, "Nothing's wrong with her. It's not that."

"No," he said, "it's not that. It's just . . ." His eyes went pleadingly to me.

Joining them at the table, I just flat-out told her. Confessed that after the last of her fertilized eggs hadn't taken, I'd used one of mine.

She listened expressionlessly, and when I was finished, I felt sure I had just lost my best friend.

But after a long silence, Tina sighed heavily and said, "I was wondering when one of you would get around to telling me."

"You *knew?*" Kevin said, astonished.

"Of course I knew," she said simply.

"How?" I asked.

"Well, duh . . . she *looks* just like you!" Tina smiled a little. "And, I guess I have a confession of my own to make. After all those failures with my eggs? I was going to ask you for some of yours . . . but I just couldn't get up the nerve. So you must have read my mind."

I got out of the chair and came around the table as Tina stood, and we both hugged.

A relieved Kevin said, "Well . . . I guess you two will want to be together."

And he discreetly made his exit.

Tina said, "Now, Baby Brandy *is* a test-tube baby, isn't she?"

"Yes! No fooling around with Kevin involved. But I still say you're a lucky girl."

"I am, aren't I? To have both of you in my life."

About an hour later I left Tina, feeling confident our friendship remained strong, and drove back to the shop, where I found Mother in the living-room area, rearranging knickknacks. Sushi was curled up on a Victorian settee—the handwritten DO NOT SIT sign pinned on the back of the love seat apparently did not apply to her.

"Dear," Mother said, looking very unlike herself in a black Bettie Page wig, "we're running low on stock—a picking trip would seem in order!"

Business had been brisk this summer, and we'd coasted along by just rearranging the goods. But the rooms were now looking a little sparse.

I joined Sushi on the love seat, the sign not applying to a co-owner, either. "I know where we can get our hands on a roomful of wonderful antiques and collectibles, and it won't cost us a dime."

"You are in jest."

"No jesting."

Mother's eyes widened behind the large lenses. "And where is this treasure trove that won't cost us a bleeding farthing?"

"It's an exotic, elegant place, but one you know well."

Her eyes grew wider still. "Yes . . . yes?"

"It's called our garage."

The stand-alone structure was filled to the rafters with stuff and things, plus things and stuff, that she had scavenged over her many years of . . . well, scavenging. But the notion of plundering it froze Mother like Lot's wife taking that one last ill-advised backward peek.

I asked, "Wouldn't it be nice to be able to put our new car in the garage this winter?"

Mother thawed a little. "Well . . . perhaps it *is* time to put those things to use. To let the darlings come out into the world and thrive!"

Into our shop, anyway.

"Great!" I said. "But this does mean I'll have to cancel my call in to the producers of *Hoarders?*"

Straight-faced, she said, "I don't do guest appearances on rival shows, dear."

"What show? We haven't heard a word in ages."

The store phone rang on the counter in the next room, and I got up to go and answer it.

"Trash 'n' Treasures," I said.

"Brandy! Phil Dean."

Wow, was our producer/director ever on cue!

"Oh . . . hi, Phil. What's up?"

"I finally have news about the pilot," he said, the tone of his voice providing no clue as to its fate.

Would Mother be doing cartwheels, or confined to her bed in deep depression?

"The show is a *go!*" Phil exclaimed.

Cartwheels, then.

Me? I wasn't so sure.

Stay tuned.

A Trash 'n' Treasures Tip

Many vendors have a cash-only policy, so hit the ATM before you arrive at a swap meet. Don't be in a position where you miss out on a bargain because you're only a card-carrying shopper. Mother keeps a spare hundred-dollar bill pinned inside her bra just like Bret Maverick used to (of course, he had a thousand-dollar bill) (and no bra).

About the Authors

BARBARA ALLAN

is a joint pseudonym of husband-and-wife mystery writers Barbara and Max Allan Collins.

BARBARA COLLINS is a highly respected short story writer in the mystery field, with appearances in over a dozen top anthologies, including *Murder Most Delicious, Women on the Edge, Deadly Housewives,* and the best-selling *Cat Crimes* series. She was the co-editor of (and a contributor to) the best-selling anthology *Lethal Ladies,* and her stories were selected for inclusion in the first three volumes of *The Year's 25 Finest Crime and Mystery Stories.*

Two acclaimed hardcover collections of her work have been published—*Too Many Tomcats* and (with her husband) *Murder—His and Hers.* The Collins's first novel together, the Baby Boomer thriller *Regeneration,* was a paperback bestseller; their second collaborative novel, *Bombshell*—in which Marilyn Monroe saves the world from World War III—was published in hardcover to excellent reviews. Both are back in print under the "Barbara Allan" byline.

Barbara has been the production manager

and/or line producer on various independent film projects emanating from the production company she and her husband jointly run.

MAX ALLAN COLLINS has been hailed as "the Renaissance man of mystery fiction." He has earned an unprecedented twenty-one Private Eye of America "Shamus" nominations, winning two Best Novel awards for his Nathan Heller historical thrillers, *True Detective* (1983) and *Stolen Away* (1991), and Best Short Story for his Mike Hammer story, "So Long Chief" (2014), completing an unfinished work by Mickey Spillane. His other credits include film criticism, short fiction, songwriting, trading-card sets, and movie/ TV tie-in novels, including the *New York Times*– bestsellers *Saving Private Ryan* and the Scribe Award–winning *American Gangster*. His graphic novel *Road to Perdition*, considered a classic of the form, is the basis of the Academy Award– winning film. Max's other comics credits include the "Dick Tracy" syndicated strip; his own "Ms. Tree"; "Batman"; and "CSI: Crime Scene Investigation," based on the hit TV series, for which he has also written six video games and ten best-selling novels.

An acclaimed, award-winning filmmaker in the Midwest, he wrote and directed the Lifetime movie *Mommy* (1996) and three other features; his produced screenplays include the 1995 HBO World Premiere *The Expert* and *The Last Lullaby* (2008). His 1998 documentary *Mike Hammer's Mickey Spillane* appears on the Criterion Collection release of the acclaimed film noir *Kiss Me Deadly*.

Max's most recent novels include *Ask Not* (the conclusion to his Nate Heller "JFK Trilogy") and *King of the Weeds* (completing an unfinished Mike Hammer novel from the late Mickey Spillane's files).

"BARBARA ALLAN" live(s) in Muscatine, Iowa, their Serenity-esque hometown. Son Nathan works as a translator of Japanese to English, with credits ranging from video games to novels.

Don't miss the next Trash 'n' Treasures mystery
by Barbara Allan

Antiques Fate

Coming soon from
Kensington Publishing Corp.

Keep reading to enjoy a preview excerpt . . .

Tinseltown Reporter, September 2015:

Antiques Sleuths, a new reality TV series scheduled to begin airing next summer, is set to go
into production this winter in the small Iowa
town of Serenity. Producing is cinematographer-
turned-show-runner Phillip Dean, stepping in to
replace late reality-show guru Bruce Spring
(*Extreme Hobbies* and *Witch Wives of Winnipeg*).

But will shooter Dean be able to fill a show
runner's gumshoes? And what motive beyond
ratings instigates the new series?

Dean, contacted for evidence at his Califor-
nia home in Holmby Hills, said, "The premise
of *Antiques Sleuths* is unique: two amateur
sleuths—a mother and daughter team—who
have solved a number of real-life murder mysteries in their quaint hometown, uncover the
mysteries behind the strange and unusual antiques that are brought in to their shop."

Mother is Vivian Borne (age not provided), a
widowed antiques dealer with a bloodhound's
nose for sniffing out murder and mayhem.
Daughter is Brandy Borne, a thirty-two-year-old
divorcée who plays reluctant Watson to her
mother's zealous Holmes, with the help of an
ever-so-cute shih tzu named Sushi.

The duo have written a number of popular
books chronicling their cases under their joint
pseudonym, Barbara Allan. The series, however,

will not focus on their amateur detecting, but on their antiques shop.

As mysteriously intriguing as this new show may sound, this Tinseltown detective deduces that in a saturated reality TV market, the verdict may already be in: *Antiques Sleuths* risks arriving DOA.

—Rona Reed

Chapter One

All the World's a Stage

Have you ever had a moment when everything was so perfect that you wanted to stop time?

Well, that moment was now. And now was me curled up with my boyfriend, Tony, on his couch in front of a lazy fire, the fragrantly nutty smell of hickory logs permeating the rustic cabin. The only sound was an occasional snap, crackle, and pop of the wood—with no resemblance to Rice Krispies, and with a counterpoint of light snoring from Sushi, my shih tzu, nestled on the floor next to Tony's dog, Rocky, a mixed breed mutt with a stylish black circle around one eye.

I was (and for that matter am) Brandy Borne, thirty-two, of Danish stock, a bottle-blonde with shoulder-length hair; at that moment, I was casually attired in a plaid tan and red shirt from J. Crew, my fave DKNY jeans, plus sparkly gold flats by Toms (because a girl always needs some bling).

My BF's idea of dressing casual was a pale yellow polo shirt, tan slacks, and brown slip-on shoes sans socks. In his late forties, with graying temples, a square jaw, thick neck, and barrel chest, Tony Cassato had taken a rare day off from his job as Serenity's chief of police, and we had spent a pleasant afternoon together in his hideaway home in the country, making a midday meal, grilling steaks and fall vegetables from his garden, which we then ate on the porch in the warm autumn sunshine.

My contribution to the afternoon was to bring the dessert and, as promised, I'd made a cheesecake and conveyed it to my car. But en route I noticed the delight that I'd placed in its pan on the passenger's seat had liquefied like Vincent Price at the end of an Edgar Allan Poe movie.

In horror and disgust, I picked up the pan and pitched it and its contents out my window, flying in the face of a possible arrest by my boyfriend. (If apprehended, I would plead justifiable littering.)

What a waste of time and money! And to think, I had a perfectly good family cheesecake recipe, but no, instead I had to take one from a "healthy food" Internet site that called for low-fat cream cheese. So cheesecake lovers everywhere, be forewarned. Ain't nothin' like the real thing, baby.

Here's what I *should* have made:

Perfectly Good Cheesecake
(No Health Benefits Promised)

1 graham cracker piecrust
4 pkgs. (8 oz. each) cream cheese, softened
1 cup sugar
1 tsp. vanilla
4 eggs

Beat cream cheese, sugar, and vanilla with mixer until blended. Add eggs, one at a time, mixing on low speed after each just until blended. Pour into crust. Bake one hour at 325 degrees, or until center is almost set. Cool, then refrigerate four hours.

My solution, at that moment, was to turn around, drive back into town, and buy a cheesecake at the Hy-Vee bakery, who had a pretty fair recipe themselves. I had left the evidence of the packaging in the car and, not lying really, allowed Tony to assume I'd made the excellent result.

I asked him, "So . . . what did you think of the cheesecake?"

Tony, his arm around me, said, "I loved it. All men love cheesecake."

"I don't think I'll pursue that one."

The fire snapped and crackled and popped. Maybe next time I'd bring Krispie Treats. How can you screw that up? (Actually, you can.)

He asked offhandedly, "How's Vivian doing?"

I twisted my neck to give him a squinty look,

like a pirate captain about to clobber his too-talkative first mate. "You're breaking our *rule*. . . ."

While at the cabin, two subjects were strictly off limits: Tony's job and my mother.

His eyebrows shrugged above the steel gray eyes. "I know, but it's been awfully quiet out there. You know, like in the old cowboy movies? *Too* quiet?"

By this he meant that Mother hadn't gotten herself (and me) tangled up in another murder of late. In other words, police business—*Tony's* business. In Mother's slight defense, sometimes she got us tangled up in the county *sheriff's* business instead. . . .

I said, "We'll start shooting the reality show in another month, and that should keep her out of mischief. Or anyway, occupied. For a change, she doesn't have murder on the mind." I lay my head back on his shoulder. "I have to admit I am *enjoying* this lull."

Which was why I wanted to stop time.

"Ditto," Tony said.

Such a way with words, my guy.

We fell into a comfortable, cozy silence.

Have you ever been at a restaurant and noticed a couple at another table hardly speaking to each other throughout their entire meal? And you thought, well, there's a marriage (relationship) in trouble. *Au contraire!* Perhaps they *prefer* silence. Take Tony and me—I was constantly being subjected to Mother's jabbering, and he had a stressful, high-pressure job, people yakking at him all day.

So we took it easy on each other.

As if contradicting that, Tony looked right at me and said, "Don't you think it's about time we talk about . . . you know—*us?*"

I squirmed.

Okay, fine—that subject wasn't Mother and it wasn't the police department, either. But the topic wasn't necessarily one I was anxious to explore. Our blossoming relationship had recently become complicated when Tony discovered he wasn't divorced.

I realize that sounds about as likely as remembering you forgot to put your clothes on before leaving the house, but let me explain.

Several years ago, when Tony Cassato was a police detective in Trenton, New Jersey, he testified against a New Jersey crime family, and his own family—that is, his wife and daughter—was forced into the Witness Protection Program. Mrs. Cassato, whom I'd never met, had been livid that Tony put them in danger, and soon served him with divorce papers, which he'd dutifully signed and returned to her lawyer.

But it turned out the papers were never officially filed. Perhaps his wife had second thoughts about ending the marriage, or wanted to maintain some kind of hold over her husband.

Whatever the reason, Tony had been unable to locate her since she and the daughter were still in WITSEC, and even after he'd left the program, Tony honored Mrs. Cassato's desire— conveyed to him by federal officers—not to be contacted by him.

"Can we talk about us later?" I demurred, explaining, "Today has been just too perfect."

Well, except for the cheesecake. The first one, I mean.

"All right, honey," he said. "But *soon*, okay?"

"I promise."

"Can't put it off forever."

"Right."

As always, first-line-of-defense Rocky heard a noise outside before we did, raising his large head off the floor to emit a long low growl, his alert eyes going to Tony.

Then I heard the snap of dry twigs and pinecones beneath car wheels, and I gave Tony a sharp look of concern, feeling his body ever so slightly stiffen.

Sushi, rousing from her slumber, emitted a high yap, better late than never from our second line of defense. Maybe third. Make that fourth. . . .

We had a right to be nervous. Last summer, Tony and I were seated on this very couch when a hired killer sent by the New Jersey mob fired bullets through the cabin windows (*Antiques Knock-Off*). We managed to escape, and the contract on Tony's life has since been withdrawn (thanks to Mother) (but that's another story) (*Antiques Con*).

Still, the memory of that night was all too fresh, and it had meant a long, lonely separation between us when Tony was hustled back into WITSEC.

I followed Tony to the window, where a powder blue four-door sedan was pulling up to the cabin's front porch.

The car stopped, and the front passenger door opened, and Mother got out.

As I breathed a sigh of relief, Tony commented wryly, "For once I'm glad it's her."

My sigh of relief was in part because Mother hadn't driven herself. She was notoriously unlicensed, her driving privilege getting lifted more times than Joan Rivers's face (RIP).

"Thanks for the ride, Frannie!" Mother called to the driver, one of her gal pals. "Toodles!"

As the vehicle pulled away, Mother headed toward the porch with the swinging arms and determined purpose of an invading army.

Sushi and Rocky, having recognized Mother's voice, scrambled over each other to get to the front door as Mother sailed in without knocking.

Mother was statuesque and still quite attractive at her undisclosed age—porcelain complexion, straight nose, wide mouth, wavy silver hair pulled back in a loose chignon. The only downside to her appearance were the large, terribly out of style glasses that magnified her blue eyes to owl-like size.

She was decked out in a fall outfit from her favorite clothing line, Breckenridge, an orange top featuring a pumpkin patch, and green slacks (no pumpkin patch, thankfully). Mother was enamored of the collection because every season was color coordinated, making getting dressed a no-brainer. (She'd had me in Garaminals until I was twelve.)

After affording each dog a quick pat on the

head, Vivian Borne said in a cheerful rush of words, "Hello, dear! And hello to you, too, Chiefie! Sorry to disturb your tête-à-tête, and I realize I risked catching you in flagrante, but I have simply *wonderful* news."

Tony and I had returned to the couch, with the resignation of defeated warriors, and Mother plopped down between us, squeezing in to make space.

She announced, with just a little more pomp than somebody about to break a champagne bottle over the prow of a ship, "I am sure you will be as thrilled as I was to hear that I have been asked . . . are you ready for this?"

Probably not.

She raised a hand in a grand, skywardly pointing finger gesture. "I have been asked to perform this coming weekend . . . drum roll, *please!* . . . at Old York! At the New Vic itself!"

When not involved in amateur sleuthery, or corunning our antiques shop, Mother was active in community theater. In case you haven't guessed. And saying she was "active" in community theater might be an understatement. How about rabidly active?

Since my idea of wonderful news was an unexpected windfall of cash from a dead distant relative, my response was perhaps less than Mother had expected. Specifically, a tepid, "That's nice."

Tony's was a tad better: "You don't say." At least he'd gotten to where he didn't automatically give her a dirty look.

Still, these two responses took the wind out of

Mother's sails, though her boat on the ocean of life never stayed still for long, and she responded with plenty of spare wind.

"*Apparently,*" she huffed grandly, "you don't understand the importance of the offer, the opportunity, that has come my way. Let me enlighten you. Old York usually imports professional talent from the Guthrie, or New York. But on this occasion, they have chosen to book *me* for their fall fete instead."

Old York was a little town about sixty miles away that fancied itself a displaced English hamlet, hence the fall fete.

"What do you mean, fate?" Tony asked, probably thinking he wouldn't mind booking her himself. "Like cast your fate to the wind?"

"It's a kind of fair," she said, "with an English accent."

That had a nice double meaning, though it probably was just an accident, and I decided not to point out to her that *fete* was French. Mother was already miffed with us and her wit was likely on hold.

I frowned. "Isn't it a little late for the fete organizers to be asking you? I mean . . . this coming *weekend*?"

Mother shrugged. "As fate would have it— that's F-A-T-E fate, Chief Cassato—influenza struck the New York troupe who'd been hired. But this late booking provides the perfect opportunity for me to perform my version of" —she cupped her hand over her mouth and whispered—"the Scottish play."

"The what play?" Tony asked.

"*Macbeth*," I said.

"Dear!" Mother blurted.

I went on: "It's an old actor's superstition, not saying '*Macbeth*' in a theater. Mother takes it a step further by never saying it at all."

Her eyes went wide and her nostrils flared. "It is not just the superstition of *old* actors! Even the young ones respect it, and I would thank you, Brandy, to honor it, as well."

"Sure," I said with a shrug.

Tony asked politely, "What's your version of the, uh, Scotch play, Vivian?"

"*Scottish* play, Chief. In my rendition, I play all the parts in a sixty-minute condensation of my own creation," Mother said proudly. "Shakespeare was a good writer, but he runs to the long-winded and needs occasional editing."

"Okay."

Her eyes behind the lenses were huge. "You've heard the old expression of someone with more than one job wearing multiple hats? Well, I take that to heart, literally. I wear a different hat for each character I'm bringing to life."

To Tony's credit, he didn't flinch. Or smirk. He just said, "Interesting."

She twisted on the couch toward him. "Perhaps you would like me to reserve a seat for you in the audience? As the star, I'm sure I'll have comps for special guests."

Behind her back, I mouthed a silent but emphatic, *"No!"*

Tony's eyes went from me to Mother. "I'll try to make it, Viv. Sounds . . . unique."

And I shut my eyes. Perhaps when I opened them, I would find I'd been dreaming.

"*Wonderful!*" Mother chirped. "Now, I'm afraid I must spirit Brandy away from this cozy nest. She and I have a lot to do before we leave for Old York! Miles to go before we sleep. That's Robert Frost, not Shakespeare, by the way."

I gave Tony a shrug and he just smiled and nodded a little.

There was never any doubt that I would be a part of Mother's "gig." First off, due to those previously mentioned vehicular infractions, Mother couldn't drive herself anywhere. And second of all, I was in charge of the hats.

Mother stood, half bowed, and made a ridiculously grand hand gesture; it was going to be a long weekend. "I'll give you two lovebirds a moment together. Or do you need longer? I can arrange a brief nature hike for myself. Just give me a window!"

What, for her to peek in?

"No," I said, "that's all right. Just a few minutes is fine."

"Splendid!"

And she made her exit.

I scooted closer to Tony. "Thanks for not suggesting she take the path that ends in a drop-off to the river."

He paused and squinted, as if that hadn't occurred to him, and he wished it had. But he said, "You're welcome."

"You're not . . . *serious* about going to Mother's one-woman *Macbeth* show, are you?"

He slipped an arm around me. "Your mother's plays are always, uh, unusual experiences . . . and the fete sounds like fun."

I nodded. "Could be at that—especially if you stayed overnight."

I gave him a kiss to seal our fate. (Okay, I promise not to do much of that.) (Straining to use the word *fate*, I mean—I'll kiss Tony as much as I please.)

Five minutes later, I was sliding behind the wheel of our Ford C-Max, with Mother riding shotgun and Sushi settled on her lap. Then I drove down the cabin's narrow pine-tree-lined lane, the setting sun winking through the bows, finally turning onto River Road to head south toward Serenity.

A captive audience of one—Sushi having curled into a ball and gone to sleep—I listened as Mother gave me a history lesson of Old York that I didn't recall requesting.

"In the mid-eighteen hundreds," she was saying, "the village was founded by several English families who drew up a charter decreeing that their British ancestry must never be 'forsaken or forgotten.' "

"Still holding a grudge about that little American uprising, huh?"

She ignored that. "Which is why to this day, visiting Old York is like taking a trip across the pond to a small English hamlet."

"Only not so expensive."

"Was that my pan?"

"Where?"

"Back there! By the side of the road. It looked just like my favorite cheesecake pan!"

I said, "One cheesecake pan looks pretty much like another."

"I would *swear* . . ."

"Haven't I been saying it's time for your optical checkup?"

Since Mother had been minding our store all day, and I had cleaned up the kitchen at home, she couldn't know the pan was hers. Not for sure.

"Yes, you have, dear," Mother sighed. "But they always try to sell me new, smaller frames, and these vintage specs are exactly to *my* specs."

She meant those oversize glasses of hers that dated back decades; at least she'd stopped having the lower half tinted a pale pink, like blush.

"Mother?"

"Yes, dear?"

"This trip to Old York? If you want me to come along and be your hat mistress, you have to promise me one thing."

"Continue."

"You'll leave your fake British accent at home."

A moment passed before she answered. "Bob's your uncle, dear."

I took my eyes off the road long enough to give her a look.

She gave me one in return—of innocence. "What? You didn't say a word about not using British expressions."

A Trash 'n' Treasures Tip

Use caution when buying a foreign antique that you know nothing about, because that lack of even rudimentary knowledge makes it harder to spot a reproduction or fake. But don't bother trying to convince Mother that her Ming dynasty vase is anything but priceless.